With these three uplifting stories Harlequin Superromance is thrilled to celebrate the mothers among us, who bring love and laughter to their children's lives.

"Mommy for Rent" by Lori Handeland

After being hired by young Dani Delgado to help plan the Mother's Day picnic, Kelly Rosholt wants to make a real family with Dani and smitten dad, Scott. But Kelly can't let herself believe that dreams might come true....

"Along Came a Daughter" by Rebecca Winters

It's love at first sight when teenager Brittany Jakeman begins to work for restaurateur Abby Chappuis. Now, if the motherless girl can only get her dad to fall for the beautiful widow…

"Baby Steps" by Anna DeStefano

Lily Brooks can't—won't—believe her dream of having a baby is over. Now it's up to her husband, Tyler, with some help from an unlikely accomplice, to help Lily see there's more than one way to become a mother.

ABOUT THE AUTHORS

Lori Handeland is a double RITA® Award winner for her novels *The Mommy Quest* and *Blue Moon,* as well as a Waldenbooks, BookScan and *USA TODAY* bestselling author. Lori lives in southern Wisconsin with her husband, two teenage sons and a yellow Lab named Elwood. She can be reached through her Web site at www.lorihandeland.com.

Rebecca Winters, mother of four and grandmother of five, has won a National Readers' Choice Award, a B. Dalton Award, many *Romantic Times BOOKreviews* Reviewers' Choice nominations and awards, a RIO Award for excellence and was named Utah Writer of the Year. When she was seventeen, she went to boarding school in Lausanne, Switzerland, which led her to study languages and eventually teach high-school French back in Salt Lake City, Utah. Her first book was published in 1978. At last count she had written ninety-eight books, ninety-four of them with Harlequin Enterprises. Rebecca welcomes feedback and invites her readers to check out her Web site at www.cleanromances.com.

Romantic Times BOOKreviews award-winning author Anna DeStefano volunteers in the fields of grief recovery and crisis care. The rewards of walking with people through life's difficulties are never-ending, as are the insights Anna has gained into what's most beautiful about the human spirit. She sees heroes everywhere she looks now. The number one life lesson she's learned? Figure out what someone truly needs, become the one thing no one else could be for that person, and you'll be a hero, too!

MOTHERS OF THE YEAR

Lori Handeland
Rebecca Winters
Anna DeStefano

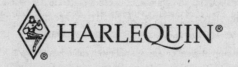

HARLEQUIN®

TORONTO • NEW YORK • LONDON
AMSTERDAM • PARIS • SYDNEY • HAMBURG
STOCKHOLM • ATHENS • TOKYO • MILAN • MADRID
PRAGUE • WARSAW • BUDAPEST • AUCKLAND

ISBN-13: 978-0-373-71482-7
ISBN-10:   0-373-71482-3

MOTHERS OF THE YEAR

Copyright © 2008 by Harlequin Books S.A.

The publisher acknowledges the copyright holders of the individual works as follows:

MOMMY FOR RENT
Copyright © 2008 by Lori Handeland.

ALONG CAME A DAUGHTER
Copyright © 2008 by Rebecca Winters.

BABY STEPS
Copyright © 2008 by Anna DeStefano.

CONTENTS

MOMMY FOR RENT   9
Lori Handeland

ALONG CAME A DAUGHTER   95
Rebecca Winters

BABY STEPS   179
Anna DeStefano

MOMMY FOR RENT
Lori Handeland

Dear Reader,

I'm so excited to be a part of the Harlequin Superromance Mother's Day anthology. Mother's Day is one of my favorite holidays. Since I am the only female in a houseful of men, I make this day count.

Of course, my favorite Mother's Day celebration ever was when we went to a baseball game. We had seats in a restaurant overlooking the outfield and they brought us drinks and food for nine straight innings. My three favorite things combined—my boys, food and sports. What a day! So when my editor asked me to write a novella incorporating Mother's Day, my first thought was baseball.

When former pro baseball player Scott Delgado lands a dream job coaching in the minor leagues, he brings his daughter, Dani, to Kiwanee, Wisconsin. Dani gets into a bind by volunteering her mother to plan the annual Mother's Day picnic. Only problem is, Dani's mom took off when she was a baby. Ever practical, Dani decides to rent a mommy. Lucky for her, there's a new business in town that does just that.

Kelly Rosholt began Rent a Mommy soon after every dream she had for her life was dashed. She was doing just fine until she came to Kiwanee and met Dani and Scott. Then she begins to dream again of the home and family she always wanted.

I hope you enjoy reading *Mommy for Rent* as much as I enjoyed writing it.

I'd also like to invite you to check out a series of books I'm writing. The Nightcreature Novels from St. Martin's Paperbacks are paranormal suspense novels featuring werewolf hunters. I like to think of them as Buffy with werewolves. *Thunder Moon* is available now.

Lori Handeland

For information on future releases and a chance to win free books, visit my Web site at www.lorihandeland.com.

CHAPTER ONE

"ARE YOU A GIRL or a boy?"

Dani Delgado contemplated the kid in front of her. About Dani's size, which meant taller than most and skinny with it, his hair was so dark it seemed to have blue streaks in the uncombed mess.

"Whaddya think I am?" she sneered. There wasn't much Dani hated more than being asked if she were a boy, but it happened all the time.

"If I knew, I wouldn't ask ya."

He wiped the sleeve of his coat across his runny nose. Two weeks into April and Dani could still see her breath on the air. What was up with that?

Sure, she'd been a little excited when her dad said they were moving from Boca Raton to Kiwanee, Wisconsin. What kid didn't want to see snow? But Dani didn't want to see it right now.

"What's yer name?" the boy asked.

"Dani."

He made a face. "That ain't any help."

Actually her name was Danielle, but she wasn't going to tell him that.

The bell rang, and all the children filed into Kiwanee Elementary. Dani hung back. This was the fourth school she'd gone to, not countin' preschool, and she was only seven. But her dad said they were here to stay—at least for a season or two.

Dad had been a semifamous pitcher for the Marlins. Then he'd done something wonky to his arm, and he couldn't play no more. For years they'd moved from city to city as he went from job to job—assistant pitching coach, head pitching coach, back to assistant again. Dani had thought they'd never stop. Then he'd gotten a job managing the minor league Kiwanee Warhawks.

Dad said this was his big break, his dream job, his life choice. Whatever that meant. All Dani knew was that he was smiling more than she'd seen him smile ever before.

Determined to fit in this time, Dani marched into Mrs. Henning's second-grade classroom. She'd been here last week with Dad. They'd walked all over the building so Dani would know where things were, then they'd met Mrs. Henning, who'd shown Dani which seat would be hers.

Dani took it, eyes narrowing at the boy from the playground. He had the desk right behind hers. She wasn't sure yet if he was mean or not, but he wouldn't be able to pull on her hair, because she'd chopped it off this morning. She knew better than to give nasty kids something to yank on.

Her dad wouldn't be happy. She'd had to sneak back to the house after he left in order to do it—he never would have let her—but Dani had been determined.

Mrs. Henning, who looked old to Dani, though Dad had said she was *only* forty—as if that were young—smiled brightly, and Dani winced. She knew what was coming.

"We have a brand-new student today."

Dani prayed the teacher wouldn't make her stand in front and talk about herself. She'd had to do that a few times already, and it never went too good. Kids would whisper and point. Dani's voice would get quieter and quieter until she mumbled. No one cared about the new kid anyway, unless it was to tease him or her.

She'd done her best to dress right today, though Dani wasn't sure exactly what "right" was. The definition seemed to change at every school she attended.

Dani had worn jeans, sneakers and one of the pink shirts her mom always sent for her birthday, even though Dani hated pink. But girls wore pink, or so it seemed. Dani wasn't very good at bein' a girl.

"Everyone, welcome Danielle Delgado, all the way from Florida." Mrs. Henning clapped, and the class joined in halfheartedly.

"You're a girl?" the boy behind her whispered.

Dani turned. "Do a lot of boys wear pink in this town?" She smirked. "Do you?"

For a minute Dani thought the kid might slug her, and her fingers curled into her palms, ready, even as she bit her lip to keep herself from saying anything else smart.

Then he laughed, smacked her on the shoulder, hard, and said, "Good one."

Dani faced front and slowly let her hands relax. She tried, she really did, to be nice, to keep her lip zipped, but she couldn't help it. Sometimes stuff just came out.

She'd been in fights at other schools, and her dad had said, "No more," and "Be a lady," but he never told her how.

Mrs. Henning finished taking attendance—the boy behind Dani was named Jeffrey Braun. People spelled their names weird here—Braun instead of Brown, Mueller instead of Miller—Dad said it was because everyone was German, but Dani didn't understand why being German gave them license to misspell. When she'd asked, Dad had sighed and rubbed his forehead. He did that a lot when she talked.

The morning went okay. She had no problem keeping up in class. Her mouth wasn't the only thing smart about Dani. But when lunch came, she thought again about how hard it was to go to a new school. 'Specially when the entire year was almost done. Everyone had their best friend already, and their second best friend and their group of friends. They didn't need her.

Dani ate alone, then went onto the playground, shivering in her too-thin coat. Who would have thought she'd need to wear a winter coat in springtime? She didn't have one anyway.

She stared at the other girls, who were all dressed in skirts and colored tights with matching sweaters and low-heeled shoes, their winter jackets unzipped to show off their outfits.

Dani glanced down at her own clothes; she'd chosen wrong

again. Not that she had a lot of skirts, or any tights or a single pair of shoes that had a heel. She was a failure as little girl.

Tears burned, and she blinked to keep them back. Dad hated it when she cried. He'd mutter his favorite line from *League of Their Own,* "There's no crying in baseball," and Dani would swallow every sob.

She liked baseball well enough. She was good at it; her dad was a *professional.* But what she really liked was dancing. What she really wanted was to take ballet lessons.

'Cept no matter how many times she hinted, Dad never got it. He just kept treating her like one of the guys. For her birthday, he'd bought her a miniature version of the Warhawks blue-and-gold baseball uniforms. She'd definitely wanted to cry then.

Dani continued to watch the girls, who stood in a circle at the edge of the playground talking and giggling. They sounded like birds flapping and squawking after being startled from the trees. She wasn't sure how to talk to them or if she should even try.

Dad always said to "just do" things—hit the ball, ride that bike, make those friends. So she walked over and said, "Hi."

They'd been discussing some picnic, she caught that much, but at the sound of Dani's voice, everyone went silent.

One girl, the one Dani figured for the leader, since she had the nicest clothes, the blondest hair and the loudest voice, lifted her eyebrows. "Does your mom want to do it?"

Instead of saying *I don't have a mom,* which, after only being in town a few days, Dani already knew made her weird, she asked, "Do what?"

"Plan the Kiwanee Mother's Day Picnic. The mom who was supposed to do it got her leg broke on the ice."

Dani frowned, trying to figure out how ice could break a leg.

"They need someone to volunteer, but all the other moms already have a job." The golden girl smiled. "Except yours."

"I...uh—"

"We have to have a Mother's Day picnic," the girl exclaimed, and all the others nodded like the wives Dani had seen in that

Stepford movie Dad hadn't wanted her to watch. "It's the best time all year."

Dani was going to tell the truth—that her mom had walked out when Dad had quit playing baseball and Dani hadn't seen her since. But when she opened her mouth, what came out instead was, "Sure, she'll do it."

THINGS WENT DOWNHILL from there. The golden girl, whose name was Ashley Wainright, let out a shriek and hugged her. Dani stood stiff and shocked as the rest of the girls patted her and cooed just like the birds she'd been comparing them to.

Stepford birds, her mind whispered, which was kind of creepy.

Then they all trooped back to school, and Ashley, the big mouth, told Mrs. Henning, who frowned at Dani—after all, Dani's dad had brought her to school and if he'd mentioned a mom at all it would have been to say that Dani didn't have one.

"But Dani, I thought—"

"She isn't here yet," Dani blurted. "She had to sell the other house."

"Oh." Mrs. Henning scrunched up her lips, then glanced back and forth between Dani and Ashley. "I see."

Dani kind of thought Mrs. Henning did see, but at least she didn't say anything more. The same could not be said of Ashley. She told everybody.

By the end of the day, twenty people had thanked Dani for her mother's help. She'd been invited to a birthday party, a roller-skating party and a sleepover.

As Dani headed to her sitter's house, only six blocks away, Ashley skipped past and called out, "I'll have my mom call your mom."

Dani waved, smiled and muttered, "Good luck with that."

She began to feel sicker and sicker. Ashley's mom would call, and Dani's dad would spill the beans, then Ashley would hate her and so would everyone else, and Dani'd never have a single friend in this town.

Why hadn't she just told the truth? Better to be the weird kid without a mom than the liar who'd invented one. Unless...

Dani stopped walking and several kids behind her scooted around. No one told her to "move it," and no one gave her a shove. First day and she was already okay, and all it had taken was volunteering her "mom" to plan a silly picnic. Maybe Dani could plan the picnic and pretend her mom was doing it.

Nah. She'd never pull that off. Somewhere along the way, someone would want to meet Mrs. Delgado, and then what would Dani do, rent a mommy?

The thought made her forget she was supposed to go to the sitter's. She gasped; she giggled; then she ran all the way home and pulled out the local paper, turning to the center and reading out loud the ad she'd seen that morning.

"Grand opening," she read. "Need help? Don't have enough hands? Time to rent a mommy."

Dani picked up the phone.

CHAPTER TWO

THE PHONE RANG as Kelly Rosholt was leaving for the day. Her partner, Paige Jensen, was on another line and didn't even glance up.

Their rule was to deal with the customer you had. They never put anyone on hold so that the caller felt devalued. People could leave a message, and Rent a Mommy would get back to them. When they did, that customer would be treated as if they were the most important human being in the world at that moment, which they were.

Kelly and Paige had turned their brainchild into a very profitable business. Catering to the twenty-first-century working mother, Rent a Mommy specialized in the kind of reliable, efficient and loving care usually found only in a mother. A mommy could be rented to cook, clean, babysit, tutor, sew or even take over a frazzled parent's shift at the local concession stand or bake sale. Anything to make life easier, Rent a Mommy did.

They'd been asked to do some pretty odd things. If the requests weren't illegal, immoral or just plain moronic, Kelly, Paige and their army of mommies did their best to oblige.

Kelly snatched up the phone. "Rent a Mommy. This is Kelly."

"Kelly! Thank God."

Kelly recognized the voice of one of her newest employees, Lisa Lindermeyer, above the background shrieks.

"What's going on?" Kelly demanded. From the volume of those screams, bloody murder wasn't out of the question.

"The kid's flipping out."

"What kid?" Kelly glanced at Paige, who'd hung up with her

client. Paige shrugged at Kelly's silent question. She had no idea where Lisa had gone, either.

"I'm in Kiwanee."

"Where's that?"

Kelly was new to Wisconsin. Originally from Iowa, this was the fifth Rent a Mommy she and Paige had opened, but the first one in this state. If all went well, they'd get the location up and running, hire a manager and move on to the next satellite agency.

"About thirty miles west of you."

Their storefront was in Madison, a booming metropolis filled with professors, lawyers, politicians, judges—exactly the type of city where Rent a Mommy would flourish.

"I told her we aren't really mommies." Lisa took a deep breath. "She didn't take it well."

Lisa must have held the receiver toward the screaming child, because Kelly could very distinctly hear, "I need a mommy! You said I could rent one."

"Who called and hired us?"

"I thought it was a grandmother or an aunt, but it must have been the kid."

"You can't tell the difference?"

"The office was a zoo. Phones ringing, people in and out. I got distracted."

Kelly sighed. This was why she worked ten hours a day—so she could man the phones. But today she'd had a meeting with the bank, and just see what had happened.

"Tell her you need to talk to her mother."

"I think that's the problem. She doesn't have one. She saw the ad in the paper and—"

"Decided to rent one. Got it. Well, find her father—"

"Not me. I'm out of here."

"What? No, you need to—"

"I quit," Lisa said. "I can't take the screaming. You want to smooth this over, you get out here and smooth. The address is on the assignment form on your desk."

"But—" *Click*. "Hell."

Kelly hung up, then tore through her in-box. The form was second in the pile. "Kiwanee," she muttered, sitting at her computer and clicking on MapQuest. "Ever heard of it?"

"Nope." Paige wasn't from here, either.

The two had met in Chicago. Kelly had been working in a day care; Paige had needed one. A single mother to a set of twins, Paige couldn't work enough hours to pay for double day care, especially when she'd barely finished high school before she'd given birth to the girls.

The father had taken one look at the identical babies and fled. Paige hadn't seen him since. She definitely hadn't seen any child support.

Kelly and Paige had bonded as women sometimes do. They'd gotten an apartment and taken to working opposite shifts—Kelly at the day care and Paige at a restaurant in the evenings. One very late night, when they were punchy with exhaustion and a few glasses of wine, Paige had said, "What I really need is a mom. Think I can rent one?"

"That's not a half-bad idea," Kelly said.

In the morning, the idea had seemed even better.

Five years later, she still thought so. Even on days like today when everything seemed to be on the fast track to hell.

Kelly's computer produced a map and she hit Print. As Lisa had said, Kiwanee was thirty miles west, on what appeared to be a two-lane highway. Kelly glanced at her watch. Four-thirty. At least she'd avoid the beltline. After only three weeks in Madison, she loathed that beltline during rush hour as much as a native.

"Trouble?" Paige asked.

"Lisa quit. I'm going to fix things. See if you can hire another mommy, one who doesn't bail at the first temper tantrum."

"Got it."

One of the many things Kelly loved about Paige was her calm in a crisis. Of course, being the mother of twins made crisis a relative term. Very few things were worse than what Paige had already dealt with.

Hiring the mommies was Paige's job. She knew people, and usually she chose very well. But there was always one or two in every town who couldn't cut it. Dealing with other people's children was so much different than dealing with your own. Or at least that's what Paige said. Kelly had no children of her own, and she never would.

She grabbed her down coat and purse, climbed into her SUV and headed for Kiwanee. The trip took about forty minutes. Driving on two-lane highways might be slower than driving on the freeway, but Kelly preferred it. She'd grown up in central Iowa, where two-lane highways were the norm. As long as she stayed alert for slow-moving farm vehicles, deer and that most dangerous of beasts, the drunk driver drifting over the centerline, she was relatively safe.

Here and there a tree sported feathery green buds, despite the chill in the air and the clouds in the sky. In the upper Midwest, two days of sun and a week of temperatures above freezing meant the daffodils would push through the still snowy earth. Anything warmer and the lilacs would bloom, the bees would awaken and leaves would pop out everywhere.

Of course, the inevitable late-spring snowstorm had yet to make an appearance. The locals expected it any day now. Bets had been made; money would change hands. There'd been snow in these parts as late as May 13, or so she'd been told. She'd believe it when she saw it.

A green sign with white lettering announced: Kiwanee 2 miles. Three minutes later, she rolled past a billboard, Welcome to Kiwanee—Population 2356.

Her MapQuest directions took her straight to the Delgado house, a freshly painted white board Colonial on a side street lined with just-budding maple trees.

"Three-fifteen Maple Street," she murmured. "Wonder what genius came up with that."

Back in her hometown, the streets had been similarly named for their most impressive feature, which had led to such gems as Hill Road, Culvert Drive and Farm Lane. Kelly felt a slash of homesickness so deep she ached with it. Since, as the cliché went, she could never go home again, Kelly did what she always did. She went on.

Strolling up the front walk, Kelly noticed the little things. The bushes needed trimming. The windows could use a good washing. Heck, they could use a few curtains. Kelly reached out to ring the bell, and the front door swung open.

If she hadn't known the child was a girl from Lisa's use of pronouns, and if she didn't understand kids well enough to realize that no little boy would ever wear pink, Kelly might have been stumped. The brown hair appeared to have been hacked off with a meat cleaver and stood up in tufts as if the child had been pulling on it. Her jeans were too big; her tennis shoes belonged in the garbage. Kelly didn't think she was wearing any socks.

But her brown eyes were shrewd as she looked Kelly up and down, then cocked her head. "So how much will it cost for you to be my mommy?"

SCOTT DELGADO WAS on the phone trying to iron out a scheduling snafu when his assistant, Vivienne—call me Vee—Schwartzman, ran in. He automatically glanced behind her for his daughter, frowning when she wasn't there. One glance at Vee's face and he said, "I'll call you back," then hung up before the other man could answer.

"What happened?" With Dani, it could be anything.

"She's not here?" Vee glanced around, her gray mop of curls swaying left then right.

"She's supposed to be with you."

"She never showed up at my place after school."

Vee had volunteered, and Scott had accepted her offer to watch Dani until he could find a more permanent solution. Since Vee had never had any kids—she hadn't even had a husband—he probably should have thought twice, but he'd been desperate to find help and help of that kind was in short supply in Kiwanee.

The town appeared to be overrun by perfect two-parent families, with equally perfect children—a boy and a girl, plus their dog. No single mother needing extra cash. No divorcée wanting to impress him with her parenting skills. He'd spent a week asking around and ended up with Vee. As she'd said, "How hard can watching one kid for a few hours be?"

When that kid was Dani Delgado, pretty damn hard. Dani had made an art form of driving sitters insane.

She didn't mean to be difficult. She was a smart aleck with a lot of energy. She was also extremely intelligent and adept at getting her way. She wheedled and cajoled, once in a while she threw a fit, though usually only with Scott. When she played, she played hard. Sometimes she broke things; so far he'd been lucky and she hadn't broken herself. Scott wasn't certain how long that luck would hold out.

Vee knew baseball not children. She'd been watching the Warhawks since their inception, twenty years past, which had coincided with her early retirement from the post office. She'd volunteered her services as an assistant five years ago, and Scott had inherited her from the previous manager.

From what he'd seen so far, Vee knew her stuff. The locker room, the equipment room, his office, the field were so orderly they made him edgy. He just knew he was going to mess them up.

"Did you check the house?" Scott asked, already slipping into his coat, which was too damn thin for this ridiculous climate. He'd figured they would have time to buy winter apparel before next winter. He hadn't realized winter was still here.

"Should I have?" Vee frowned. "She was supposed to come to me."

"Where did you look?"

"The playground, the park, the route from the school to my house."

Well, that made sense, although the house should have been the next step. He debated calling, then decided against it. He'd go home, see if Dani was there and, if not, he'd call then wait for the police. Wasn't anything he hadn't done before. He'd just hoped he wouldn't have to do it again, or at least not this soon, and not here.

For the first time since he'd arrived in town, Scott wished he'd driven his car to work. In Kiwanee, there wasn't much need for a vehicle unless the temperature was below zero, you had a lot to haul or you were leaving town. The city was one mile square. Scott had been walking the seven blocks between his house and the ball field each day. Today he retraced them at a run.

A strange SUV was parked out front. For an instant Scott panicked, though he wasn't sure why. After all, a kidnapper wouldn't linger. A kidnapper would have snatched Dani and been gone. Maybe his ex-wife had finally gotten tired of searching for a new, rich and famous husband and decided to pay some attention to her daughter.

Nah. Never happen.

So who belonged to the shiny gas-guzzler? Hard to say since everyone in town except Scott had one. According to Vee, in the winter you needed them or you wouldn't be going anywhere.

Which made him think that the car belonged to a neighbor and had nothing to do with him or Dani at all.

He raced up the front walk and burst in the door. A woman stood in his kitchen, speaking calmly and quietly to Dani.

Tall and slim, she wore a light gray business suit with a pale peach silk blouse beneath. The skirt ended at her knee revealing a very nice set of calves and ankles. Her blond hair had been twisted and pinned so it was hard to tell how long it was, though definitely not short.

Speaking of which…he glanced at Dani. What the hell? When he'd dropped her off at school that morning, she'd had hair.

"Dani," he began, his voice coming out louder and angrier than he'd meant for it to.

The woman glanced up, and he was startled by the shade of her eyes. Grass-green when he'd expected sky-blue.

Then his daughter turned, and the tears shimmering on her cheeks made him forget everything but her.

"What did you do?" he demanded.

"It wasn't her fault," the woman began.

Scott lifted his gaze from Dani's to the stranger's. "I wasn't talking to her."

CHAPTER THREE

"YOU THINK I DID something?"

Scott moved farther into the room. "Did you?"

The woman's spine stiffened; her head lifted. The movement caused her suit jacket to separate as her breasts thrust forward.

He averted his gaze. He had no business noticing her breasts. Not only because his daughter was watching every move he made with those sad, teary eyes, but because breasts were off-limits. Just look at the trouble he'd gotten into the last time he'd been interested in a pair.

He glanced at his daughter and softened. At least he'd gotten Dani out of the deal. Otherwise his marriage would have been a total loss.

"I take it you're the father."

"Got it in one," he said. "And you are?"

"Kelly Rosholt." She stepped forward, high-heeled pumps clicking on the vinyl floor, as she offered a perfectly manicured hand. "Rent a Mommy."

Scott shook her hand as he asked, "Rent a what?"

"We're a new service, out of Madison. We help with the kids, the house, the school, pretty much anything you need."

"Why are you here?"

"Your daughter called and hired us. She seems to be under the mistaken impression that we're actually mothers for hire."

"That's what the paper said." Dani wiped her eyes.

She hardly ever cried. Of course, he couldn't bear it when she did, so he always made a joke about there being no crying in baseball. Dani loved baseball. She'd been playing it with him since she could swing a bat.

"Let me get this straight," Scott said. "You called and hired a service to be your mother?"

Dani dug the toe of her ratty old sneaker—he could have sworn those things had been new a month ago—into the floor. "Yeah."

He glanced at Kelly Rosholt. "No offense, lady, but you don't seem like much of a mommy to me."

Something flickered in her eyes, and he could have sworn her lips trembled before they tightened. But when she answered, she was all business. "I'm the owner. I came out here when your daughter threw a screaming fit and the employee who'd taken the job quit."

Dani refused to look at him. He'd deal with her later.

"You often accept jobs from munchkins?" he asked.

"It was a mistake, which is why I came."

Something she'd said made Scott pause. "Wait a second. Your employee left, *then* you came? That's a thirty-minute drive."

She tipped her chin. "Give or take."

"You hire people who just walk out and leave kids on their own?"

"Dani was alone when my employee got here, Mr. Delgado. I wouldn't be throwing stones in that glass house. The crash just might catch the attention of social services."

"She wasn't supposed to be alone."

"Uh-oh," Dani muttered.

"Yeah." He fixed her with a glare. "Why didn't you go to Vee's?"

"I didn't wanna."

Scott resisted the urge to smack himself in the forehead. She didn't wanna. What was he going to do with her?

"You don't like Vee?"

At first Dani didn't answer, then she lifted her head and stared at him defiantly. "I need a mommy."

When had this started? It was natural that Dani would miss

her mother, though he had to say Kara had never been much of one. She'd hired a nanny the instant Dani was born, and when she'd left, there'd been no question of custody. Dani had been Scott's from the beginning.

Kara never called—forget about visiting—and maybe every other year she remembered to send a gift at Christmas, though for some reason she thought it was a terrific idea to send a pink shirt for every birthday. Scott had believed he was doing a pretty good job being both mom and dad, but maybe he'd been wrong.

"You have a mother," he said.

Dani snorted and rolled her eyes. Scott nearly gaped. She might have a bit of a smart mouth—she got it from him—but she was rarely a brat in front of company. Yet, according to this woman, Dani had thrown a screaming fit this afternoon.

Had she hit puberty already? He thought it was too early, but then again, he didn't know much about little girls. She was his first. He had hoped she wouldn't be his last, though, with the way she was acting, maybe he should rethink his dream of a houseful of kids.

"I don't understand this," Scott murmured. "You never cared about having a mother before."

Kelly Rosholt shot him a look. He got the impression he'd said something wrong, though he couldn't figure out what.

Dani sighed. "I volunteered my mom to plan the Kiwanee Mother's Day Picnic."

Now Scott snorted. Kara planning a picnic. He doubted she'd ever been to one.

"Honey, you know your mom—" Scott stopped. He wasn't sure what to say, especially in front of Ms. Rosholt. Dani's mom wasn't going to plan a picnic. They'd be lucky if she showed up for anything less serious than a lifesaving bone-marrow transplant.

"I didn't mean for my *real* mom to do it," Dani said. "I'm not stupid."

Scott winced. Well, so much for keeping family secrets a secret.

"You called us to plan the picnic instead of your mother?" Ms. Rosholt asked.

"Kind of. I didn't exactly tell them I didn't have a one."

"What *did* you tell them?" Scott asked.

Dani hunched her shoulders. "That she was on her way."

Scott counted to ten to keep from shouting. Shouting worked pretty well with baseball players, not so well at all with little girls. He knew that much.

"You're going to admit the truth tomorrow," Scott said, thrilled at the calm, level, sane tone of his voice.

"But, Dad, there's no one to plan the picnic, and it's the biggest thing of the year, and everyone will be upset if they don't have it."

"I'm sorry about that, but there's not much I can do. I have all I can handle with a new job and you."

Ms. Rosholt cleared her throat. They both glanced at her. "I could plan the party."

"Yay!" Dani shouted, making Ms. Rosholt jump. "It wouldn't be so bad if I could at least say I had someone to plan the party."

Scott didn't want to reward Dani's deceit. She'd lied about having a mother who was on her way to town. However, he could understand why she'd done it. Still—

The phone rang. He picked up the handset, glanced at the caller ID. *Vee.* Damn, he'd forgotten to call and tell her he'd found Dani.

"Excuse me," he murmured to Ms. Rosholt, then answered, "She's here," skipping hello.

"Thank God. What got into her?"

"I'll tell you later."

"Wait," Vee said. "I called about something else, too. You need to go to Fargo tomorrow."

"Can't."

"You have to. The new pitcher is balking at coming to hicksville. The boss man wants you to go and convince him personally."

"A guy from Fargo is calling Kiwanee hicksville?"

"He's never seen the neon on Paramount Street." She began to talk with an exaggerated country twang. "Doggone stuff purt near lights up the whole county."

"Funny."

"I thought so. I can watch the kid while you're gone, but she's going to have to come to my place. I have my mahjong club to-morrow night."

Scott's head reeled at the thought of telling Dani she had to stay at Vee's and listen to the mahjong tiles clack until he got home around midnight, if he was lucky.

His gaze went to Kelly Rosholt. "Never mind. I might have a solution."

He disconnected. "Excuse me one more time," he said, then speed-dialed an old friend as he walked into the living room.

Five minutes later, he knew what he needed to. His college roommate had become a private investigator, which could be quite handy at times. Justin had done a quick check on Rent a Mommy, and the business had a stellar reputation, as did Kelly Rosholt.

"Sorry about that," he said as he returned to the kitchen. He fixed Dani with a stare. "Vee was worried about you."

She looked down.

"You can call and apologize later."

"Yes, sir," Dani said.

That was more like it.

Scott turned to Ms. Rosholt. "I'd like to take you up on that offer of party planning."

"Great."

Her smile was purely professional. He wondered if she prac-ticed in the mirror. Kara always had, though her smile had been a different kind of professional.

"I'd also like to hire you to take care of Dani and help around here for a week or so. I just took the job as manager of the Kiwanee Warhawks. I need to find live-in child care, but I haven't had the chance. Until I do, can I count on you?"

"Certainly. When should we start?"

"I have to leave town tomorrow." Dani made a soft sound of distress. "Just for the day. But I won't be home until you're in bed, Dani."

Her face eased. He was going to have to find someone she bonded with, and soon, because this job was going to involve a lot of days, as well as nights, on the road.

"I'll have someone here before school gets out tomorrow," Ms. Rosholt promised.

"Not you?" he asked.

"I don't work in the field anymore." She glanced at Dani and her face seemed wistful. "Someone has to be in charge."

Scott had to admit he was relieved. He wanted Dani to be taken care of by a motherly type—someone who would bake cookies, read stories, tuck her in—all the things her real mother hadn't been capable of doing. Kelly Rosholt didn't appear capable of them, either.

Oh, he was certain she was an excellent businesswoman. She had to be to have begun Rent a Mommy only five years ago and already made such a success of it. But her demeanor, if not her blond hair and curvy figure, reminded him too much of Kara for comfort.

Scott reached into a kitchen drawer and withdrew a key, handing it to Ms. Rosholt. "If your employee could be here by three, so Dani doesn't come home to an empty house."

"Of course." Her eyes met his, and Scott experienced a dangerous tingle. "You can count on me," she said.

Strangely, he felt that he *could* count on her. Not that he wouldn't send Vee over to check on things tomorrow.

He might be a fool, but he wasn't stupid.

KELLY DROVE toward Madison, happy she'd averted the crisis, thrilled to have a new client, saddened by what she'd seen.

Kiwanee reminded her so much of the place where she'd grown up, the memories nearly overwhelmed her. But Kelly had spent years forgetting. She wasn't about to let a single visit to one tiny town bring everything back. She was stronger than that.

Still, she felt sorry for the kid. She understood where Dani was coming from. Kelly would make certain she sent the perfect "mommy" to watch over Dani until the father found a more permanent solution.

Kelly spent a few seconds thinking about Scott Delgado. She couldn't help it. From the moment he'd burst into the house, she'd had a hard time keeping her eyes off him and her mind on the discussion.

She vaguely remembered his name from his pro-baseball days, but that wasn't what intrigued her. She had been drawn to his thick, dark, slightly curling hair and equally dark eyes, which were complemented by tanned skin from a lifetime outdoors. Just over six feet, with wide shoulders and narrow hips, he walked with an athlete's grace. He no doubt had an athlete's pecs and abs, too.

Her fingers clenched on the steering wheel as she guided her SUV around a sharp curve of the highway. What was wrong with her? She hadn't been attracted to a man since her divorce. Broken hearts were not easily mended; broken lives took even longer. Kelly's heart, her life, her very dreams had been crushed. She didn't think she'd ever recover.

Initially, the children she'd watched over had helped; then they'd begun to hurt. Being with them only emphasized Kelly's inadequacies and brought home the fact that she'd never be a mother. *Never.*

So Kelly had remade herself into a businesswoman. She walked the walk, talked the talk, wore the clothes, the makeup, the hairstyle. The first step to a successful franchise was looking the part.

Kelly pushed her memories of the past into the past as she exited the highway. Instead of returning to her apartment, which was filled with boxes and little else, Kelly went to the office. She needed to find someone to send to the Delgados' tomorrow, but, according to the computer, all available mommies were otherwise engaged.

She called Paige. One of the twins answered.

"It's Auntie K," she said. "Where's your mom?"

"Giving Maggie a talk."

"Uh-oh. What'd she do this time?"

Paige's twins, Mary and Margaret, might be identical, but they were as different as two girls could be. Margaret, or Maggie, loved animals, dirt and sports, not necessarily in that order, while Mary craved frilly socks, brightly colored pencils, crisp white paper and books.

"Someone said I was a priss. She walloped 'em," Mary said matter-of-factly.

The two girls, despite their differences, were inseparable, and woe to anyone who messed with either one of them.

"Then they fell in the mud and rolled round and round," Mary continued. "Mom was not amused."

Kelly smiled, hearing Paige's voice coming out of her daughter's mouth. "I bet not. Was Mags hurt?"

"Nah. But she's suspected."

"Of what?"

"Can't go to school for two days."

"You mean, suspended."

"Okay. I gotta go. Mom's yellin'."

"You better let me talk to her."

The phone hit the counter with a painful thud. "Mom! Auntie K wants you."

Seconds later, Paige came on the line. "Why did I have twins?"

"Because triplets would have been too cruel?"

She sighed. "They'll be the death of me."

"Something has to be."

Paige made a derisive *psst* before asking, "What's up?"

"I need a mommy to help a single dad in Kiwanee."

"I'm interviewing this week. Should have someone by Friday."

"She's supposed to be there by three tomorrow."

"Ain't happening."

"I already promised."

"Unpromise. We were down to one mommy—Lisa—then she bugged out. Pickings are a little slim right now, but we have our standards."

Those standards were what had made Rent a Mommy thrive. They didn't hire just anyone. Their employees were empty-nesters, mothers of high-school-age children and, in the summer, teachers or education majors.

"As soon as school's out, we'll have an influx," Paige continued. "And again in the fall when the moms need more to do. Right now we haven't got a huge roster to choose from."

"But—"

"Don't look at me, either. Princess Hits-a-Lot got herself suspended. I'll be here for the next two days."

"Crap."

"I know much better expletives than that."

"Too bad you can't use them." The twins repeated everything.

"No, but I can think them, over and over and over again."

"Does it help?"

"Not one bit."

"I promised this guy," Kelly said. "Lisa screwed up and he's desperate."

"You'll have to do it."

"No!" Kelly blurted, her heart thumping like the wheels of a speeding freight train at the thought of spending any time in Kiwanee.

"Then you'll have to back out of the job."

Kelly chewed her lip. She couldn't do that, either. The quickest way to bad word-of-mouth was to leave someone in a lurch with child care. Besides, she had promised.

"Hell," she muttered.

"I knew you'd see it my way," Paige replied. "Have a nice day."

Paige hung up. Kelly ran through all the expletives she knew in her head, and discovered her friend was right.

It didn't help.

CHAPTER FOUR

KELLY DIDN'T GET MUCH sleep. She went to the office early so she could take care of business, then left at one in the afternoon, ran home and changed out of her suit and into a pair of khaki slacks and a fitted peach sweater that conveniently matched her nails. She added taupe pumps and finished off with silver earrings, a necklace and bracelet. She left her hair in its French twist. A little overstated for the outfit, but at least it would be out of her face. Before two o'clock, Kelly was on the way to Kiwanee.

The second trip took her five minutes less than the first. She knew her way now. In a few days, she'd know the way much better than she wanted to, but she was determined to make the best of the situation.

She'd gone into this business to use her talent at being a wife and a mother to lend a hand to families and children who needed her. She'd also had little choice in the matter. She hadn't known how to do anything else.

She could have become a teacher, but that would have involved moving in with her parents and continuing to live in the same town as her ex-husband while she got her degree, and that Kelly could not bear. So she'd left her home, her family and her dreams behind, and she hadn't returned. She couldn't.

The sign Welcome to Kiwanee flashed by, and though just the sight of the town invoked unpleasant memories, she was also glad she'd arrived. She could get to work, occupy her mind, try to face her demons and forget about the past.

"Please, God, let me forget about the past," she prayed as she parked in front of the Delgados'.

Inside was quiet, not exactly neat, but not messy, either. The house was lived in. The place felt like a home.

Shoes had been kicked into a corner. A raincoat and sweatshirt hung on a coatrack, along with a baseball hat that sported the letters *KW* and a strangely vicious-looking bird strutting along the base of the brim wearing a miniature version of the same hat.

Cereal bowls, a juice glass, a coffee cup had been rinsed and set in the sink. Kelly loaded them into the half-full dishwasher. From the slime on the plates inside, she surmised that last night's dinner had been spaghetti. Kelly hit the rinse button, hoping it wasn't too late to avoid staining the white plates forever.

A note lay on the countertop.

> Thank you for coming. Dani gets out of school at two-thirty, so she should be home no later than three. Please feed her, help with the homework and put her to bed by nine. No TV until the homework's done. No cookies until she's eaten a fruit or a vegetable. (I mean it, Dani!) My cell number is 555-4253.
> Scott

Kelly set the sheet back on the counter, then glanced into the refrigerator where she discovered defrosting chicken breasts, lettuce, tomatoes and plenty of fruit in the bin if salad wouldn't cut it.

A quick check of the clock revealed she had plenty of time to walk to the elementary school, meet Dani and make certain she found her way to the right house today.

At work that morning, Kelly had found the address of the school, as well as the directions. Kiwanee Elementary lay only four blocks away on the other side of the small downtown area that made up the business section.

As she strolled down Paramount Street, she said hello or nodded to everyone she passed. Most faces were curious. She was obviously a stranger, just as obviously not a tourist, so who was she? If they saw her more than once, they'd ask. But for now, she was an intriguing mystery in a town that had few of them.

Paramount Street catered to the tourist crowd that would arrive with the beginning of baseball season. Several restaurants, an ice-cream salon, bookstore and craft/souvenir shops lined the sidewalks. Kelly turned on School Road just as the final bell shrilled.

Within seconds the doors slammed open and children spilled out. Kelly stood at the edge of the playground, her mouth curving as she watched the kids run off. Shouts and laughter filled the air.

The sun shone today, but the temperature hovered below average, darn close to freezing. She frowned when Dani appeared, wearing jeans and yet another pink T-shirt—how many did she have?—with nothing more than a lined windbreaker and no hat.

She was talking to a group of girls who reminded Kelly of the crowd in *Mean Girls*—dressed not only too well, but too maturely, for their age. Short skirts, long hair that appeared to be highlighted—at seven? Were they nuts?—with heels on their boots and hoops in their pierced ears. Kelly half expected to see the glint of a belly button ring peeking out of the too short hem of their tops.

"Dani!" Kelly called, and lifted a hand when the girl glanced her way.

Dani's eyes widened. She turned to the girl next to her—the tallest, blondest one—and said something before hurrying over. "I thought someone else was coming."

"I wanted to."

Not even close to the truth, but the kid had abandonment issues already—no shock there—Dani didn't need to know that Kelly would have done anything to avoid this, if she could have.

Dani's lips tightened. She was about to say something when Barbie's little sister showed up.

"You must be Mrs. Delgado." Her voice was so high and she spoke so fast that Kelly wondered if the kid had been sucking helium when no one was paying attention. She opened her mouth to correct her identity, but the girl kept talking.

"We didn't think you'd get here so soon. But this is great. You can start planning the picnic right away. I'll have my mom call. Tonight!"

She ran off, blond hair streaming, heels clopping along the sidewalk like a Clydesdale's hooves.

"Skipper," Kelly muttered.

"What?" Dani was staring at her with a mixture of fear and curiosity. Kelly probably did sound nuts.

"Skipper is Barbie's little sister, right?"

"Who's Barbie?"

Kelly cut her a glance. "You're kidding."

"The only Barbie I ever heard of was some doll. But how can she have a little sister?"

"Why can't she?"

"Because she's not real." Dani rolled her eyes. "Duh."

"Never mind that," Kelly said. "You didn't tell your friends that your mom wasn't coming, did you?"

Dani looked away. "They're not my friends."

"Seemed pretty friendly to me."

"They might be—" she slid a glance toward Kelly "—if they got to know me and liked me before they found out I was weird."

"Who said you were weird?"

"I haven't seen my mom in years. You don't think that's weird? Especially around here?"

Kelly thought it was criminal, but she'd just keep that to herself.

"Sweetheart, your mom's behavior has nothing to do with you."

"You ever live in a small town?"

"Oh, yeah."

"Then why are you lying?"

Kelly contemplated Dani for several seconds. She wasn't going to be able to get much past this child. Not much at all.

"Okay. You're right. Some people might think it's strange you don't have a mom, but they'll get over it."

"Maybe you could just pretend—"

"No, I couldn't."

"Why not?"

"You think your dad wouldn't notice people calling me Mrs. Delgado?"

Dani winced. "I suppose he might."

"Exactly. So you'd better come clean with the locals, angel face, or I will."

"All right." Dani turned and started toward home, dragging her feet.

Kelly ignored the annoying *scritch-thump* of shoes against the pavement. If she commented, she'd only be giving Dani a reason to keep it up.

She kept walking, purposely moving ahead of Dani, letting the girl have some time to herself. Kelly had nearly reached Paramount Street when she realized the *scritch-thump* had stopped, but it hadn't been replaced by anything else.

Spinning around, half-afraid Dani had made a break for it— and wouldn't that just be special, losing the child her first day on the job?—Kelly nearly collapsed in relief to see Dani in front of a big store window a hundred yards away.

Kelly opened her mouth to call out, then noticed the intent expression on Dani's face. Instead, she retraced her steps.

The window was blocked by drapes but printed on the glass in large, flowing, pink script was Michelle's School of Ballet.

Kelly hadn't seen such longing since she'd caught her own reflection in the glass outside the hospital nursery.

"You like ballet?" she blurted.

Dani spun on her heel and walked away.

JUST SEEING the ballet school made Dani feel funny, both sad and happy, like she wanted to cry and she wanted to run and jump and laugh at the same time.

God, she *was* weird. Some days she could hardly stand to listen to the thoughts inside her own head.

Dani loved old musicals. She couldn't get enough of watching the ladies in the beautiful clothes swaying to the music. Sometimes, at Christmas, there'd be ballets on the PBS stations, like *Swan Lake* and *The Nutcracker.*

Dani had tried some of the steps in front of the mirror in her room, humming the tunes as she danced. They'd never stayed in one place long enough for her to take lessons, even if she'd had the guts to ask. One thing Dani remembered about her mother was that she'd loved to dance.

She reached the house long before Ms. Rosholt. The door was locked, so she took the key she wore around her neck and unlocked it, dumping her backpack on the coffee table and heading into the kitchen for milk.

She saw the chicken, the salad and made a face. She didn't like salad, wasn't crazy about chicken, either. But she didn't think Ms. Rosholt would let her eat pizza and Oreos. Not unless it was her birthday, or maybe if she was dyin'.

The front door closed. Dani drained her glass, rinsed it, then set it on the counter. As Ms. Rosholt came into the kitchen, she headed for the living room.

"Homework?" Ms. Rosholt asked.

Dani nodded. She didn't like the way Ms. Rosholt looked at her, as if she could see everything Dani felt and thought. She wasn't used to people staring at her like that. Until now, it had been just her and Dad, and he was so clueless it wasn't even funny. She had a feeling Ms. Rosholt was as far away from clueless as anyone could get.

Dani finished her homework, ate her dinner, managing to choke down the salad after she'd doused it in French dressing, then headed upstairs for a shower.

"You need any help?" Ms. Rosholt asked.

"Not since I was four."

Ms. Rosholt laughed, which startled Dani. Most of her sitters told her to watch her mouth when she said stuff like that. Why she kept saying it, she wasn't quite sure. Probably because she just couldn't help herself.

Dani went to her closet. She needed to figure out what to wear tomorrow, and it had to be something better than what she'd worn so far.

Today, Ashley had stared Dani up then down and said, "Well, I guess that's understandable since your mom just got here. All your good stuff must still be packed."

Ouch.

Dani yanked out the only skirt she owned—her funeral skirt, which was straight and black—then tossed it on the bed. She couldn't wear that to school unless she wanted to go Goth.

Next she searched through her pants. She had jeans and khakis. That was it.

She had enough T-shirts to open a store called Baseball's My Life. Her dad had brought her one from every team he'd played against when he'd played and every team he'd managed against while managing. Would he notice if she burned them?

Then there were the pink shirts her mom sent. Pink made Dani look like a pale little boy too poor to wear anything but his older sister's hand-me-downs.

Dani kicked the wall, then noticed her shoes. They were falling apart. She needed new sneakers, then maybe she could talk Dad into some sandals with a little bit of heel. If it ever got warm enough to wear sandals around here.

She began to pull things out of drawers, holding them up in front of the mirror, then tossing them over her shoulder. Within minutes, her room appeared as if a tornado had hit.

She found some ribbons her mom had sent her once upon a time. "Fat lot of good these'll do me with no hair."

Dani tossed them over her shoulder. When she turned at a noise, it was to see Ms. Rosholt in the doorway, multicolored ribbons trailing from her hand.

KELLY TOOK IN the trashed bedroom. There were clothes everywhere, but this didn't appear to be a temper tantrum. Kelly'd seen those before. Everything got thrown around, not just clothes.

Dani was scowling into the mirror as if she didn't like what she saw.

"Who cut your hair?" Kelly asked.

"I did."

Kelly wasn't surprised.

"Why?"

"So no one could yank on it."

"Kids yank on your hair a lot?"

"Not if it's short."

This wasn't getting them anywhere. Kelly moved farther into the room. "I heard a thud up here, so I came to make sure you hadn't hit your head in the tub."

"I didn't get there yet."

"Were you looking for something?"

"Can't find what you don't have," Dani muttered.

"Which is?"

"Girl clothes."

"What are girl clothes?" Kelly asked, but she already knew. Clothes like the ones the Barbies wore.

"You know." Dani waved her hand at the piles on her bed and floor. "Not these."

"Mmm. Seems like you've got some nice things."

"Gack." Dani mimed throwing up.

Kelly stifled a smile. "Do you want some help?"

At first Dani didn't answer. Then she lifted her head and her dark, serious gaze met Kelly's. "Can you teach me to be a girl?"

Kelly's smile faded. *Poor baby.* "You are a girl, honey."

"I don't know how to dress. I don't know how to walk or talk or—" She threw up her arms. "Anything. I know baseball. Big deal."

"In a few years, a girl who knows baseball is going to be a good thing to be."

"Why?"

"Boys like baseball."

She wrinkled her nose. "Boys are dumb."

"Sounds to me like you know quite a bit about being a girl

already." At Dani's confused glance, Kelly continued. "'Boys are dumb' is the password for the little girls' club. At least until you're twelve." Then it became "boys are dreamy," or the twenty-first-century equivalent.

Dani gave a wan smile. She understood that Kelly was kidding. For seven, she was very intuitive.

"Ashley thinks all my clothes are still in boxes. She's gonna expect me to wear something better now that my mom's here."

"Except I'm not your mom."

Dani sighed. "And I don't have anything better."

Though Kelly didn't want Dani dressing like the other girls, she understood her need to fit in, and with that she could help.

"We can put something together that'll work."

"We can?"

"You bet." Kelly shook her fistful of ribbons. "These aren't just for hair anymore."

"What?"

"Put on your favorite jeans."

Dani dug through the pile and found a faded, slightly threadbare pair. Though Kelly wanted to tell her to choose again, she didn't. People paid good money to buy jeans that scuffed up.

Kelly turned around while Dani slipped them on, then she held up the lengths of ribbon next to Dani's face. "With your coloring, you should wear bright shades—red, purple, orange. Forget pink."

"No problem," Dani muttered.

Kelly withdrew two long red ribbons from the cache, then chose a purple one. She threaded them through the belt loops of the jeans, tied them in a big, bold knot and let the ends hang down. "What do you think?"

Dani's answer was a grin.

"Do you have a white blouse?"

The girl pulled one out of the closet and put it on. Kelly rolled up the cuffs to just below her elbows, then tied the tails into a knot at the waist. To cap off the ensemble, she braided more colorful ribbons and wrapped them around Dani's right wrist.

"One more thing." Kelly ran downstairs and withdrew a travel-size tube of hair gel from her purse. Then she put Dani in front of the mirror and showed her how to fluff her hacked-off locks into a professionally jumbled do.

"Wow," Dani said. "My hair actually looks like it was meant to be this way."

"I think it was," Kelly said. She was darn pleased with herself.

"Thanks, Ms. Rosholt," Dani breathed.

"Call me Kelly."

The phone rang; Dani answered. The joy on her face faded, and Kelly took a step forward, worried there'd been an accident.

Dani waved her off, then took a deep breath. "There's been a mistake, Mrs. Wainright. My mom's not coming." She listened a second. "No, she won't be here next week. She won't be here at all. Ever." Pause. "I'm sorry, too. But I have a…" Her eyes met Kelly's. "A friend who's going to plan the picnic. I'll put Ms. Rosholt on."

Dani held out the phone. Kelly couldn't help herself; she leaned over and kissed Dani on the forehead.

While the girl took a shower, Kelly spoke with Ruth Wainright, agreeing to meet her later in the week and learn the particulars of the picnic.

They were just saying their goodbyes when Kelly had a thought. "Does Ashley take ballet lessons?" she asked.

"There aren't very many girls in Kiwanee who don't," Ruth said. "At the annual Fourth of July celebration, they ride in the parade, then perform. It's adorable."

"Do you happen to have the phone number?"

Ruth did, so as soon as Kelly hung up, she dialed Michelle's School of Ballet and registered Dani for her first class.

CHAPTER FIVE

SCOTT HAD a good day. He'd calmed the nerves of his new pitcher merely by showing him a map. Madison, aka Mad Town, was only half an hour from Kiwanee. If the guy wanted, he could live there and commute. Several players did, though Scott couldn't understand why. After spending one day in Madison, he'd wanted to hop the next plane to the nearest deserted, tropical island.

It wasn't so much the weather that bothered him. Even though he'd grown up in California and spent years in Florida, snow and cold weren't the issue. What drove him nuts were the people, the cars, the buses, the bikes. One look at the streets of Kiwanee, and Scott had known he belonged there.

As he drove into town late that night, Scott cataloged every amenity. School only a few blocks from home. Home only a few blocks from work. Local merchants selling just about everything a person could want. All of his life he'd dreamed of raising a family in a place like this. Now he was here, and it was just him and Dani. He doubted there'd ever be a big family for him. After Kara, he didn't trust people.

Especially curvy, blond people who put themselves ahead of everything else.

He pulled into the driveway, warmed by the lights in the windows, the knowledge that his daughter was here, sleeping in her own bed, instead of someone else's, where he would have to either leave her overnight and go home to a dark, empty house alone, or drag her sleeping body from a couch and juggle her and her things into the car, *then* drive home and do the same thing until he got her inside. He hated that.

He scowled at Kelly Rosholt's SUV, which was parked at the curb. What the hell was she doing here? She reminded him too much of Kara, right down to his annoyingly predictable reaction to her.

Scott climbed out of his car and let himself in the back door. A plate of chicken and pasta sat on the counter, covered with a plastic microwave cover that he hadn't even known he owned. In the refrigerator sat a salad, covered with Saran Wrap. Not very Kara-like at all.

He stepped into the living room but no Ms. Rosholt. After checking all of the downstairs areas, he found her on the second-floor landing, turning away from Dani's room as if she'd just looked in on the child. As he loomed at the top of the steps, she gasped and took a step backward, putting herself between him and Dani.

"It's just me," he said quickly.

"I didn't hear you come in." Her voice trembled a little.

"Everything okay?"

She nodded, then indicated with a flick of her wrist that they should go downstairs to talk. He moved aside, and as she went past he got a whiff of her hair—summer wind with a hint of wild-flowers.

He followed her down, admiring how her legs brushed against the khaki fabric of her pants. Her sweater rode up, revealing a slice of skin a shade lighter than the peach material.

She'd kicked off her shoes somewhere and her feet, clad in sheer stockings, whispered against the carpet. With her matching peach toe- and fingernails, her silver jewelry and her upswept hair, she was overdressed for this job, this town, this house. He needed to remember that while clothes might make a man, they defined a woman.

Kelly Rosholt's definition read: *Don't touch! That means you, Scott.*

"I made you a plate." She retrieved her shoes from where she'd left them under the coffee table.

He gave them a quick once-over and wasn't surprised to see gray-brown pumps with heels too high to chase children. Not that Dani would need chasing. Hopefully.

"Thanks," he said. "Appreciate it."

"No problem."

She gave him a quick rundown on the day. What Dani had eaten, what homework she'd done, the progress on the blasted picnic—as if he cared. Then she hesitated, biting her lip and studying his face.

"What else?" he asked. "Did she break something, take something? Did she get mud on you, herself, the furniture and the walls? Did she dissect a golf ball again? Or was it a football this time? Did she try to boil your purse?"

"What? No." Her expression sharpened. "Has she done those things before?"

"Most of them twice."

"I see."

"What do you see?"

"She wants attention."

Scott shrugged. "All kids do."

"Exactly. Which is why I signed her up for ballet lessons."

Scott blinked. He put his finger in his ear and wiggled. Then he shook his head and gave up. "Why?"

"The other girls go to ballet lessons."

"Dani isn't like other girls."

"Maybe she wants to be."

"Since when?"

"I'm not sure. But she seems to think she's a bad girl."

"She can be."

"Not a 'bad'—" Kelly made quotes with her fingers in the air "—girl, but a bad *girl*. As in, she doesn't know how to be one."

"That doesn't make any sense." He glanced upward, toward where his daughter slept. "She can't not be what she is."

"She's a little girl in a new town, trying to make friends with other little girls. It doesn't work out very well when you're different."

"Being different is special."

"Of course it is, but she needs to find that out for herself. It won't help if her being different means she's alone. You want her to like it here, don't you?"

More than anything.

Scott felt terrible that he'd dragged her from city to city while he worked his way up in the ranks of minor-league management. Dani had acted up; he couldn't blame her. He hoped Kiwanee could be the place where she'd fit in. But he didn't want her to do so at the expense of who she was.

"So I'm supposed to stand by while she behaves like all the other bozos?" he asked. "Does drugs, gets drunk, has sex?"

"They usually frown on that in ballet class."

He stuffed his hands in his pockets and looked away.

"What's wrong with you?" she asked. "It's ballet not thug school. Vee thought it was a good idea."

Slowly, Scott glanced back. "You discussed this with Vee?"

"Seemed the thing to do when she showed up a few hours ago and didn't want to leave." Ms. Rosholt smirked. "Checking up on me?"

"Not really." Her eyebrows lifted. "*You* weren't supposed to be here," he muttered. "Why are you?"

"Careful, I might start to think you don't like me." His gaze flicked to hers, but all he saw was amusement. "Relax," she said. "I'd have done the same thing. Dani's your most precious possession. Making sure she's safe, by whatever means you've got, has to be your number-one priority."

Scott frowned. She didn't seem the type to agree with that. He cast a quick glance at her perfect clothes, her tightly wrapped hair. She seemed more the type to put her career, her condo, her car in front of her child. Then again, if she were going to make a success of her business, she'd have to know and spout the appropriate propaganda.

Man, he sounded cynical. Probably because he was.

"Why are you here?" he repeated.

The earnest expression fled, replaced by a professional mask. "We're short staffed."

"You could have backed out."

Her chin lifted. "Rent a Mommy keeps its promises."

Though Scott wanted to send her on her way, he needed the help. He could put up with how she made him feel—by turns angry, frustrated, annoyed and aroused—for a week, maybe two. Besides, she was here to take care of Dani, the house and the picnic. When he came home, she should go. Like now.

"Well, I won't keep you…" he said.

She made no move to leave. "So you're okay with the ballet lessons?"

"Not really."

Ms. Rosholt let out a frustrated huff. "You should have seen her face when she was staring into the window of the school. She wants this."

"We can't always get what we want."

"Well, Mick, I think she needs it, too."

He sighed and looked upward again.

"What's so bad about ballet lessons for a little girl?" she asked softly.

Scott closed his eyes, remembering how Kara had danced. Graceful and sure, she'd spun and spun in front of the mirrors he'd had installed to make a studio just for her. The first time he'd seen her, Kara had been dancing, bending, kicking, twisting her lithe, perfect body in that skintight leotard. He'd been toast.

"Mr. Delgado?"

He opened his eyes. She'd moved closer. Too close. He could see the brilliant green of her irises, the amazingly long and dark lashes, a sprinkle of freckles across her nose that she'd tried to hide with makeup but been unable to. Why did she have to have freckles?

Her lips, painted the same peach as everything else, were pursed; she seemed worried. How long had he been standing here remembering? Long enough to make her think he was halfway to losing his mind.

"Call me Scott," he said, then wished he hadn't when his voice came out hoarse and low.

"Scott," she repeated, her focus skimming over his lips before jerking back to his eyes. "I'm Kelly."

He took a giant step back as his body responded with a familiar jolt. This was such a bad idea.

"My wife danced," he blurted.

"Ah."

He stiffened as every lustful thought fled. "What does that mean?"

"Nothing."

"You think I pushed my daughter into becoming a tomboy, that I dressed her like a boy, and I taught her to play baseball so that she's nothing like her mother."

Silence fell between them. Instead of losing her temper, instead of meeting his raised voice with her own, Kelly retrieved her purse and coat, then opened the door before pausing to look back. "Sounds to me, Scott, like you think that."

KELLY DROVE away from Kiwanee, once again wishing she didn't have to return. She'd felt something tonight—not only for Dani, but for the father, too—something extremely dangerous. She'd liked him.

Kelly didn't like men.

No, that wasn't true. She *liked* them, as you might like a pleasant acquaintance or a genial elderly uncle, but she never inched closer to them as their eyes fluttered closed and their face took on the glaze of memory. She didn't breathe in their smoky, cinnamon aftershave and stare at the five-o'clock shadow just darkening their jaw. She especially didn't long to comfort them, or to kiss them.

What was it about Scott Delgado that called to the part of herself she'd buried back in Iowa?

"Dammit!" She smacked her palm against the steering wheel.

If it wasn't for Dani, she'd make any excuse so that she didn't have to return to Kiwanee, even if it meant giving up this satellite location for lost.

However, Dani needed her, and a child in need was not something Kelly could ever turn her back on.

She'd just have to stifle whatever bizarre urges she'd felt in that living room with Scott. He was *so* not her type.

"Walking, talking, available," she murmured. Three strikes right off the bat.

Her cell phone rang, blessedly ending her conversation with herself. She glanced at the caller ID and quickly answered. "Paige? What are you doing up at—" she checked the digital display on her dashboard "—one o'clock?"

"The twins have a fever."

"Both of them?" Paige groaned. "Stupid question." The two did everything together, including illnesses. "Guess it's good that you'd already planned to be home for the suspension of Maggie."

"Yeah, things worked out *great,*" Paige muttered. "How are you?"

"Eh."

"That good?"

Kelly smiled. Paige knew her so well. Quickly she told her about Dani, Kiwanee and Dani's dad.

"I haven't heard you talk about a man in that tone of voice in—" Paige broke off. "Come to think of it, I've never heard you talk about a man. At least not like he's a man. You only discuss them in relation to their positions in the food chain—dad, son, brother, grandpa, accounts payable."

Kelly didn't answer. Paige was right.

"All men aren't like your ex," Paige continued. "Someday you'll meet one who has a brain that isn't located between his—"

"I'll talk to you tomorrow," Kelly interrupted, then hung up.

Kelly's story wasn't a new one, although it was probably no longer as common as it had once been, say in the 1950s.

She'd been married at nineteen to her high school sweetheart, not because she'd had to be but because she'd wanted to be. All of her life she'd dreamed of being a wife and mother. Maybe a strange dream for the twenty-first century, but it was her dream.

As a child she'd babied her dolls. When she'd gotten older, she'd been the one all the girls came to for sympathy and advice. She'd enjoyed cooking and cleaning the house. It made her feel good to see wash hanging on the line, soaking up the Iowa summer sun.

Her father had been a farmer; so had her husband. Both Kelly and Pete had wanted a life just like their parents, so shortly after graduation they'd settled into their very own farm, fashioned from a section of Kelly's dad's and Pete's. They'd been happy—at least the first year—then things had begun to go badly.

"You're not pregnant," Pete said.

"Not yet."

"We've never used anything to prevent it. We do it all the time."

She'd laughed and kissed him. "Let's do it again."

So they had—a lot.

Another year passed. They'd gone to the doctor, and Kelly's whole world collapsed. She was barren.

Such an old-fashioned, cold word for such an up-close and personal diagnosis.

She'd spent a week in bed, staring at the ceiling. Pete spent that week in the guest room. She'd been too upset to notice that he could barely bring himself to look at her. But she'd dragged herself upright, and she'd forced herself to be cheerful, to search for another way.

Kelly could still remember what she'd made for dinner that last night—all of Pete's favorites. Pork roast and sauerkraut. Mashed potatoes and gravy. Green beans with baby onions and bacon. She'd bought a bottle of wine in town. They were going to toast their new life.

Pete had other ideas.

From the moment he'd sat at the table, he'd perched on the

edge of his seat as if he wanted to run away. Kelly ignored the warning bells in her head that said something was terribly wrong.

She poured wine, chattering brightly about her day in town, then with a flourish, she handed him the brochure from the adoption agency she'd visited. Strangely enough, he presented her with an envelope at exactly the same time.

Kelly had laughed, thinking how wonderful it was to be so in tune with someone. She'd actually thought Pete was giving her the same brochure. Then she'd opened the envelope and seen the word *divorce*.

While she'd been lying in bed mourning their lost dream, he'd been hiring a lawyer and ending their marriage.

"I want children, and you can't give them to me," he'd said.

"But—" She'd tried to show him the adoption brochure.

He'd tossed it to the ground. "I don't want other people's castoffs. I want children of my own."

"They'd *be* our children."

"No," he'd said coldly. "They wouldn't."

Kelly had packed a bag and gone to live with her parents. Before the divorce was final, Pete was engaged.

Kelly couldn't live in the same town and watch his new wife bear child after child, while she remained alone. She couldn't stand the whispers, the silent, pitying stares. So she'd left everyone she'd ever loved behind, vowing she'd never open herself to that kind of heartache again.

CHAPTER SIX

SCOTT SPENT A RESTLESS night, tormented in turn by flashes of Kelly Rosholt's peach lips and horrific scenarios of muffed double plays and a double-digit error count. Tonight would be his first game as manager of the Warhawks.

Dani was already dressed and slurping cereal when Scott came downstairs.

"What gives?" he asked. Usually he had to pull the covers off her bed and threaten an ice-water shower before she woke up.

She shrugged, a gesture so adult and so Kara-like he winced. He took in the ribbons around her wrist and through her belt loop, the gunk in her hair. She looked adorable—a combination of little girl and fashionista.

"How did you—?" He waved vaguely at her outfit.

"Kelly helped me."

He should have known. At least the woman had managed to make Dani's shorn head appear less like a bad prison haircut.

"Kelly said that you asked her to teach you to be a girl."

Dani hunched her shoulders and practically put her nose into her bowl. "So?"

"I didn't realize..." He paused, tried again. "I didn't know—"

She glanced up. "How could you? You're a *guy.*"

When had that become a bad thing?

"It's okay then?" Dani continued.

Scott blinked. Had he missed something?

"Ballet? I can go, right?"

"If that's what you want."

Her face lit up. "More than just about anything."

How had he not known that? More and more he was beginning to feel he didn't know diddly-squat.

"I need new shoes." Dani stuck out her foot, covered in gray, ripped tennis shoe.

Boy, did she. Another check in the "I suck at being a dad" column.

"I can't tonight," he said. "My game—"

"Kelly can take me. I have to get ballet stuff, too, before class."

"But my game—"

"I'll be done by five. Your game is at six."

Scott reached for his wallet and doled twenties onto the counter. After Dani left, he wrote a note to Kelly, detailing what she needed to buy Dani, then asking her to bring his daughter to the game.

He thought of Kelly Rosholt arriving at the baseball diamond in her too-high heels and her too-perfect suit. Just seeing her there should make him realize once and for all that a woman like her had no place in his life.

BY NOON, Kelly was back on the road to Kiwanee. She'd gone to the office, dealt with what required dealing with and rerouted the calls to Paige's home phone. The twins' fever had broken, but they were tired and cranky. So was Paige.

Kelly had set up a meeting with Ruth Wainright to get her notes and files on the picnic. Since Ashley and Dani both had ballet class at the same time, Kelly arranged to meet Ruth there.

She managed to hustle Dani through the shoe store and purchase new tennies, ballet slippers and a pair of white sandals with tiny etched flowers across the straps.

Then they speed-shopped at the family-owned department store. When Kelly grabbed the required black leotard and pink tights, Dani made a face at the color but didn't argue. Kelly also found a winter coat, on clearance, several pairs of winter leggings and a short yellow skirt, which Dani said was the exact shade of

Warhawk gold. They made it to Michelle's with just enough time to spare so that Dani could change into her dance outfit.

Kelly had expected Michelle to be an anorexic ex-dancer with a pretentious French accent. Instead, she discovered a local mom who'd loved to dance and been good enough that she'd attended the UW for a degree in the same. But Michelle had no desire to head to New York, or even Chicago. Instead, she'd returned to Kiwanee and opened her own school. Girls came from all the neighboring small towns to learn both art and grace.

A small, separate room fronted a large window through which the mothers could watch, since none were allowed inside during lessons. Many brought younger children, who toddled off to play with a pile of toys or pretended to read the well-worn stack of books. The waiting moms said hello to Kelly, then settled in to read a book, knit or watch their children through the window.

Kelly and Ruth took two chairs in a far corner of the room. Ruth was a tall, slim, efficient woman who told Kelly to call her if she had any questions. Kelly took a quick look through the file and was impressed with her notes.

"This seems pretty comprehensive to me," she said.

"The file I got was pathetic. I swore the next person wouldn't have such a rough time."

"I was thinking of going with a Mexican fiesta for the theme," Kelly said.

Ruth's forehead creased. "Theme?"

"You don't have a theme for the picnic?"

"Mother's Day."

"That's an occasion, not a theme."

Ruth shrugged. "I was lucky to get the balloons ordered and the games organized."

"Food?"

"Hot dogs and brats. I bought them from the Save U. Had the men grill."

"Has anyone ever done anything different?"

Ruth tilted her head, narrowed her eyes and thought back. "Once we grilled chicken."

"In other words, you grill," Kelly said.

"The point of a Mother's Day picnic is that the mothers don't cook. Which means—"

"Someone has to, and the men know how to grill."

"Exactly." Ruth beamed. "Plus, we need to stay within the budget the city gives us."

"Kiwanee pays for the picnic?" Kelly had figured everyone who attended contributed a little, and whatever was taken in was used for the next year.

"It's tradition. After Kiwanee was founded, they always had a spring get-together, a way for everyone who'd been inside and isolated all winter to reconnect before the summer planting season began. Eventually the spring get-together became the Mother's Day picnic."

"What's the budget?" Kelly asked.

Ruth pointed to a number on the first page. "That's for everything. Food, decorations and entertainment."

"Entertainment? Like games?"

"Or music, a magician, maybe a family-style comedian. Something to make the day special."

"Okay." With that budget, the Mexican fiesta was out, but she'd think of something.

Absently, Kelly turned toward the window. All the mothers had left their seats and now stared through the glass. A few whispered, others pointed, several more glanced in her direction, then quickly back.

Panicked, Kelly got to her feet, ignoring the file that spilled to the floor. She hurried across the room and peered in, terrified she'd find Dani on the floor broken, bleeding or both while she'd been discussing the merits of piñatas.

However, Dani wasn't on the floor. No one was. The class danced and, at first, Kelly couldn't tell which girl was Dani. They all moved so smoothly. When she did find her, she was amazed.

"Wow," Kelly whispered. Not only had Dani caught on to the

steps her first day, but she'd caught on better than anyone in the room.

She was wonderful, stunning, a talented natural.

When the song was over, Dani appeared dazed, as if she hadn't known she could do that. She caught Kelly's eye. The joy on the child's face started a warm glow in Kelly's chest. She gave Dani a thumbs-up.

For the rest of the lesson, Kelly watched the tiny dancers, trying to stop her heart from breaking at the thought of all she'd lost that she'd never even had.

DANI COULDN'T BELIEVE she was here, in ballet class. And she was *good*.

But that wasn't what made her stomach all floopy. Turning around and seeing Kelly in the window had.

She hadn't expected her rental mom to watch her. Kelly was meeting with Mrs. Wainwright about the picnic. But when Dani had finished the first dance and known that she'd nailed it, she'd wanted Kelly to see. When she'd turned, Kelly had been there, and her face had looked as happy as Dani felt.

The class ended. Ashley and her friends gathered around Dani. "You want to come to my house?" Ashley asked.

"My dad's first game is tonight."

"You're going to watch baseball?" Ashley's nose wrinkled as if Dani had admitted to rolling in swamp water because she liked the smell.

"Yes."

Dad would be upset, maybe even mad, if she didn't go to the game. If he got the same great feeling from seeing Dani in the stands when he did his favorite thing as Dani had gotten from Kelly watching her do hers, she understood why he always wanted her there. She couldn't take that away from him, and she didn't really want to.

"Hey, twinkle toes." Kelly motioned for Dani to hurry up.

Dani grinned. She liked all the names Kelly called her, especially *sweetheart* and *honey*. Kelly said them as if she really meant them, too.

"You were amazing." Kelly helped Dani into her new coat, then handed her the new tennies. Dani couldn't walk around town in the ballet slippers, even if it wasn't cold enough to freeze her feet off if she tried.

"Thanks," Dani murmured, uncertain how to handle the attention, uncertain what to say to such compliments. She *was* amazing, but if she said that, everyone would call her stuck-up, which was almost as bad as people asking if she was a boy.

"We need to hurry home so you can change, eat and get to the field."

Hearing Kelly use the word *home* gave Dani a wiggly, warm feeling in her chest, one she'd never had before.

At the house, Kelly made her a grilled-cheese sandwich and heated tomato soup while Dani tried to figure out what to wear. She knew her dad wanted her to come in the kid-size baseball uniform, but she just couldn't stand to dress like a boy again. So she stared at the blue-striped pants and told herself she wouldn't cry.

"Something wrong?" Kelly stood in the doorway.

Dani looked at Kelly then back at the outfit on the bed.

"Oh," Kelly said.

How did she know what Dani was thinking without her saying a word? It was both spooky and fantastic.

"What should I do?" Dani asked. "I don't want to hurt Dad's feelings."

"Of course not. Sometimes men are—"

"Stupid," Dani muttered.

Kelly laughed. "Well, let's say slow. They try, but they miss."

"Just a bit outside," Dani said in her best Bob Uecker voice.

Kelly's forehead creased. "What?"

"*Major League*. Baseball movie. It's Dad's favorite."

"Oh, yeah. I saw that. Good stuff." Kelly fingered the baseball pants. "Let's mix and match, hmm?" At Dani's confused expression she picked up the blue-and-yellow jersey. "You were right about that skirt being the same shade."

Dani started to see where Kelly was headed. She removed the new skirt from the bag and slipped it on, tugging first a turtle-neck, then the jersey over her head. Kelly had already pulled yellow and blue ribbons from the pile and made another bracelet. She handed Dani a pair of blue tights, then found a pair of white socks in Dani's drawer and showed her how to fold the tops over and over into anklets. Last but not least, came her shiny new tennies and the baseball cap.

"Wear it backwards." Kelly set the hat on her head.

Dani's eyes met Kelly's in the mirror, and together they grinned.

As they drove to the baseball field, Dani remained silent. It had never occurred to her that she might want a new mom. She'd been too busy hoping the old one would show up.

But she had to admit that wasn't going to happen, and she didn't much care anymore. She couldn't imagine her mother watching her at ballet, planning the Mother's Day picnic, show-ing her how to dress in a way that was a mixture of girl stuff and Dani, so that Dani felt both comfortable and pretty.

Kelly understood her better in a day than her real mom could understand her ever. Dani knew this, even though she couldn't remember hardly anything about her mother at all.

Dani glanced at Kelly and discovered something else. She wanted a mom, and not just for a day, a week, even a month. She wanted one forever.

She wanted this one.

CHAPTER SEVEN

"O'ER THE LA-AND of the free. And the home of the brave."

The crowd erupted into cheers as the last notes of "The Star Spangled Banner" faded on the crisp evening air.

Scott was impressed with the number of spectators. He'd been told that a large percentage of the town showed up for games, but he hadn't really believed it. By his estimatation there had to be two hundred people in the stands. Considering the temperature hovered in the vicinity of forty degrees he wondered if everyone had lost their marbles.

Scott was scanning the bleachers when Kelly arrived with Dani. He lifted his hand, waving them over, but Dani tugged on Kelly's arm, whispered something, and they went to sit behind home plate. It was then that he saw Dani wasn't wearing the uniform he'd had made for her, or at least not all of it. Instead, she resembled a minicheerleader. He'd be concerned that she was going to freeze in that skirt, but she had on blue leggings and a turtleneck sweater that appeared pretty toasty.

"I'll be right back." He handed the roster to Vee and hurried over to Dani and Kelly. Leaning down, he tweaked his daughter's nose. "You look great."

"I do?" Her eyes widened.

"Always."

She beamed and straightened her bracelet. The ever-changing rainbow of ribbons around her tiny wrists were starting to grow on him.

He turned to Kelly. "I didn't mean for you to stay. Dani can sit behind the dugout."

"I love baseball."

"You do?"

Kelly laughed. "Don't sound so shocked. We'll have a great time. Won't we, kidikins?" She turned to Dani, and the two of them shared a smile that somehow made Scott feel left out.

"Okay," he said, backing up. "I'll talk to you after the game."

"Go, Warhawks!" the two of them shouted, and the entire crowd echoed the sentiment.

Scott had thought just seeing Kelly in his environment would force him to realize she was not meant for this town or for him. Unfortunately, it had the opposite effect.

Though she'd worn jeans today, she'd donned boots in deference to the cold. They were black, high-heeled, shiny things that drew the eye to the slim length of her calf. What was it about high heels that made a woman's legs go on forever?

She'd also let her hair down so that it spilled around her shoulders in a fall of gold. Her blue sweater managed to be both bulky and clingy, the material soft and fleecy. He wanted to touch it, and then he wanted to touch her.

Gritting his teeth, Scott turned away.

Years of discipline allowed him to do his job each and every inning, but in between he was distracted by the sound of her voice. Instead of standing out like the outsider she was, Kelly talked with everyone; she laughed. She cheered on his team and she seemed to know every player's name, which wasn't as amazing as it sounded, considering the program in her hand.

Several other little girls arrived and ran straight to Dani, giggling and shrieking. What was it about little-girl shrieks? They seemed to have a decibel range all their own, one that made Scott want to howl like a tortured dog.

Just when he was about to make Vee put a stop to the noise, Kelly organized the throng into a pint-size cheerleading squad. She taught them several cheers, and within a few innings he found himself enjoying the rhythmic chants. Scott had to admit, they were damn cute and Dani, right in the middle of them, seemed happier than he could ever recall her being. He'd made the right move in coming here.

He'd believed that, but he'd also been uncertain. Had he made the decision based on his own needs and wants and not Dani's? He'd been worried she wouldn't fit in, that she'd be miserable. But they'd only been here a week, and she'd already made friends.

Of course she'd changed quite a bit in that week, and he wasn't sure how he felt about that. She'd been his baseball buddy, his best pal. Now she was a little girl, heading far too fast toward young woman and making him realize how very little he knew about the species.

"Yer out!"

The umpire's exclamation had everyone on the bench leaping up. Vee pumped Scott's hand enthusiastically, then said, "What the hell?" and hugged him, too. All the little cheerleaders started shrieking again.

Scott had won his first game as a minor-league manager.

KELLY STARED at the dugout. The happiness and pride on Scott's face made her chest go as tight as it had when she'd seen Dani's expression after her first dance. She was getting too involved with the Delgados.

She needed to remember that she was only a rental. This wasn't her family, and it never would be.

She'd made a mistake staying for the game, but she did like baseball. She'd also wanted to make sure that Dani was all right. Leaving her charge on the bench behind the dugout wasn't responsible, even though she knew the child would be fine considering she had over two hundred babysitters. The people of Kiwanee had accepted the Delgados as if they'd lived here all their lives.

Most small towns were a little standoffish. However, Kiwanee depended on the income brought in by the Warhawks. Which meant they welcomed anyone associated with the team—players, managers, coaches, office staff—as if they were born-and-bred Kiwaneeans.

"Kelly!"

Dani threw her arms around Kelly's waist and pressed her sweaty little head into Kelly's chest, leaving a damp imprint on her sweater. Though she'd just vowed to pull back emotionally, Kelly found herself hugging the child, never wanting to let go.

"That was the best!"

"Glad you had fun." Kelly forced herself to release the girl. "We'd better get you home."

"Are you coming tomorrow?" Dani asked.

"Tomorrow's Saturday. Your dad will be home."

"So?"

"You won't need me. I'll be back on Monday."

The weekend had come at an opportune time. The separation would do all of them good.

"Did everyone hear?" Kelly turned to the woman in the stands—Susan Something—with whom she'd shared chatter and cheers during the game. "There's a snowstorm on the way."

"How much?" Kelly asked.

"A foot by morning." Susan lifted her face to the sky and inhaled. "Can't you smell it?"

Kelly didn't smell anything but trouble.

By the time she turned into the driveway, fat flakes were tumbling down.

"You'd better get dressed for bed," she said, staring out the window with a frown.

"I don't *have* to go to bed, do I? Can't I wait for Dad? It's Friday night."

"I suppose that would be all right. Just get into your pajamas, and we'll watch TV until he comes."

Dani couldn't have been upstairs ten minutes. When she came down, she joined Kelly at the window. "Holy cow!"

An inch of snow already covered the green grass and dusted the bright yellow daffodils shivering in front of the house across the street. The thought of driving to Madison, on a two-lane highway in this mess made Kelly shiver, too.

"Can I go out and play?" Dani asked.

"No."

"Why not?"

Kelly could tell by the tone of Dani's whine that she was over-tired. If she could get the child to sit down for five minutes, she'd fall asleep.

"Your dad will want to take you out the first time. We'll wait for him."

Dani pouted, but only for a second. "Can we watch *Beauty and the Beast?*"

"You bet."

The two of them curled together on the couch, tugging a blanket draped at one end over their legs. The next thing Kelly knew, she heard a bang in the distance, then felt a sudden chill. A shadow fell over them, and she pulled Dani closer.

But the shadow lifted the girl and took her away. Kelly reached out, but she was alone. She was always alone.

She awoke with a gasp. The movie was over; the screen had gone blue, and Dani was gone. Beyond the window the world was a swirl of white.

The stairs creaked. Scott appeared in the entryway to the living room.

"I put her in bed," he said softly. "She didn't even move."

"Big day." Kelly swung her legs onto the floor and stood. "I need to go."

"You can't."

"It's that bad?" she asked, though she knew it was.

"Took me twenty minutes to get home. You can stay in the guest room tonight."

"Thanks." Though being here with Scott in the dark made her nervous, the thought of driving through the storm, probably ending up in a ditch or worse, terrified her.

He went to the window and peered out. "Vee said they won't plow until the storm's gone through, probably sometime tomor-

row. By evening the temps are supposed to be in the midfifties."
Scott turned away from the glass. "Dani's never seen snow. Tomorrow will be fun for her."

"For you, too."

"I've seen snow, even made a few snowballs in my time."

"In California?"

Scott shook his head. "When I was still pitching, we had
spring games in Chicago, Milwaukee, even St. Louis, and sometimes we'd get caught in one of these freak storms. The team
would go out and—" He stopped, then shrugged sheepishly.

"You played in the snow."

"We didn't have much else to do when we were stranded in
a strange town. Plus, a lot of us were from warmer climates—if
not the Southern states, then the Caribbean. We didn't get too
many chances to build a snow fort."

The thought of Scott Delgado building a snow fort, or having
a snowball fight with other major-league players in snowbound
cities across the upper Midwest made her smile. The image was
charming. Too charming.

"Have you had a chance to contact any nanny services?" she
blurted.

"No."

"Do you want me to?"

He moved closer. "You that anxious to leave us?"

Something in his voice made her pause. He sounded almost
sad, but what did he have to be sad about? From the beginning
she'd gotten the impression he didn't really like her much at all.

"Rent a Mommy is only a temporary solution," Kelly said.
"You need permanent help."

"Something permanent would be nice," he murmured.

He was now so near she had to tilt her head to see his face.

"Dani and I haven't had anything permanent in our lives
except for each other in so long I'm not sure what permanent
means anymore. Any nanny I hire won't be permanent in the true
sense of the word."

"That's true."

Kelly experienced a twinge of unease at their isolation, along with an unexpected thrill of awareness as his body hovered inches from hers.

The blanket of snow just outside the window caused a silvery glow to filter in, casting his face in blue shadow. She could see the fine rasp of his beard, the glint of his dark gaze. She felt the heat of his skin, a contrast to the chill that frosted the air outside.

"I want Dani to feel safe and loved," he said.

"She does."

His head came up; their noses brushed. Kelly caught her breath as their eyes met, and something wild flared between them, something born of this storm, birthed in the isolation of this night.

She kissed him, or maybe he kissed her. She could never be sure. It didn't really matter. She hadn't been kissed in so long, her legs nearly gave out from the sheer pleasure of it.

His mouth was warm and soft. His big, rough hand cupped her head, tilting her so he could explore every corner with his tongue.

She should have stopped the embrace immediately, but she couldn't. She would later realize the idea never even crossed her mind. All she'd thought was "yes," all she'd wanted was more.

Tentatively she touched his tongue with hers, running her fingers through his hair, knocking his goofy Warhawks hat onto the floor.

She wasn't sure how far things would have gone if the wind hadn't battered the house, taking hold of the screen door and rattling it as if someone were coming inside.

They sprang apart like teenagers caught necking by their parents, then stood staring at each other wide-eyed as the snow tumbled down.

Kelly found her voice first. "Where the hell did that come from?"

"I don't know."

"I didn't think you even liked me."

"I didn't think I did, either."

"What happened then?"

"You," he began, then stopped. "We...well, I—" He leaned down and snatched his hat off the floor, shoving it back on his head with a scowl. "Hell."

"That about sums it up."

"Can you stay another week?" Her eyebrows lifted at the sudden, out-of-place question. "I have to go to Nebraska. It would really help if you were here for Dani."

And because she couldn't say no to that, Kelly had to say, "Yes."

CHAPTER EIGHT

MORNING DAWNED, and the snow still fell. Kiwanee had bypassed the predicted foot about half a foot ago.

Since he hadn't fallen asleep for hours after he'd kissed the rental mommy, Scott slept late.

He'd always been somewhat disgusted by men who had affairs with their nannies. What kind of guy did that?

A desperate, pathetic one.

He had no excuse. He *was* desperate and pathetic, and he'd been unable to stop himself from touching her as they stood bathed in the eerie, white reflection of the snow.

Snow in April. He'd known it could happen. But last night the storm had seemed surreal, making everything that happened the same. Had he really kissed Kelly Rosholt?

Scott glanced down, unsurprised to find the quilt across his lap bowed like a pup tent.

Yep. He'd not only kissed her, but he'd wanted very badly to do more than that, had dreamed of it, along with the freckles across the bridge of her nose, the entire three hours that he'd managed to sleep. He couldn't stop thinking about those freckles, her lips, the—

"Stupid," he muttered. How was he going to face her this morning without remembering what he'd dreamed of doing to her last night?

"Dad!"

The door to his bedroom slammed open, and he flipped onto his stomach, biting back a curse as he landed on the center pole of his steadily deflating pup tent.

"Kelly's making pancakes. She says get up. Time to build a snow fort."

In spite of himself, Scott smiled. The idea of making a snow fort with his daughter—hell, with Kelly Rosholt—was too enticing to resist. He took in his daughter's pajamas. "You'd better get dressed."

"You, too." Dani scampered from the room, thundering down the hallway with the grace of a wounded water buffalo.

"And she wants to be a ballerina," he muttered as he turned on the shower.

Ten minutes later, he hesitated outside the kitchen door. The scent of coffee and pancakes, the sizzle of bacon made his mouth water. He could hear Dani chattering to Kelly about what kind of fort they were going to make. It sounded complicated. He took a deep breath and walked in.

His gaze went to Kelly's. He waited for the narrowing of the eyes, the tightening of the lips, the cold shoulder. Instead, she smiled, and something in his stomach jittered. He couldn't help but smile back.

Kelly poured a cup of coffee and set it on the table, then picked up her own and sipped. She contemplated Scott over the rim.

"This looks great," he managed. "Thanks."

"Anytime." Kelly sat at the table, and the three of them ate breakfast. There was no awkwardness. If Scott didn't know better, he'd think he'd imagined the whole thing.

Dani finished and jumped up. "I'm going to get my boots."

"Plate in the sink," Kelly said.

"'Kay!" Seconds later thumps and thuds sounded from the hall.

"About last night," Scott began.

"Forget it."

Scott wasn't sure he could. "But—"

"Let's just have a nice day in the snow without worrying about anything else."

Dani appeared in the doorway. "Come on! It'll melt before you two are ready."

Kelly laughed. "Okay. We're coming."

Quickly they cleaned the kitchen. Scott loaded the dishwasher; Kelly wiped the table, counter and stove. They worked together easily and well, as if they'd been doing it for years.

Kelly kept a winter coat, snow boots, gloves and a hat in her SUV. "You never know when you might need them," she said when Scott lifted a brow.

Which made him incredibly nervous. What if he were driving somewhere with Dani and the car broke down? What if the temps went below zero, and they had no gloves or hats? What if a freak snowstorm stranded them, and they died from exposure?

He'd never had these ghoulish thoughts until he'd had a child. Now he had them constantly. He was the only person between Dani and disaster. His parents had died before she was born; he had no brothers or sisters. Kara certainly couldn't be counted on. No, Scott had to be prepared.

He made a mental note to stow extra winter apparel in his own car—he also made a mental note to buy some—along with umbrellas, bottled water, a first-aid kit....

He was probably going to need a bigger car.

They tumbled into the chilly morning air. The sun ricocheted off the carpet of snow and sent sharp shards of light into his eyes. Scott staggered to his car for his sunglasses.

The temperature was already climbing. By tomorrow the snow would be well on its way to water.

"What first, ladies? Snowman or snow fort?"

A snow*ball* hit him in the head.

He tilted his chin toward his chest and stared at a wide-eyed Dani over the tops of his glasses.

"Oops," she said, and then she ran.

The snowball fight involved many shrieks and giggles, Kelly proving that she could still hit that extra decibel, particularly when Scott closed in with a handful of snow.

She was also sneaky, and she could wind up and pitch a snowball nearly as well as Scott could. Within half an hour, Kelly was declared the winner.

By then the yard was trampled so badly it seemed as if a herd of whitetail had wintered there. They opted to build a snowman instead of a snow fort, since most of the snow had been tossed through the air, with a good portion of it exploding in the street and on the roof.

"Are you cold?" Scott asked, taking in Dani's red nose.

She shook her head, then bit her lip as she tried to roll the base of the snowman evenly as Kelly had shown her. Wherever the great, white ball rolled, Dani left a track of wet, green grass behind. The snow was melting fast.

Scott watched Dani and Kelly. The two of them chattered and laughed. They consulted on the best way to lift the body of the snowman onto the base, then argued about how big the head should be. Their voices rose and fell, their giggles blended. People walking by on the sidewalk waved, greeting them all by name and smiling fondly. Scott looked at the town, the house and his daughter.

The only thing missing was a wife.

DANI HAD WANTED to see snow. Now that she had, she loved it. Although she could understand where a whole winter of white might get boring.

But today the piles and piles had been nothing but fun. By the time they went inside, they'd had a snowball fight, and they'd built a snow family—a dad, a mom and a kid. Dani had wanted a snow dog, too, but Kelly had put her foot down about that.

"I'm not that talented, girlie-Q." Then she'd kissed Dani on her ice-cold nose and said, "Who wants hot chocolate?"

After Dani had taken a warm bath, she sipped hot chocolate while Dad made their first fire in the fireplace. He wasn't very good at it. Kelly had to help him.

At first they'd laughed together, then they got kind of quiet. Then they kept looking at each other for a long time without talking, then they'd look away and both would talk at once. It was strange.

The three of them spent the rest of the day playing games and watching movies. Outside, the snow melted off the roof with a steady *drip-drip*. When the sun went down, their snow family was leaning so far to the right that by morning they'd topple over.

Dani fell asleep with her head on Kelly's leg about halfway through the Brewers game. The Milwaukee-based team had no problem playing baseball during the snowstorm since they'd put in a retractable dome the last time they'd built a stadium. The announcer did say, though, that the stands were nearly empty, the locals opting to stay off the roads or maybe just too busy shoveling.

"Bed for you." The world tilted as her dad lifted Dani into his arms and took her upstairs.

She'd always loved being carried to bed. Sometimes, when she was little, she would pretend to be asleep just so Dad would have to hold her.

They reached her room, and he bent to place her on the bed. Dani clung to his neck.

"Hey." He sat on the mattress. "Thought you were out for the count."

"I woke up." She pressed her cheek to his.

"You upset because I have to leave tomorrow?" His arms tightened, and he pulled Dani into his lap. "I'll be back at the end of the week."

She shook her head. "I'll be okay."

"Of course you will. You can call me anytime you want."

Dani hesitated. There was something she wanted to ask, but she wasn't sure how.

"Dad?" she began, and he tilted his head, waiting. "I like Kelly."

"Me, too," he said.

"Can we keep her?"

CHAPTER NINE

THE DAYS SCOTT SPENT away brought Dani and Kelly closer together. Kelly had suspected it would, but she hadn't been prepared for just how much she would come to love the girl, the community, the life that wasn't really hers.

Ever since she and Scott had kissed, she'd been pretending it hadn't happened. She wasn't sure what else to do. Kissing her employer. Sheesh, what had she been thinking?

She hadn't been. She'd only been feeling—for the first time in years.

Scott left late Sunday morning, and because of her confusion, Kelly wasn't sorry to see him go. She threw herself into the job and pushed the feelings, the memories, ever deeper.

Sunday afternoon, she went grocery shopping for the week; Sunday night, she helped Dani plan her outfit for the next day. More ribbons, another pink T-shirt, jeans and her new sandals. The snow was gone. High temperature for Monday would be in the low seventies.

"Kelly, will you come and watch my softball practice tomorrow?"

"Of course, pumpkin. Can't wait. You like softball?"

"Sure. Although it's dumb that girls have to play softball instead of baseball. But it's fun enough."

At practice, held in the same park that would host the Mother's Day picnic, the sun shone so brightly it seemed to mock the few piles of snow still lurking beneath bushes and on the curbs lining the parking lot.

Kelly sat with the other mothers and enjoyed the warm spring breeze and the companionship. She'd spent the past five years with only Paige for a friend. Not that there was anything wrong with that.

Dani wound up and pitched the huge white ball over the plate. The batter swung and missed. Dani appeared as comfortable covered in mud as she did in a leotard, and she was fitting into Kiwanee better every day. Despite Scott's fears that the other girls would corrupt his daughter, she seemed to be the one doing the corrupting.

At ballet, several of the girls wore multicolored ribbons as bracelets. At softball practice, two of the ballerinas showed up in the outfield and another occupied second base.

Dani's circle of friends grew. The night before Scott was scheduled to return from his trip, she was invited to a slumber party at Ashley's house.

Kelly dropped her off, choking up when Dani hugged her, then kissed her on the lips, before shouting "See ya!" and running for the house.

Kelly made a detour past the park. She had most of the picnic planned. This year there'd be a pig roast instead of a brat fry or a chicken grill. Paige knew a guy, who knew a guy, who had a pig farm and managed a roasting business on the side. Still, she needed to come up with something…

"Special," Kelly whispered, staring through the window at the spring-green park. She still had nothing and time was running short.

Kelly returned to the house and tried to watch television. Then she tried to read a book, but she was restless, so she dialed Paige.

"I was just going to call you," her friend said. "I found a nanny."

"I didn't ask you to."

"That's why I'm so good at this job. Before you've even asked, I've already done it."

The thought of turning Dani, of turning Scott, over to a stranger made Kelly a little sick to her stomach.

"You're embarrassing me with all that sloppy gratitude," Paige said.

"Sorry," Kelly muttered. "Thanks."

"What's wrong with you?" Paige demanded. "You didn't want to go there. You didn't want to stay. I thought you'd be jumping and dancing."

Mention of dancing made Kelly want to cry.

"I am," she lied. "I'll tell Sc—" She paused, then tried again. "I'll tell Mr. Delgado about the nanny, see when he can do an interview."

"Great. Did you talk to the pig farmer?"

For a second, Kelly's mind blanked. Why on earth would she talk to a pig farmer? Then she remembered the picnic, the pig roast.

"Yes. Everything's set. It was the perfect idea for this project."

"I knew it would be. So, what did you think of the guy?"

"What guy?"

Paige's long-suffering sigh came over the wire. "What guy do you think? The pig farmer."

"He seemed to know his business."

"He's hot."

Kelly had an image of a sweaty man in striped coveralls next to a blazing fire pit full of pig. Who wouldn't be hot?

"The farmer," Paige said, when Kelly didn't answer. "He is a grade A, choice cutie. And he's single. Want him?"

"Me?" Kelly squeaked. "No thanks. Hey, if he's so great, why don't you take him?"

"Not my type."

"But he's mine?"

Just because she'd been married to a farmer once didn't mean she wanted to be married to one again. Hell, she didn't want to be married at all.

Liar, her mind whispered.

Her mind was right. Despite everything, deep in the most secret part of her, she wanted to be married with children as much now as she'd wanted it then. That it wasn't going to happen only made her want it all the more.

"It's time you started dating, Kelly."

Kelly doubted it would ever be time. She just couldn't open herself to the disappointment, the inevitable pain. Besides, lately, thoughts of dating, of men, of sex all led to one thing.

Scott.

Kelly rubbed her forehead.

"I'll talk to you tomorrow, Paige." She hung up even though her friend was still talking.

The house was clean, no child to watch. Television sucked, and her book was boring. She might as well go to bed.

Kelly wandered through the house, turning off the few remaining lights. She stood in the living room for several minutes, letting the quiet wash over her. Just as she headed upstairs, a thump sounded on the back porch. It was long past the time for visitors.

"Probably a cat," she murmured, even as she inched closer to the kitchen.

A shadow drifted beyond the window—tall, hulking, man shaped—and Kelly began to back toward the portable phone she'd set on the coffee table.

Before she could get there and dial 9-1-1, the doorknob turned. Kelly's breath caught.

She'd locked that. She was certain of it.

Frantically she glanced around for a place to hide. Her gaze landed on Dani's softball bat. She snatched it up just as the click of the latch was followed by the muted thud of footsteps on the kitchen tile.

Her gaze went to the front door. No time to run, no time to hide. Only time to—

Kelly wrapped both hands around the bat and waited.

SCOTT HAD MISSED Dani. He'd missed Kiwanee, his house, his office. If he were honest, he'd missed Kelly, too.

So he'd hopped an earlier plane out of Omaha. Some of his

team had came back with him, and some opted to stay one more night in the hotel and return as planned in the morning.

Of course, the flight was late leaving Nebraska, even later landing at Dane County Regional Airport. By the time he'd retrieved his bag and his car, then driven to Kiwanee, all the lights in his house were off. Well, at least he'd see Dani first thing in the morning.

The trip had been a good one. The Warhawks had only lost one game of five. For a road trip, heck for a home stand, that was impressive.

Scott paused to dig out his house key, then opened the kitchen door. The place was eerily silent.

He stepped inside and crossed the room, planning to go upstairs and check on his girls. The thought made him pause. When had he begun to think of Kelly as his?

Had it been when he'd kissed her? Or maybe when he'd dreamed of doing more.

He heard a muffled screech, like a bare foot on hardwood. He stepped from the kitchen into the hall, saw movement, felt a whoosh of air and ducked.

The bat smacked into the wall behind him.

"Scott!" Kelly's voice was horrified. "I thought—I'm sorry."

The tremor in her voice made him panic. "Where's Dani?" he demanded.

"She's—"

Terrified, he snatched the bat from her limp hands and tossed it onto the carpet. Then he grabbed her wrist and yanked her against him. "What happened?" He tightened his grip. "What's wrong?"

All sorts of horrors ran through his head in hideous, living color. Were there murderers, kidnappers, bank robbers on the loose? Drug dealers? Zombies? Aliens? What could possibly have happened to make his cool, calm rental mommy flip out?

"N-nothing," she managed.

"Where's Dani?" he asked again.

"At a slumber party."

He searched her face. The house was dark, the only light that of the full moon shining in through the front windows. Still he could see her expression fairly well, and she seemed to be telling the truth.

"You're alone?"

She nodded. "I got spooked. The back door, it was locked and then—" She stopped. "What are you doing here, Scott?"

"I—" He took a breath, released her and leaned against the wall, trying to calm his racing heart. She'd scared the crap out of him.

"Scott?" Kelly moved forward.

"I'm okay." He lifted a hand to ward her off. Instead, she took his in hers, holding on as if he were a single slim rope in a wild and stormy sea.

Reaching out, she touched his cheek. Suddenly he couldn't breathe again.

She felt it, too, the strange connection between them. The certain and yet bizarre knowledge born in the solitude and the darkness of this night, that they'd been destined to meet, to love Dani, perhaps to love each other. The surety that they were meant to kiss—right now, right here, like this.

CHAPTER TEN

KELLY HAD TO kiss Scott. She had to touch him to make certain he was real. She had to press her mouth to his and make everything all right.

They'd scared each other badly. Foolishly, true. But foolishness didn't make her legs tremble any less or her heart pump any slower. The only thing that could was him.

She still held his hand, their fingers linked together, palm to palm. He still leaned against the wall as if he needed its sturdiness at his back just to remain standing. Kelly moved in, trapping him there—he didn't seem to mind—his eyes fluttering closed as her body skimmed the surface of his.

The taste of him was familiar, his scent one she already knew. His free hand found the curve of her waist, pulling her more firmly against him.

Her arm looped his neck; her head tilted just so and he opened to her, his tongue sliding along the fullness of her bottom lip before he tugged at it with his teeth. The sensation shot straight to her toes, stopping at key points along the way, making parts of her tingle that hadn't tingled in years.

She'd always been tall, been mortified by it as a teen, not wild about it as an adult, but now, being tall was great. Because it meant she could press against him without even rising onto her toes and multiply those tingles where it mattered the most.

He disentangled their hands, and she moaned a protest into his mouth, one that turned into a moan of pleasure when he grasped her hips and yanked her more tightly against him. She leaned into his body, pressing him into the wall, increasing the pressure until they both gasped.

Scott dragged his lips away, stilling her with a gentle hand. "Whoa," he muttered, then leaned his forehead into hers. "Hold on, or we'll be done before we start."

Her gaze met his, so close his eyes looked black in the shadows of the night. "*Are* we going to start?" she whispered.

"Yes," he said simply.

"It's been a long time for me."

"Me, too."

She straightened, capturing his hand again. "Let's not wait any longer."

Together they climbed the stairs, and he drew her into his room. She was both nervous and excited. She wanted him, and then again, she didn't. What if—?

She cut that thought off before it could form. If she kept thinking about the future, that would lead to thoughts of the past—a definite mood killer.

Before her mind could run away with her resolve, she began to unbutton her blouse.

"Let me," he murmured, nudging her fingers aside.

Slowly her shirt opened. He watched her emerge, inch by inch, his face reflecting a fascination that called to her own. When his dark head lowered, and his lips followed the path of his fingers, goose bumps rippled across her skin, and she shuddered with delicious abandon.

He popped the catch on her jeans, holding her gaze as he lowered the zipper, then slipped his hand inside and stroked her just once through the satiny slip of her panties. She arched into him, and he kissed her, hard, mouth open, tongue searching for hers.

Clothes flew after that, each of them helping the other. They fell onto the bed in a tangle of arms and legs, touching, exploring, tasting.

Fascinated with the sleek expanse of his skin over the rippling muscles in his chest and abdomen, she memorized the feel of his body with her fingertips, the curve of his hip with her tongue.

When he rolled away, rustling in his bedside table, then muttering and tossing things to the floor, at first she didn't know what he was searching for. She'd never been with anyone but her husband, and they'd had no use for condoms.

The rasp of the packet made her flinch. She bit her lip to keep from saying he didn't need one, because he did. She knew that. She might have been sheltered once, but she wasn't stupid. Just because there was no possibility of pregnancy didn't mean there wasn't a possibility of something else.

He came back murmuring her name, nuzzling her breasts, and she welcomed him into her with a gasp of surprise and joy. She'd needed this; she'd needed him, and he was there.

Slow and deep, they rocked together. When the climax came over them, their lips met, and they held each other until every last sensation fell away.

Face against her neck, body still buried in hers, he whispered, "I never thought I'd feel like this again."

Kelly wasn't certain what to say. Did he mean he never thought he'd have such great sex again? Or something more?

The connection she'd felt with him since the first time they'd kissed had only deepened tonight. She could love this man; she probably already did. In his arms, she could easily imagine creating a perfect family of three, but what did he feel?

He kissed her, quickly, lightly. "I'll be right back."

He hurried into the adjoining bathroom. The water ran, the toilet flushed, and then he was tumbling onto the bed, his face shining with a happiness that echoed the hope in her heart.

Gathering Kelly against him, Scott tucked her head beneath his chin. "I've been looking for you all of my life, Kelly. I've always wanted a home, a family. The way you are with Dani. She's so happy now, so confident and sure. Because of you."

"I didn't do that much."

"You did. I'm good at the basics—feed, clothe, play. We were buddies. Then we came here and—" His shoulder moved beneath her cheek in a shrug. "I didn't know what to do for her anymore."

"You love her. She knows that."

"She needs a mother." Kelly's heart stuttered at those words, then fell at the next. "She needs brothers and sisters. I've always dreamed of filling a house with kids. Kara didn't want any more children. She didn't want the one we had. I couldn't stay married to a woman who didn't share my dream. My fault for not finding someone like you in the first place."

Kelly couldn't move; she couldn't speak. The sense of déjà vu was overwhelming.

Luckily Scott's trip, the lateness of the hour, and the sex all combined and his next words slurred as he fell toward slumber. "Boys, girls. Doesn't matter as long as they're ours."

As soon as he was asleep, Kelly fled.

CHAPTER ELEVEN

THE SOUND OF the front door opening and closing woke Scott. Something was missing, and at first he wasn't sure what. He was home, in his own bed, then he remembered.

"Kelly?" he called.

Her clothes weren't on the floor. She wasn't in the bathroom. When he heard footsteps on the stairs, he stepped into the hall, then had to duck into his room and shut the door as he'd been waltzing around buck naked.

"Dani, what are you doing here?"

She didn't answer the question, instead asking one of her own from the other side of the closed door. "Where's Kelly? She was supposed to pick me up, but she called and asked Mrs. Martin to drop me off instead." Dani's voice faded as she went toward the guest room. "Is she sick?"

The creak of the door was followed by a gasp. Scott shoved his legs into his jeans without benefit of underwear and ran. "Is she okay?" he asked.

All of Kelly's things were gone. The bed was made. Not a single speck of her remained.

Dani turned toward Scott, folded her arms and tapped her foot. "What did you do?" she asked.

KELLY LEFT Dani a note on the dresser, explaining that she'd been called away and she'd get in touch just as soon as she could.

Once back in Madison, she made sure there was an available

mommy to take over with Dani come Monday, and she contacted the nanny applicant and gave her the Delgado's contact information so she could arrange an interview.

Then she went home, unplugged the phone and crawled into bed. She never wanted to get out.

She had vacation days coming, and she took them, leaving a message for Paige. But she should have known her friend wouldn't be satisfied with that.

Two days later, Paige showed up on her doorstep. She rang the bell until Kelly thought her head might explode. So she opened the door, even though she hadn't taken a shower or brushed her teeth in…Kelly couldn't remember.

"What is wrong with you?" Paige demanded before Kelly had even shut the door. "You look like hell."

"Which matches how I feel." Kelly went into the kitchen, put her head in the refrigerator, decided she didn't want to eat and walked back into the living room. There were still moving boxes all over the place, and she just couldn't bring herself to care.

After what had happened with Scott, she wasn't sure she could bring herself to stay here, though she didn't know if she'd ever work up the energy to move her body, let alone all her furniture to another town.

"You're sick?" Paige put her hand to Kelly's forehead.

Kelly slapped it away. "In the head."

Paige wrinkled her nose. "You kinda smell, Kel."

"Whatever." Kelly collapsed on the sofa and put her arm over her face.

She heard Paige go into the kitchen, and run some water in the sink, then she returned. Kelly figured her friend was either going to drink the water, or try to get Kelly to. Instead, she poured it on Kelly's head.

"Hey!" Kelly sat up sputtering and choking. Water had gone up her nose, some dripped off the end. "My couch."

"It's leather." Paige handed her a dish towel. "Now, are you ready to tell me what happened at the Delgados'?"

Kelly paused in the act of blotting the liquid off her couch. "Who said anything happened at the Delgado's?"

"You're there, then you're here. You send in a new mommy for no reason. You suddenly need a vacation—" Paige lifted a brow "—though all you seem to be doing is perfecting your couch-potato skills. The kid and the dad have been calling non-stop. The dad even showed up at the office and practically took the place apart trying to find out where you lived."

"He did?" Kelly cursed the hope in her voice. There was no hope.

"He seemed pretty determined. He never showed up here?"

Kelly shook her head. She had an unlisted number; still, he could have found her if he'd kept trying. She sighed. Even to her, the sound was pitiful.

"Spill it," Paige demanded.

And because this was Paige, Kelly did.

When she was done, her friend sat on the coffee table and took Kelly's hands in hers. Kelly braced herself for a sorrowful agreement that this was for the best. She'd get over him. She'd find someone else. All those things were probably true, but they didn't feel true. They felt like the biggest lie of all.

"You're a moron," Paige said gently.

Kelly blinked for several seconds, then she yanked her hands from Paige's. "What?"

"Maybe the term *idiot* would apply." Paige tilted her head. "Dumb-ass?"

"Why do I tell you anything?"

"Because I'm such a good listener." Kelly narrowed her eyes, and Paige smirked. "Definitely because I give great advice. Talk to the man."

"No." The very thought made Kelly's hands shake.

"You're condemning him because of something someone else did. Not all men are like Pete."

"He said—" Kelly's voice broke as she again heard Scott's

final words before he'd drifted off to sleep, *Doesn't matter as long as they're ours.*

"Whatever he said was without knowing your situation," Paige continued. "You can't end everything before you tell him the truth."

"Yes, I can."

"Dimwit."

Exasperated, Kelly began to pace. "Do you know what it's like to have the man you love tell you you're defective? That he wants to replace you, like he'd replace a toaster, with a working model?"

"You don't know that's how Scott will feel."

"I don't know that he won't."

"You love him."

"Who said that I love him?"

"You did. You said, 'do you know what it's like to have the man you love tell you…'" Paige made a circular motion with her forefinger. "Blah, blah, blah."

"I meant Pete."

"No, you didn't. Besides, if you didn't love him, you wouldn't be so devastated."

Kelly looked away. Paige was right again.

"Love doesn't come around as often as people think, Kelly. You might never get another chance. So take one. Tell him the truth."

Kelly thought about it, but not for long. Having her heart broken once in a lifetime was quite enough for her.

"I can't," she said.

"Coward."

Kelly thought she liked that better than *moron.* But as Paige got up and walked out of the house, slamming the door behind her, she murmured, "Then again, maybe not."

HOURS BLENDED into days blended into a week and beyond. Kelly returned to work. But she didn't sleep well; she didn't eat any better. She was twitchy whenever she went into the office, afraid Scott would show up, afraid he wouldn't.

She missed Dani with a longing that settled as a physical pain just below her heart. She kept in contact with cards and e-mail, but it wasn't the same. Dani was hurt and upset. Finally Kelly couldn't stand it anymore.

The next Saturday, she checked the schedule at Rent a Mommy. The nanny had obviously not worked out, since Scott still used their services. She saw that one of the mommies was working that day, which meant Scott must be out of town. Kelly climbed into her SUV and headed for Kiwanee.

The sight of the town made her eyes sting. She missed it, too, and how could that be? She'd never wanted to set foot in a place so small, so rural, so much like her hometown again.

At the Delgados', she was relieved to see one car in the driveway, and it wasn't Scott's.

Dani answered the door, then threw herself into Kelly's arms. "You came back," she whispered.

Uh-oh.

Kelly drew away, peering into Dani's face. "Just for a visit, not to stay."

Dani's lip trembled.

"Hey, I'll always be your friend. You can call me anytime."

"Why did you go? I love you. I want you to be my mommy."

Kelly's eyes burned. She wanted that, too.

"Dad misses you. He sighs a lot. He won't say your name. He won't talk about it. What did he do?"

Kelly had a sudden flash of what he'd done, what they'd done. What she really, really wanted to do again.

Abruptly, she stood. "Nothing, smoocheroonie. It wasn't him, it was me."

"He said it wasn't you, it was him. What kind of crap is that?"

Kelly choked on a startled burst of laughter. "Are you supposed to say *crap?*"

Dani rolled her eyes, then tugged Kelly into the house.

Kelly waved at the rental mom, who glanced out from the kitchen.

"She's okay," Dani whispered. "But she isn't you."

"Thanks."

Dani pulled her into the living room. "I wanna show you something." She picked up a notebook from the table and handed it to Kelly.

Figuring the girl had started keeping a diary, or perhaps a book of drawings, Kelly opened the cover, then frowned. The first page was filled with a list of words. Upon closer inspection she saw they were all the silly nicknames she'd used for Dani while she was here.

"One more." Dani took the notebook and painstakingly wrote *smoocheroonie* on the last line. "I really liked it when you called me those things."

Kelly ran her hand over Dani's hair. "I liked calling you them."

"But—" Dani bit her lip.

"But what, baby cakes?"

Dani wrote it down, then handed Kelly the notebook again. "Turn to the second page."

At the top had been written "What I Wish Kelly Would Call Me," then beneath were the words: *my daughter, my child, mine.*

"Oh, kiddo," Kelly began.

"You could adopt me. Adopting would make me yours, right?"

"Right, but—"

"Dad's always talking about adoption."

Kelly stilled. "What?"

"Did you know he was adopted? He really, really wants lots of kids. He says he needs to help others like he was helped."

Kelly's mouth moved, but no words came out. She had to sit, so she did. Then she had to move, so she got up. "Where is he?" she asked.

"At some adoption party. He's a sponsor of—" Dani scrunched her face up, trying to remember. "I don't know. He left the name in the kitchen."

Kelly turned on her heel and headed in that direction.

"Where's Scott?" she demanded of the mommy in residence, who handed her the contact sheet.

"Parents Through Adoption," she read. "Fund-Raiser at the University of Wisconsin Union."

She glanced at her watch. She'd just have time to make it.

CHAPTER TWELVE

"ADOPTION ISN'T for everyone, but what better way is there to share your love, share your life than with a child who needs you so badly?"

Applause lifted toward the ceiling. There had to be three hundred people who'd paid fifty dollars for lunch and the chance to hear Scott speak, maybe shake his hand. Scott enjoyed these talks. *Usually.*

Today, well, lately pretty much every day, he enjoyed nothing.

He missed Kelly, and knowing that he'd probably never see her again, or if he did, it would be some accidental meeting where they'd either pretend they didn't know each other and move on, or try and make nice, then end up so uncomfortable they'd have been better off pretending, only depressed him more.

He'd tried to find her. He'd wanted to talk to her to at least discover what he'd done, why she'd run. He'd nearly called his old roommate the P.I. to ferret out her address, but then he'd had a revelation.

His talk of a home, a family, children, had spooked her. He'd been wrong again about the woman he'd fallen in love with. Though Kelly had seemed the polar opposite of Kara, in the end, she wasn't. She was a businesswoman who'd wanted something from him, and once she'd gotten it, she'd left.

Kara had wanted the attention that had come from being married to a major league ball player, and she'd wanted the money.

So what was Kelly's excuse? He was no longer a big-deal ball player, which meant the money wasn't rolling in anymore, either.

In the first painful days after she'd left, he'd wondered if she'd only wanted sex. He'd found that hard to believe, but he was also finding it hard to come up with any other options.

Scott stepped away from the podium and greeted the dozen or so people who wanted to talk to him. For the next half an hour he chatted, he explained, he promoted the agency he supported with all his heart. If it weren't for adoption, he wouldn't be the man he was. Scott firmly believed that.

As he said goodbye to the last guest, he saw Kelly sitting at an empty table. He wasn't sure what to do, what to say. Then he saw the expression on her face, the one he remembered from when they'd been all tangled up together, the one that had made him think she loved him, too.

He took one step toward her, then he stopped. He'd been wrong before, and both his heart and his daughter had suffered for it. He wasn't going to take that chance again.

He crossed the short distance between them slowly. She rose as he approached. They stood a few feet apart silent and unsure.

"What are you doing here?" he blurted at the same time she said, "Scott, I'm sorry."

"For what?"

"I should have told you."

"That you didn't love me? That you only wanted one thing and you'd be gone?"

"Huh?" she said.

"You took off after I told you my dream, after I said I wanted a family with you. What was I supposed to think?"

"I don't know." She looked away. "There's something I have to explain, if you'd just hear me out."

Scott motioned for her to take a seat, and he joined her.

The story of her life, her marriage and her idiot husband made Scott's hands curl into fists. When she was through, she stared at her lap.

"Kelly," he said, and reached for her.

Her head went up and hope lit her eyes. She curled her fingers around his and held on.

"You obviously know why I'm here." He waved absently at the banners proclaiming Adoption Is For You!

She nodded.

"I love you, not just for myself, but for Dani, too. She needs you. I need you. The children who could find a new and better life with us need you. When I said I wanted kids, I just meant—" he lifted one shoulder, then lowered it "—kids."

"You said it didn't matter as long as they were ours."

"They'd *be* ours. We'd adopt them together." He took a deep breath. "Marry me?"

Joy spread over her face, and he kissed her. She was the one he'd been searching for. He was the one she'd been destined to find.

Suddenly Kelly pulled away. "Oh!" She stood and paced a few steps to the left, then to the right, then back to stand in front of him. "I've got it. The perfect event to make the Mother's Day picnic special."

"I've asked you to marry me, and all you can think about is the Mother's Day picnic?"

She lifted his hand to her mouth and kissed his knuckles. "You'll like this thought."

When she did that, he pretty much had only one thought, but he managed to control himself. "Okay, what's the perfect thing to make this year's picnic special?"

"A wedding."

EPILOGUE

EVERYONE AGREED that the Kiwanee Mother's Day Picnic that year was the best ever.

The day dawned clear and sunny, the sky a bright blue. The temperature hovered in the low seventies. The park smelled of flowers, fresh-cut grass and barbequed pork.

Kelly had worked nonstop, but with the help of Paige and all the mothers in Kiwanee, she was able to pull off a wedding to rival any that had required years to plan.

At eleven o'clock in the morning on Mother's Day, Kelly walked down a sidewalk covered in rose petals, wearing a tea-length dress of ivory lace, with her parents at her side.

Paige was her maid of honor. The twins and Dani, who had decided at their first meeting that they were best friends forever, stood as bridesmaids. They all wore crowns of white roses with multicolored ribbons streaming to their shoulders.

She'd given up her apartment and moved her things into the house just yesterday. When the Madison satellite location was up and running, Paige would move on and Kelly would remain as the manager. Her days of traveling were over. She was home.

In the gazebo, she became Kelly Delgado, wife of Scott, mother of Dani. They'd already filled out all the paperwork to begin the process of their first, but definitely not their last, adoption.

Dreams really did come true.

* * * * *

ALONG CAME
A DAUGHTER
Rebecca Winters

Dear Reader,

Who can forget the teenage years when our emotions carried us to the heights of joy one minute, only to plunge us to the depths of despair the next? We experienced agony and ecstasy on a daily basis. Have you ever wanted to go back to that precarious time? Frankly, I'm not sure my heart could take it unless I relived it through a good story.

Along Came a Daughter will touch your heart as this vulnerable teenager gets her first job and ends up bringing her father and her new boss together. Love is kindled and bursts into flame. Becoming a family is the only thing that will satisfy them, but it takes this lovely girl to make it happen.

Enjoy!

Rebecca Winters

CHAPTER ONE

DON'T EVER CUT YOUR HAIR, *mon amour.*

Every time Abby Chappuis stood in front of the mirror in the morning, she remembered what her husband had said. André came from a family of French-Swiss blondes. Maybe that was why he'd loved her ash-blond hair. That's what it was. Long, unruly hair unsuited for work in a restaurant.

Years ago, she'd learned how to confine it in a fat French braid that hung down her back. André would undo it at night as a prelude to making love.

Getting it cut would be like severing a tie to her husband's memory. She couldn't do that any more than she could remove her wedding ring.

After darkening her lashes to make her translucent green eyes stand out, she applied a generous coat of coral lipstick. Pink didn't do a thing for her.

She took the gold studs out of her ears and fastened her edelweiss earrings, André's first gift to her. The white flowers matched the ones embroidered among the colored flowers on the black weskit she wore over her dress. A dash of floral perfume and she was ready for the day.

On her way out of the bedroom she tied a clean white apron around her slender waist. The staff wore royal-blue dresses for the lunch crowd and red for dinner. Abby worked in comfortable low heels. Being five foot seven, she didn't need the extra height.

Once she'd locked the door to her apartment, she went downstairs to open the front double doors of the restaurant. The sun hadn't burned off the morning mist yet, as she breathed in the invigorating ocean air.

From the entrance she could watch the locals and tourists going out on the fishing boats. Sailboats would dot the horizon the moment the fog rolled out.

Abby loved Oceanside, California. She considered herself fortunate to be at this place in her life, owner of her own business, able to be paying back the bank loan. If there was a vital part of her personal life missing, she'd learned to live without it, because there would never be anyone like André.

She waved to Wally, who ran the frozen chocolate-banana concession next door. His wife, Sheila, came around with her children most days, and had become a good friend.

Farther down she spied Art setting up tables out in front of his seafood restaurant. Instead of being cutthroat competitors, with a dozen different places to eat and shop down here on the wharf, it felt as if they were all a family.

"Mrs. Chappuis?" A deep, unfamiliar voice sounded from behind her. Abby turned to see a tall, fit man in his mid-to-late thirties approach with a definite sense of purpose.

Dressed in cream trousers molded to—clearly—powerful thighs and a matching sport shirt covering very broad shoulders, she knew she'd never seen him before. She would have remembered. But he knew who she was. He'd even pronounced her name correctly.

The stranger had been blessed with a virile masculine presence that would stand out in any crowd. Abby even had to admire his short-cropped hair—more black than brown. He was one of the most striking men she'd ever seen.

That was saying a lot considering the number of male diners who frequented her restaurant year after year. However, he didn't seem to reciprocate her appreciation. In fact, his midnight-blue eyes were almost accusatory, putting her on her guard.

"Yes—may I help you?"

"I'm looking for the owner of the restaurant. Is he around this morning?"

André had been gone six years. "You're looking at her."

The man's charged gaze searched hers as if she were some sort of puzzle that wanted solving. "My mistake," he muttered. "I was led to believe you were the manager."

By whom? "I'm both." Abby derived a certain amount of pleasure in setting this particular man straight. "What can I do for you?"

"My name's Richard Jakeman."

Ah. "You're Brittany's father." Now that she thought about it, she could see the resemblance.

Abby had taken the girl at her word when she'd told her she lived with her father in one of the luxury high-rise beachfront condos Abby could see on the other side of the bay. That explained why he'd come along the pier from the direction of the harbor street.

There'd been no mention of a mother during the interview. Abby didn't pry. She assumed the girl's mother had either passed away or Brittany's parents were divorced and she lived with her father. Maybe she was visiting for the summer.

When the teen had come by last week asking for a summer job, the only thing she'd mentioned about home was the fact that getting to work on time would be a cinch. A two-minute walk from the complex.

His jaw tightened. "I understand you've hired her."

And you're not happy about it. No mystery there.

Most parents would be happy to know their child had the drive to go looking for a job. If Abby had children, she'd be thrilled if they were as resourceful.

She extended her hand. "Welcome to Chez André, Mr. Jakeman." She registered his firm grip. "Why don't we go inside where we can talk in private."

"If you have the time," he said, before relinquishing her hand.

Was it her imagination that he was angry with her? Or was she reading something that wasn't there?

"I'll make time for *you.*" She checked her watch. "It's only ten o'clock. The restaurant doesn't open for business until noon. Come in."

He followed her inside to one of the tables. The staff hadn't arrived yet to put on the tablecloths and setup. To Abby's surprise he helped her into a chair before sitting opposite her. That hadn't happened to her for a long time.

The tantalizing smell of the soap he used reached her nostrils. She didn't like being this aware of him.

"My daughter applied for work without telling me," he declared.

Uh-oh.

"I can see why. I feel like I've entered an authentic Swiss chalet. Your place is very charming."

"Thank you."

"But—"

"But Brittany didn't say anything to you until *after* I let her know she was officially hired."

He folded his hard, muscled arms. "She didn't inform me of her *fait accompli* until this morning while she was getting ready for school."

Today was Monday. Brittany had worked Wednesday through Friday last week without telling him?

"I'm sorry you didn't hear about it before now."

"Believe me, I am, too."

Abby wouldn't blame him if he were fuming. Being a parent, he had every right to be upset. She could hardly reconcile the well-mannered teen as a person who would keep this from her father.

"I'm here to get her unhired. She won't be coming in anymore."

"I see."

"We have plans for the summer. Whatever she might have told you, she's in school to keep up with the rest of her class. Brittany's too young to work—she's never had a job before."

"You mean, except for babysitting and helping you at work on the odd occasion."

That seemed to take him by surprise. He nodded. "No formal training."

"I wouldn't expect it of a girl who'll be celebrating her sixteenth birthday next month. Sometimes no experience is better. Then I don't have to untrain a person. You would know all about that since Jakeman Commercial Real Estate Developers is one of the most successful companies in Southern California."

His eyes glittered. "If she told you that to impress you, I'm sorry."

"Actually *I* was the one who connected the dots. In fact, I was impressed because she *didn't* name-drop. Take it from me—your daughter was hired on her own merits."

He gave her a frank stare. "Which are?"

"She's a smart, lovely young woman who said she needed a job."

"*Needed* a job?"

"Her exact words."

"Nothing could be further from the truth."

In terms of money, maybe not. Unfortunately, Abby couldn't betray Brittany's confidence. A confidence that might hurt her father.

"You can be proud of your daughter, Mr. Jakeman. She's been a welcome addition around here. Everybody likes her—she's eager to learn and willing to take directions without complaint."

There was more to it than that. First of all, Brittany had been hurt by a boy who'd viewed her as daddy's little rich girl. The label had stung. She'd wanted to get a job like any normal girl. But Abby wasn't prepared to give away that confidence. Secondly, Abby felt drawn to his daughter and liked her a lot. The decision to hire her had been based on instinct, and Abby's had rarely let her down.

"I'm glad to hear it. But, Brittany knows our move to my Oceanside branch is an experiment of sorts so we can spend more time together," he explained. "Did she tell you we're only going to be here until fall?"

"She did. As it happens, summer is my busiest time. I need

the extra help. Brittany indicated she was out of school at five to twelve and would be free to work weekdays from noon until you get home from work at six every evening."

The furrow deepened between his dark eyebrows. "Shouldn't you ask for parental consent before you go ahead and hire a fifteen-year-old?"

Brittany was one month shy of sixteen, but Abby wasn't willing to get into this with him. The man had issues. How he'd produced such a pleasant child was an enigma to her.

"The law doesn't require it. In my opinion, any presentable teen who comes to my restaurant asking for a job shows all the signs of being mature enough to take on adult responsibility. What goes on between you and your daughter is your business, not mine."

Abby pushed herself away from the table and stood. "Please tell Brittany it was a real pleasure to meet her, and I wish her well. I'll send her paycheck in the mail tomorrow. Now, if you'll excuse me, my suppliers will be here any minute. Have a lovely day, Mr. Jakeman."

She walked through the restaurant and down the hall, never turning around to see if he'd gone. He'd upset her on several levels, but right now she was more concerned about Brittany's feelings. Abby could only imagine the teen's disappointment.

She'd been so anxious for a chance to prove herself. To prove a certain senior back in Escondido that he was wrong about her.

As Abby thought back to the girl's confession, she remembered Brittany had even fought back tears, talking about the guy she'd had a crush on. "He said I was a spoiled rich girl who had maids waiting on me all day long. After he said my dad gives me everything I want so I don't need to work, I told him I earned money babysitting. He laughed and said that wasn't a job. He told me to get real."

At Brittany's age those remarks would have hurt Abby, too.

"Everyone needs to work," she'd said in a quiet voice. "Especially rich girls who might not always be rich one day."

Her comment had made Brittany smile.

"Are you willing to wash dishes?" Abby asked her.

"I'll do anything!"

"I pay eight dollars and fifty cents an hour."

Abby was jerked from her thoughts by the sound of a truck backing up to the service doors.

She could cry for Brittany, the girl had been so excited about her first job. Over the past few days the teen had gotten off to a great start. How sad.

Abby would miss Brittany's spirit, but the situation was out of her hands. The gorgeous, wealthy Richard Jakeman was in charge. Did he have any idea what a lucky man he was?

CHAPTER TWO

A LONG TIME AGO, Rick had learned there was no secret shortcut to getting home early on a weeknight in five o'clock traffic. Now that June had come to California, the Pacific Coast Highway reminded him of Moses's exodus from Egypt.

Even Oceanside, which wasn't quite as popular with tourists as Laguna or San Clemente, seemed to be overrun. From now on he would leave his office by three-thirty to get home at a decent hour.

He gripped the steering wheel with impatience, eager to reach the condo and show Brittany his surprise. Even poor old Buddy, who was on his last legs, would like it. That is if Rick ever made it home.

His cell phone rang for the dozenth time. He checked the caller ID, hoping it was Brittany. But his distraught daughter hadn't returned any of his calls. Liz Wright. He'd phone her back later. The attorney he'd been seeing on and off for the past few months hadn't been happy about his move. Rick couldn't help that. Brittany would always come first.

They'd made the decision to live by the water for the summer in a furnished condo. She would invite her friends to stay over. He would cut down his workload to spend more time with her.

It had all sounded fine in theory, then came the first crisis when Brittany declared they didn't need Jennifer, their house-keeper, anymore. Had insisted she was grown-up and could run things by herself once they settled in Oceanside.

Rick didn't doubt her ability. He just didn't like her to be by herself for hours at a time, so he'd brought Jennifer with them.

Things hadn't been the same since. His normally affable Brittany had become quiet and standoffish.

He'd thought they were making it through the teenage years without too many problems. But after learning his daughter had gotten a job without discussing it with him or asking his permission, he realized he'd been living a fantasy.

Since she'd kept Jennifer in the dark about her after-school activities, too, the news had hit him particularly hard. He'd never known his daughter to lie like this deliberately. Wanting a job seemed to have come out of nowhere.

Worried over the change in his one-and-only offspring, he made another call to her on his cell phone. When she didn't pick up, he left another message.

"Guess what, kiddo? I'm three blocks from you." He'd probably get home faster if he parked and walked the rest of the way. "You're really going to like my surprise."

After hanging up, he called Jennifer. "I'm almost home. Would you ask Brittany to come to the phone, please?"

"I would, but she went out a little while ago."

"Is she still upset?"

"*Devastated* is the word I'd use. After school, she stayed in her room and cried her heart out. When she finally came out, she refused to eat and said she was going to take Buddy for a walk. That was about an hour ago. Isn't it amazing how much that job meant to her?"

Not really. But then Jennifer would have had to meet Mrs. Chappuis to understand part of the appeal. He frowned, not liking the direction of his thoughts. "We moved here to enjoy the ocean."

"I know, and I think it's a wonderful idea for both of you. Give her some time."

Time wasn't exactly the problem. Rick didn't want Jennifer to know part of his daughter's rebellion stemmed from having a housekeeper around. He hoped Brittany wasn't acting out because he'd told her she was still too young to be home alone. It crossed his mind that if she got upset enough, she'd meet up with the wrong kids. He didn't want to think about the trouble she could get into.

"Is our picnic fixed?"

"All packed and ready to go."

"Thanks, Jennifer. You're a saint. I'm heading into the garage. See you in a minute."

Relieved to be home at last, he parked the car and got out, nodding to a couple of his new neighbors. The over-thirty brunette with the dark tan he'd seen before entered the first elevator with him. He pushed the third-floor button.

She leaned in front of him, brushing his shoulder, and pushed four, then smiled. "Hi. Since we're neighbors, we might as well get to know each other," she said flirtatiously. "I'm Pam Brooks."

"I'm Richard."

"Nice to meet you. You must have moved in recently."

"About ten days ago."

Her gaze drifted to his ringless left hand. "Is there a Mrs.?"

The woman wasted no time, but her aggressiveness turned him off. "No."

Rick enjoyed women as much as the next man. He'd had his share of relationships in the past, but he liked to do the chasing. Before he could tell her he was seeing someone else—or had been—he didn't know if he wanted to keep it alive with Liz— the elevator stopped and the doors opened. Relieved, he stepped out.

"Brittany—" he called to his daughter, who was walking toward their condo with her head down, Buddy at her heels. They must have come from the stairs.

In a few swift strides Rick reached her and gave her a hug, one she didn't reciprocate. Buddy barked a greeting. The woman in the elevator forgotten, he ushered his family inside.

"We're all home!" he announced to Jennifer.

"Now I can stop worrying!" she called back.

Brittany pulled away from him and dashed to her room with Buddy. Rick followed slowly and closed the bedroom door so they could talk in private.

She sank down on the bed and undid the dog's leash, still re-fusing to look at Rick.

He pulled a chair over and sat opposite her. "You and I are all we've got, honey. If you stop talking to me, then we're in real trouble. I tried calling you several times. Where have you been this afternoon?"

She lifted her head. Rick was shocked at her pallor. "I went to the restaurant to thank her and to apologize for not telling her you didn't know anything."

He'd thought she might have gone over there. "That was the right thing to do."

"She said that since you'd been to see her this morning, it wasn't necessary, but she was glad I did. She gave me my pay-check right there." She strangled back a little sob. "She said that if you ever changed your mind, the job was always open. Abby's the nicest person I've ever known."

Abby already? Not Mrs. Chappuis?

"Everyone loves her, Dad. So do I."

He scratched behind the Scotch terrier's ears. For a daughter who used praise stintingly, even over her favorite teacher, those were strong words to describe someone who'd been a total stranger a few days ago.

She didn't say any more because she'd broken down sobbing. The sound went straight to his gut.

"Brittany, I had no idea you were so unhappy at home you got it in your head to look for a job. We moved here to have fun this summer. I thought you and I made a great team."

She wiped her eyes. "I thought we did, too. How come you had to bring Jennifer with us?"

"We've been over this before. I've never left you alone. You need someone to take care of you when I'm at work."

"I'm not a baby!"

"Everyone needs someone, I don't care how old you are. It's not good to be by yourself in an empty house for hours on end. I don't like it when *you're* gone and I'm alone. Is it Jennifer you object to? Be honest with me."

"No. I like her a lot."

"Then what is it?"

She put her arm around Buddy, who'd jumped up on the bed to comfort her. "Nothing."

That was a lie, but it was going to take time to get the whole truth out of her.

"Guess what? I bought that sailboat we looked at last week. It's waiting at the marina for us to take out right now."

She raised her face from the dog's black fur. "You go ahead without me if you want. I'm going to bed."

"Brittany—"

"Sorry, Dad, but I don't feel like doing anything. If you want to move back to Escondido, it's okay with me." Tears trickled down her pale cheeks. "We shouldn't have come here. I bet Abby thinks I'm an idiot."

The pain in her eyes disturbed him as much what she said. He'd seen her upset before, but she always snapped right back. To fall into a depression this severe was totally unlike the daughter he'd raised almost since she was born.

"Mrs. Chappuis would never have hired you if she'd thought that. The only thing that concerned her was the fact that you didn't clear it with me first."

Her eyes filled again. "I was afraid to ask you in case you said no."

He heaved a sigh. "Am I that much of an ogre?"

"No."

"Then what?"

She shook her head. "It doesn't matter. It's too late now anyway. I just want to go to sleep."

Rick had reached an impasse with his daughter.

"All right." He got up and moved the chair to the table. "I'll look in on you later."

He walked into the living room where the middle-aged housekeeper was talking to someone on the phone. Probably her sister. She covered the mouthpiece and looked up at him. "I take it she's still upset?"

Brittany wasn't the only one. "Yes. Did she tell you anything?"

Jennifer shook her head.

He sucked in his breath. "Will that picnic keep until tomorrow?"

"Of course. I'll put everything back in the fridge."

"I appreciate it."

"What about your dinner? Can I fix you something?"

"No thanks. I'm not hungry." He reached for the newspaper, grabbed a cold beer from the fridge and wandered out onto the deck.

From the railing he could view the northern end of the bay where his new sailboat was moored. If he looked in the opposite direction, he saw the pier-side shops and restaurants still bustling with activity. One eating establishment in particular caught his attention.

By the time he called it a night and went to bed, he'd made a decision. Only time would tell if he lived to regret it, but he couldn't allow the situation to go on like this any longer.

THE NEXT MORNING, as Abby started down the stairs of her apartment, she heard the buzzer at the service entrance around the back of the restaurant. She checked her watch. Ten to ten. Fabrice was a little earlier than usual today. She hurried around to unlock it.

"*Bonjour,* Fabrice," she said as she pushed the door wide so his bread cart would clear the opening. *"Ca va aujourd'hui?"*

"I don't know how Fabrice is, but I'm fine."

Her head flew back.

Richard Jakeman! Wearing a light gray suit that fit his body to perfection. He smelled as good as before, his black hair still damp from the shower.

The blood pounded in her ears. She hadn't expected to see him again.

"I didn't mean to startle you, Mrs. Chappuis."

"That's all right."

"When you didn't answer the phone, I knocked at the front door. Then I took a chance you might be around back. I remembered you told me you have deliveries at this time."

She took an extra breath. "That's true. The vendor from the *boulangerie* will be here any minute."

His scrutiny made her nervous.

"I heard the phone ring, but I was in the middle of something. The answering machine picks up all my calls. I would have returned yours."

Abby groaned. She was talking too fast, running on and on. She needed to get a grip.

Something was wrong at home for him to show up here this morning. Disturbed by the situation with Brittany, Abby hadn't slept well. The teen had made such a sincere apology, she'd moved Abby to the point of tears.

"Is your daughter all right?" she ventured.

He stared hard at her. "What do you think?"

Just as she'd surmised.

Abby averted her eyes. "Come in."

Locking the door again, she showed her surprise visitor to the office on the other side of the stairs.

By the time he stood opposite her desk where she'd sat down, she'd hoped to have recovered her equilibrium, but no such luck. His presence seemed to dominate the tiny room. If she could just avoid that all-encompassing gaze. No doubt he had too much pent up energy to sit.

"Did you mean it when you told Brittany the door would always be open?" he asked without preamble.

Abby's pulse rate picked up. Once again she found herself looking into those intense eyes. The faint shadows beneath them hinted that he'd spent a restless night, too.

"Of course. Does this mean you've changed your mind about her working?"

He studied her features for a moment. "Let's just say the situation warrants a second look. But you may not be agreeable when I ask you to cut down her hours."

She stirred restlessly. "What did you have in mind?"

"If you need her the full six hours a day, then it can't work, because I've converted to summer hours and will be home by four-fifteen."

"I don't see that as a problem."

He put his hands in his pockets. "We're going to take advantage of the water and go sailing together as often as we can."

She gave him high marks for being a loving father. When she'd first met him, she hadn't thought him capable of compromise, but he'd had a change of heart for his daughter's sake.

"That sounds wonderful for both of you. Under the circumstances four hours a day works for me."

He looked relieved. "You're being very understanding about this."

"Four hours a day is enough for anyone starting out on their first job."

"My thoughts exactly. I'll go back and tell Brittany." His eyebrows met in a frown. "She stayed home from school this morning because of a bad headache. When I tell her she has her job back, I'm sure she'll get well in a hurry and be here at noon."

Abby rose to her feet. "If she still feels too ill today, tell her I'll be expecting her tomorrow."

Their eyes met. "Thank you." He shook her hand. Before he let it go she felt warmth creep through her arm to her entire body.

"You're welcome. I'll be glad to get her back."

A brooding look stole over his face. She had the impression he wanted to say something else, then thought better of it. What was wrong now?

But before she could recover her wits to ask him, he'd left her office and was out the self-locking rear service door.

CHAPTER THREE

BY SOME FLUKE Rick managed to beat his daughter home from work on Friday afternoon. They were going to get Chinese on their way to the boat. He'd given Jennifer the afternoon and evening off to do what she wanted.

Buddy followed him while he changed into shorts and a T-shirt. When Brittany still hadn't arrived, he riffled through his mail on the kitchen counter. Then he reached for the newspaper. After staring at the headlines without reading them, he tossed the paper aside and began pacing.

Brittany should have been home by now. She'd kept to their bargain all week. They had an agreement. Four o'clock sharp. It was almost quarter after now. He had half a mind to go over to Chez André and find out what was keeping her.

"Come on, Buddy. I'll take you out." He attached the leash to the dog and they left the condo. He'd almost reached the door for the stairs at the end of the hall when it opened.

"Dad! Hey, Buddy—"

The dog tried to break away from his leash to get to her.

"Sorry I'm late. Some firemen came to the restaurant to do a demonstration on the new extinguishers. We all had to be there and watch in case we ever have to use one."

Rick had come to a standstill, barely taking in her explanation. Except for the same jeans and blouse she'd put on for school that morning, he almost didn't recognize her. It was her hair. She'd pulled it back into a French braid. Exactly like…

"What do you think?" She twirled in front of him. "Abby said I had to do something to keep it confined or wear a hairnet."

He tugged on the end of it. "You look lovely." More sophisticated. He wasn't prepared for the change.

She beamed. "Thanks. Abby showed me how to do it."

Rick had guessed as much.

"Do you think I could get my ears pierced?"

Another first. The power Abby Chappuis already had over his daughter alarmed him.

"Let's talk about that on our way to the harbor."

"It's hot out. Give me time to change into my shorts."

"Okay. Buddy and I'll wait outside."

"I'll hurry."

A few minutes later, she joined them. They walked a short distance to the Chinese take out near the pier, then gravitated to the patio to eat. She was so excited, she didn't even notice he'd bought her favorite *char-shu*.

"How was school?"

"I aced my math test. Abby taught me a way to remember the double negative and I got a hundred percent."

Abby again. "I'm proud of you."

"Thanks for letting me keep my job. I love working!" she said, pushing at her food with her chopsticks. "Chet has been teaching me how to stack the dishes in the machine. There's a real science to it. He's says I'm a little on the short side, but not too short."

His five-foot-three daughter took after her mother in that department.

"How old is Chet?"

"He's a senior in college getting his degree in business. There's another guy, Tony, who washes dishes too, mostly at dinner. Anyway, Chet wants to own a restaurant like Abby's one day. He knows a lot already. Between you and me I think he's got a huge crush on her."

After meeting Mrs. Chappuis, Rick was tempted to tell his daughter Chet would be lucky to get in at the end of a very long line behind the woman's husband.

"Did you know they only serve one thing so they don't have menus?"

He finished off another deep fried shrimp. "I *didn't* know that."

"It's called *fondue au fromage*. The *u* has to be pure."

"You sounded French just now." If ever anyone was a quick study, it was his daughter.

"Thanks. Abby taught me some other French words, too. She says I have a good ear and ought to sign up for it at school in the fall."

Was that so?

"Of course she speaks with an accent from Lausanne. Chet said her husband, André, was from there, but he died."

Rick stopped chewing. "What happened to him?"

"Chet said they were in a bad car accident on the Santa Ana freeway and he was killed."

"That's tragic."

"I know. It's so sad. She met him on a tour in Switzerland while she was in college. His family runs a restaurant over there. Chet says she never got over losing him."

That explained the ring she still wore.

"The restaurant's named after him."

André Chappuis...

"I'm learning how to pronounce the wines. You should see their huge wine cellar! Not that it's really a cellar. They import three kinds from Switzerland. The Neuchatel and kirsch, for making fondue."

The revelation that Abby's husband had died made it difficult for him to concentrate on what his daughter was saying.

"The other one is a white wine for drinking with it. I can't remember the name. Chass something. It comes from the vineyards in Sierre, Switzerland, where they speak French and German. I'm trying to learn everything as fast as I can so I can become a waitress."

Didn't he know it! "Slow down, honey." He prodded her with his elbow, indicating the fast-cooling take-out carton she'd barely touched. "These are early days yet."

Brittany ignored him. In fact, she was oblivious of their surroundings. The patio had become more crowded since they'd sat down. He had an idea his daughter's chatter was amusing the people at the table next to them. "On Monday, Abby's going to show me how the fondue is made. You have to use special cheeses she imports from this town called Gruyères, except I'm not saying it right."

Rick wondered how long Abby's husband had been deceased as he swallowed the last of his spring roll.

"There's a big painting of it over the fireplace in the restaurant. It's the most adorable mountain village you've ever seen with this fabulous castle. You can't drive cars there."

"Where?" Rick asked, still deep in thought.

"*Gruyères.* I want to go to Switzerland, Dad. I'm going to save up my money. Abby says—"

"You know something, kiddo?" he interrupted her. "You haven't touched your food."

"I'm not hungry. Abby let me eat some French bread and cheese on my break. It's really good. She gets it from an authentic French bakery in San Diego. They deliver it fresh every day."

Yes. Rick had found that out the first morning he'd gone over to talk to Mrs. Chappuis.

"All the employees eat it, but no one seems to gain weight because they work too hard."

Rick took a moment to drink some of his water. "What do you think about the rest of the staff?"

"Everyone's great. Even though they're older than me, they treat me like I'm one of them."

"I'm glad you're enjoying this."

"Abby's the best!"

He grated his teeth. Waving away a seagull that was brazenly edging too close along the patio railing, he asked, "Do you have homework from class?"

"A little. I'll get it done later."

"Anything you need me to help you with?"

"D-a-d. I think I've got it covered. Oh, hey, I invited Danice for the weekend. Is it okay if she comes in the morning?"

"I was about to suggest it." His daughter needed to concentrate on someone besides the owner of the restaurant.

"Good. I'll call her right now. I want to introduce her to Abby. She said I could."

"Brittany?" he called after her, but she'd jumped up and walked away from him down the sidewalk and was already speaking into her cell phone. Rick grimaced. It appeared Chet wasn't the only one who'd developed a crush on the boss.

His daughter had grown up with several wonderful housekeepers over the years. Rick couldn't have made it without them. But apparently they weren't anything like Abby Chappuis.

After five hours of sailing, he returned to the condo with an exhilarated daughter in tow. Normally Rick would have been on a high, too. But while he'd tried to explain the basics of sailing to his daughter, she'd treated him to a nonstop litany of her boss's virtues.

He looked down at the dog and tossed him a treat. "You know what, Buddy? I need to pay Mrs. Chappuis another visit pronto."

After meeting with her on Monday morning, Rick had no idea he would have to set more ground rules this soon. It was a good thing he wasn't doing anything with Liz this weekend. Maybe next.

Once he'd showered and changed, Rick asked Jennifer to keep an eye on Brittany, who'd settled down to watch a TV program with Buddy on her lap. The restaurant stopped serving at ten. He checked his watch. It was quarter to ten.

Minutes later, he rounded the bay, crowded with tourists enjoying the warm evening.

The delicious smells of a variety of foods wafted over him. A few steps brought him closer to the restaurant where his ears picked up the strain of a festive polka.

What with the red cloths on the tables, the Swiss flag stirring in the gentle breeze and the chalet's window boxes overflowing with flowers, he could almost believe he was in Europe.

The place was packed. A couple of waitresses dressed in their red uniforms moved in and out of the doorway to serve tables.

But he was looking for one particular woman who, he grudgingly admitted, would be enticing if she wore sackcloth.

Tonight couldn't have come soon enough. And not just because of Brittany. In the past few days, something had happened to him. After all these years on auto pilot, he felt something stirring, something emotional. Toward Abby.

He needed to see *Mrs*. Chappuis again, to prove she wasn't a figment of his imagination.

She radiated intelligence and confidence—with such alluring magnetism. And beautiful? It was apparent no one was safe around her. Least of all Rick.

He decided to walk to the end of the pier and wait until diners began leaving.

On his way back, he stopped to buy a frozen chocolate banana. Brittany raved about them. After one bite he understood why. As he turned away from the counter, he and the owner of Chez André caught sight of each other at the same time. She'd been chatting with one of the last customers, who was just leaving.

Rick stayed where he was until she was free. "I've been waiting for you," he called over. "We need to talk."

"Has the week been too much for Brittany?" she asked as they walked back into her restaurant together. "Four hours a day doesn't sound like a lot, but it's hard work. Maybe too hard?"

"On the contrary," he muttered. "She's never been more alive."

"Then—"

"I'm the one who's having a problem."

Her glance flew to his in puzzlement. "Give me five minutes."

Rick nodded before walking over to the fireplace to examine the painting Brittany had described. Someone had turned off the music. Somewhere out of sight he heard employees talking and laughing. They seemed a congenial enough group as they closed up the place for the night. A couple of them eyed him curiously on their way out.

Little by little the restaurant emptied. The owner eventually reappeared carrying a stack of newly laundered napkins. "Peace at last." She sat down at one of the tables to fold them.

He sat opposite her. "I see your work is never done."

She reached for another napkin, giving him a knowing smile. "That's what Brittany says about you."

Brittany... The reason he was here.

"Does my daughter do a lot of that?"

"What do you mean?"

"Talk incessantly about me the way she does about you?"

Before she could respond, a sandy-haired guy who looked college age came out from the back. He gave Rick a speculative glance.

"Hey, Abby. I'm leaving now. Anything I can do for you before I go?"

"No thanks, Chet. See you on Monday."

Unsmiling, Chet stared at the two of them a moment longer before he disappeared out the front doors. Rick sensed a certain amount of hostility emanating from the guy.

"I understand he's the one training my daughter on the dishwashing machine."

"Yes. I don't know why you're here, so I didn't introduce you. He'd tell Brittany you'd been to see me. Under the circumstances I thought it best."

"I appreciate that." Rick cocked his head. "How much has she told you about her mother?"

Abby blinked but kept folding. "Only that she died when Brittany was one."

"Rachel had lymphoma."

He read the sadness in her green eyes. "I'm sorry about your wife," she said. "I know what it's like to lose a spouse."

"My daughter told me about your husband. I'm sorry for your own loss. But as far as Brittany goes...she doesn't remember her mother. In fact, we've been doing fine until now."

"When I was her age, I wanted more independence, too," Abby said. "It goes with the territory of being a teen, I guess."

"Now that she's met you, I'm afraid it's a little more complicated than that. Over the years, there've been a series of exceptional housekeepers in our lives, but she never bonded with any of them."

Abby's mind made the leap. "You think she has with me. Is that what you're saying?"

He rubbed the back of his neck. "I *know* she has."

The unexpected news thrilled Abby, who'd been inexplicably drawn to the girl from the first day she'd met her. *Get a grip,* she told herself. *You have no right to get too caught up in Brittany's life.*

"My daughter's young and impressionable," he continued. "Whether you're aware of it or not, you've taken on more than an employee. I came here to warn you."

She seemed to be getting mixed signals from him. Was he angry with her? Or his daughter? Or both?

Abby sat back in the chair, refusing to feel guilty about extending the opportunity to Brittany. Many sixteen-year-olds held jobs. Abby had herself.

"What would you like me to do?"

"I wish I knew."

While she attempted to digest what he'd just said, he pushed himself away from the table and stood. "Funny—when she first told me about Chet, I th◌ ht I was going to hear she had a crush on *him.*"

Years of love and nuturing lay behind that remark. Brittany's father was hurt, and that hurt Abby. "Did you ever admire another man besides your father?" she asked.

He gave a slow nod. "But that's all it was. I didn't see any of them as a replacement."

Replacement? His comment touched a chord.

They were getting into deeper water. He wasn't the only who didn't know what to do about the situation. Abby more than liked Brittany. The girl was very precious. Already she couldn't imagine not having her around.

Anxiously, she gathered the napkins and got to her feet. "If you feel that strongly, perhaps you should tell her you've changed your mind about her taking a summer job after all. I'm sure you could come up with a valid reason. I would back you up if it came to that."

Lines formed grooves around his mouth. "Surely I don't have to tell you that it would cause a breach with my daughter I could never repair."

"You're her hero, you know," she said under her breath, but he heard her.

"If I intervened, I'd lose that coveted title."

Hardly able to breathe, she said, "Is there a woman in your life right now?"

"Yes and no."

Abby *did* ask. "How does Brittany feel about her?"

"Doesn't the fact that I'm talking to you answer that question?"

Troubled, Abby shifted her weight. "I think you're making too much of this. She's excited about the job, but the novelty will wear off."

"One can only hope." She heard no levity in his voice.

"I like your daughter. I want to see her succeed. I'll make a conscious effort to keep the relationship professional."

He shrugged his shoulders. "I can't ask for more than that, but I'm left with another dilemma."

"What is that?"

"While we were out sailing this afternoon, she made me promise to come here after she gets off work on Friday. She wants the two of us to have dinner together, no doubt to impress me with her knowledge of *fondue au fromage*. And the proper wine to drink with it," he added.

Hoping her voice sounded steady, she said, "Cheryl's one of my best waitresses. I'll ask her to wait on you." Abby would make herself scarce. "I'll tell her to bring a bottle of Grapillon for Brittany."

He raised his eyebrows. "Grapillon?"

"A nonalcoholic grape drink from Switzerland that goes well with the cheese."

He studied her features for a moment. "That's probably the only thing she hasn't told me about yet."

Long after he'd left, Abby stood alone in the dim light of the empty dining room. There was a dark side to this man. He was complicated. She'd have to watch every step with his daughter.

When he said he'd come to warn her, he'd meant he didn't want her to enable his daughter any more than she already had. The last thing she wanted was for Brittany to get hurt.

CHAPTER FOUR

ON FRIDAY EVENING, Rick walked to the restaurant. It was the second time in a week. After negotiating for a new commercial property for Oceanside, he'd left his office an hour early to shower and shave.

He'd been tempted to phone Liz and ask her to come, but decided against it. She would see it as an encouraging sign. It wouldn't be fair to her or Brittany.

This evening, they'd given sailing a miss because his daughter was too eager to share her new world with him. Of course that world included her boss who'd be on the premises throughout the evening.

He'd been too intense with Mrs. Chappuis earlier. He had a suspicion she wasn't happy about him coming here tonight. In truth, he was surprised she hadn't reconsidered keeping Brittany on staff.

Knowing she had access to the job application his daughter had filled out, he'd half been expecting a phone call at his office telling him this wasn't going to work. As a result, his week had been a complete wash.

The only good thing to come out of it was that he'd figured out what had caused his unwarranted behavior. He was jealous of his daughter's attachment to Abby.

Before now no one had given him reason to believe. So it had come as a shock, one he hadn't handled well because the object of Brittany's unprecedented affection was a formidable foe.

Charming, warm, compassionate, utterly desirable....

He intended to apologize to Abby. If at all possible, he'd take her aside tonight.

"Dad—"

He jerked his head toward his daughter, who was waving to him from one of the restaurant's outside tables bordering the pier. She was wearing her school clothes. He wondered how long she'd been trying to get his attention.

"I thought you'd never notice me," she complained, as he reached her.

He sat down next to her. "You were right about this place. I feel like we've been transported to Switzerland. How did things go today?"

"I learned how to set up the tables." She handed him the drink list fashioned in wood. It gave the background of the two drinks served: nonalcoholic Grapillon, and fendant, their white Swiss wine made from Chasselas, an old varietal.

"Abby hand-painted all these flowers. They match the ones on the leather straps holding those huge cowbells."

Rick had seen them hanging from the rafters. "She does beautiful work."

"If you read on the back, it tells you about fondue." She turned it for him. "Fondue comes from the French word, *fonder,* which means 'to melt.' It refers to cheese being cooked at the table with its own heat source."

He was trying to pay attention, but he couldn't stop looking around for Abby.

"Traditionally if you drop the bread off the fork and into the pot, you have to kiss the person next to you. Gross, hmm?"

Loving this daughter of his, he kissed her cheek, as she tried to squirm away. He couldn't help wondering how many times Abby's husband had used that ploy.

"Dad—you're not supposed to kiss me yet."

"I felt like it, kiddo."

She rolled her eyes. "Guess what else? Tonight I arranged the chocolate truffles on the dessert plates with the doilies. You have to use special gloves to handle them."

Rick was half listening as he unfolded the cloth napkin and smoothed it over his lap.

"They're made in Switzerland, too. Abby let me eat a couple. You won't believe how good they are."

He could believe it. Anything to do with Abby was out of the ordinary.

He stifled a groan. Now *he* was starting to think of her as Abby.

"Good evening, Brittany," a voice broke in on them.

"Hi, Cheryl. This is my dad, Richard Jakeman."

"Welcome to Chez André, Mr. Jakeman. Your daughter is such a treat to work with."

Rick glanced at the good-looking, auburn-haired waitress who put two plates with French bread on the table.

"Thank you. Everyone's made her feel welcome."

"I've been here three years, which tells you I wouldn't want to work anywhere else. Have you decided if you want wine or Grapillon?"

"We'll have one of each."

"I can't wait to be a waitress," Brittany confided after the other woman walked away.

"You're kidding," he teased.

"Dad—" She kept looking around. "I wonder where Abby is? I was hoping she'd come out and sit with us."

After his talk with Abby earlier, it was evident she'd decided to leave the father and daughter alone. "With a crowd like this, I imagine she's too busy." Brittany frowned.

The drinks arrived just before a pot of bubbling fondue. He could smell the distinctive odor of the cherry wine mixed with the garlic.

"*Bon appétit,*" Cheryl told them.

"Thank you," he said, but he was afraid his appetite was gone.

Brittany took over. "You break your bread into quarter-size pieces and put one on the end of your fork. Then you dip it in the cheese like this."

He copied her example. The first bite told him all he needed to know.

"This is incredible," he muttered.

"Abby'll have to come out here sometime. Let's save a little for her." His daughter was still convinced she'd be joining them.

Brittany had no idea he'd eaten fondue before since it wasn't commonly served. But he had to admit he'd never tasted anything this good. A few more bites and he said, "Excuse me, honey. I'll be right back."

"Okay. Don't be long." She always said that.

He made his way through the restaurant to the restroom area. En route, he searched for Abby. She was nowhere to be found. His gut tightened. By sheer strength of will he didn't go into the kitchen.

"Mr. Jakeman?" Cheryl called when he was on his way back to Brittany.

He turned.

"Brittany asked me if I'd find Abby and tell her to come to your table," the waitress said, shifting her hold on two trays of food. "But one of the girls just told me Abby took the night off. Will you please let your daughter know? I've got tables waiting."

It felt as if a tight band constricted his lungs. "No problem."

So that was that. But his daughter wasn't going to like it.

CHAPTER FIVE

ABBY'S BEDROOM window overlooked the harbor. An hour ago she'd seen Brittany's father taking long strides toward the restaurant. Like a stallion in a herd of geldings, he'd been easy to pick out of the crowd. No other man compared.

Just watching him sent a yearning through her body.

At one point during the evening she'd thought she'd at least go outside and say hello to Brittany and her father to be friendly.

Bad idea. She couldn't bring herself to do it. Not after he'd come expressly on Monday night to warn her off. The things he'd confided had tormented her all week. But she had to admit she would have liked to eat dinner with them.

Her adrenaline kicked in again when she looked and saw the two of them leave the restaurant. Brittany turned frequently to her father to say something. He didn't pause or take time to enjoy the harbor. If he did any talking at all, Abby couldn't tell.

She pressed her forehead against the pane. What would it have been like to get to know him if they'd met under different circumstances? She longed for him to treat her like a woman who interested him—without issues or complications.

In two short weeks, the man and his daughter had worked their way beneath her skin. Since he'd told her he would be coming this evening for dinner with Brittany, he'd never been out of her mind.

Abruptly, she turned away—to be confronted by a photo of her husband propped on the bedside table. André seemed to be staring at her with accusation in his eyes.

She felt consumed by guilt. A part of her wanted to run after those two people moving farther and farther away. Brittany's father made her feel things she hadn't felt for so long....

"Forgive me, André. Please forgive me."

Disturbed by thoughts she shouldn't be having, she wheeled around and went into the bathroom. Removing her "Heidi" dress—as Brittany called it, which was how Abby would always think of it now—she took a long shower and washed her hair. Afterward she put on a robe and wandered into the living room.

Nothing on TV interested her. She turned it off and lay on the couch with her feet up while she worked on a crossword puzzle. Normally it helped her to relax before bed. Not tonight. She felt wound up like a top.

Dropping the crossword magazine on the floor, she happened to see another photo of her husband on the end table next to her begonia. She sat up and reached for his picture.

His friends and family back in Lausanne thought he could pass for Switzerland's ski champion Didier Cuche, and she could concede there was a superficial resemblance to the blond downhill skier.

Chez André was his baby. André had been a restaurateur like his father and grandfather before him.

She'd gotten caught up in the business with him. First at a strip mall farther inland. After his death she had taken a huge financial risk and moved to this coveted spot by the pier.

If André were alive, he'd be thrilled to see that his dream was materializing.

If the car crash hadn't happened, their unborn child would be six years old.... Abby couldn't help but wonder what her little boy would have looked like by now. He'd be a first-grader. Probably a towhead like André. Maybe green-eyed like herself?

Brittany had inherited her father's blue eyes. Yet where his were dark and intense, hers were full of sunshine. If Abby had a daughter, she would want her to be just like Brittany. Something about the girl wouldn't leave her alone.

Abby delighted in their conversations. Though Brittany expressed the usual amount of teenage angst, it was her father she ended up talking about the most. As she was leaving the restaurant earlier today she'd said, "My dad would live at his work if he could. But he's got me so he *has* to come home."

With a smile Abby had said, "I'm sure that's no penance. He's a fortunate man to have you waiting for him. Are you on your way home now?"

"Yes. I have to let Buddy out."

"Who's Buddy?"

"Our dog."

"What kind?"

"A Scottish terrier. He's blind in one eye. Dad says he won't be with us much longer."

Abby had to clear the sudden lump in her throat.

"See you tonight. I hope." Another quick smile and Brittany had hurried out.

Abby felt a pang in her heart because she hadn't been able to grant her that. It had been difficult to keep her distance from the teen this week. But, she must have done something right because she hadn't had another visit from Richard Jakeman. To her chagrin she'd hoped he would find a reason, any reason, to drop by. He never did.

Too restless to lie there, she got up to put the photo back on the table. This time she was afraid to meet André's gaze. She shuddered involuntarily to realize her thoughts of late had been taken up by another man. Somehow the impossible had happened.

She walked back to the bedroom to finish drying her hair. For once the sound of the polka music drifting up from the restaurant irritated her. She needed to get out. It was only eight-thirty. And Sylvia was in charge tonight.

She put on an aqua cotton top and pleated taupe pants, then tied her hair at the nape with an aqua chiffon scarf. She slipped on a pair of bone-colored sandals, grabbed her purse and left the apartment. Amid the hustle and bustle downstairs, she was able to disappear out the service entrance without anyone being aware of it.

The alley behind the restaurant led to the main drive. The evening air had a velvety texture, increasing the ache inside of her. Avoiding the harbor where she knew the Jakemans moored their sailboat, she walked two blocks to the Coast highway.

Bad mistake. There were so many families on vacation together. Couples were out in droves, some with their arms around each other, many holding hands. Once in a while she glimpsed lovers standing against palm trees in passionate clinches. A steady stream of cars passed by loaded with surfboards, music blaring.

Summer had come to Southern California, and with it too many memories of when she'd loved and been loved, and life had been full of possibilities. The emptiness she was feeling tonight was unbearable.

She made a few purchases at the drugstore, then retraced her steps to her one-bedroom apartment. She'd never lived there with André. The apartment itself held no memories of him, no vestiges of the baby nursery in the place where they used to live. She found it to be a safer refuge than anyplace else. Despite André's pictures.

Once inside, she went over to the desk in the corner of the living room and got on the computer. There was a barrage of e-mails. She saw one from her mother-in-law and opened it first, reminding her that André's parents would be celebrating their wedding anniversary on the twenty-sixth of June.

Abby had already made plane reservations a month ago, but she still didn't know if she wanted to put herself through another experience which was always emotional. If she did go, it would have to be a quick trip. She couldn't handle anything longer than a couple of days.

For the past five years, she'd spent her two-week vacation with them, closing the restaurant for part of October, her slow month. But she always came home depressed.

Unable to give her mother-in-law a definite confirmation just yet, she began reading her other posts.

RICK POKED HIS HEAD inside his daughter's bedroom. She was lying on top of her bed, talking to Danice on the phone. Buddy lay sprawled next to her.

"I had a great time tonight," he whispered.

"Me, too," she whispered back without conviction, holding her hand over the mouthpiece of the phone. The moment he'd told her Abby had taken the night off, all the excitement had gone out of her. As for Rick, the news had been like a kick in the gut.

"See you in the morning, honey."

He shut her door and went to the kitchen. "Jennifer? I'm going for a walk before I turn in."

"It's a beautiful night for it."

Tell me about it. "I couldn't agree more. If you need me, call me on my cell."

Brittany had told him Abby lived above the restaurant. If he had any hope of talking to her in person, he needed to get over there before the restaurant closed.

He checked his watch. Only ten minutes left before the doors were locked. Not wanting to phone and give her the chance to turn him down, he would wing it and see what happened. He was already *persona non grata* with her, so he had nothing to lose.

Determined not to be thwarted, he entered the restaurant and headed straight for the hallway. The dinner crowd was thinning out. People would think he intended to use the restroom.

After startling Abby at the service entrance the other morning, his impromptu arrival tonight would probably guarantee his death sentence. But he was beyond caring and sprinted up the stairs.

"Hey, you! No one's allowed back here," a male voice called after him. "Come down or I'll call the police."

Rick knocked on the door, then turned to discover the man behind him was Chet. The younger man had recognized him, yet he'd still followed him halfway up.

"As you can see, it's just me, there's no need for the police."

"Unless Abby gives the word, you have no right to trespass."

Brittany's powers of observation were dead-on. The dish-washer had a big thing for the boss. That was too bad.

"Let's let her decide, shall we?"

He knocked again and the door opened.

The sight of her took his breath away. Rick had never seen her in anything but her uniform. He'd never seen her hair un-braided. She stared back at him in shock, her eyes very green in contrast to the turquoise scarf.

"I know it's getting late, but I need to talk to you."

"Abby?" Chet called to her from below. "Is everything okay?"

She couldn't believe Brittany's father had come back to the restaurant. It made her slow on the uptake.

"Everything's fine, Chet." She opened the door wider. "Come in," she said to Richard. To her dismay her voice sounded shaky.

As Rick moved inside, Chet said, "Abby? Could we talk for a minute?"

She eyed Brittany's father. "Excuse me. I won't be long."

"I'm in no hurry."

His remark came close to buckling her legs. She shut the door behind her and went down a few steps. "What is it, Chet?"

"You can tell me to butt out if you want, but it was obvious there was tension between you two the other day. I don't care if that guy's built. If he's bothering you, I'll get rid of him. I know a few moves. All you have to do is say the word."

She should have introduced them before now. "Thanks, Chet, but it won't be necessary. He's Brittany's father." Abby had no doubts that in any physical confrontation, Richard Jakeman would emerge the winner with both hands tied behind his back.

Chet's eyes flared in surprise before his expression closed up. "I had no idea. Sorry if I overstepped."

"You didn't. It's nice to know you keep a close eye. Makes me feel safe. Have a good night."

Abby hurried back up the stairs where she found her unex-pected visitor thumbing through the crossword puzzles. He looked up, eyeing her intently. Her pulse raced.

She took the magazine from him and put it on the table. "After a hectic day they help me unwind."

"Maybe I'll buy one and see if it works for me."

"I thought sailing was your cure."

"You'd think so." He stood with his powerful legs slightly apart, hands in the pockets of his white cargo pants. In a coffee-colored silk shirt, the man looked sensational.

"Brittany told me you've been weird all week. When you didn't come to our table tonight, it convinced her you must be sick. Yet it appears you're perfectly healthy."

She rubbed her palms against her hips, a gesture he took in. "I thought it might be better if the two of you ate alone."

He raised one of his eyebrows. "Was that because you didn't want your staff to see the three of us enjoying ourselves together?"

Abby frowned. "Of course not. You know the reason."

"I'm not certain I do. You still go by *Mrs.* Chappuis, and you wear your wedding ring like a shield. How long has your husband been gone?"

She stared at him, taken aback by his blunt question. "Six years. Now, if that's all, I've got a busy day coming up tomorrow."

He ignored her. "Pieces of your husband are everywhere in the restaurant and up here. Having been there myself, I recognize the signs."

Conflicted by several different emotions all tearing her apart at the same time, she said, "You're the one who warned me to keep a professional distance from your daughter."

He pursed his lips. "About that. I came to apologize for creating an untenable situation. It's apparent my daughter has a fatal case of hero worship where you're concerned. I've been trying to fight it, but there's no contest."

She stared hard at him.

"The truth is, I've never had to share her affection. It's something I'd better get used to or I won't survive the teenage years."

His confession humbled her. "Brittany's easy to love. You've raised a wonderful daughter, Mr. Jakeman."

He studied her upturned features. "The name is Rick."

A shiver traveled down her spine. "I'm Abby."

His lips twitched. "Yes. I know. I hear it in my sleep."

"Oh, dear."

"For Brittany's sake, please go back to being yourself around her. Hopefully it's not too late to repair some of the damage."

She didn't understand. "Is there more?"

"Yes. My daughter's not the only one in the Jakeman family who you've affected. I'm having a hell of a time obeying my own instincts to stay away from you. That's what I came to say."

In the next instant he was gone, closing the front door behind him.

His admission staggered her. Without conscious thought, she locked the door, then leaned against it. Men flirted with her all the time. It went with the job. But Brittany's father wasn't flirting or anything close to it. He didn't want to be attracted to her. He resented her because of his daughter's growing attachment to her.

Abby hadn't been wrong about those mixed signals coming from him. He was trying to deal with his frustration in the only way he knew how. If he'd picked up on her attraction to him, that made everything so much worse. Especially for Abby, who had to live with this unexpected turn of events.

Suddenly she felt exposed and vulnerable. All those barriers she'd erected over the years to guard her precious memories had been trampled like so much dust.

CHAPTER SIX

AFTER WORK Monday evening, Rick happened to get on the same elevator with Pam Brooks. They pressed the buttons to their floors. She flashed him a smile that turned him off. No matter how hard she was trying, he wasn't interested.

When the elevator stopped on three, the doors opened and there stood his daughter rocking expectantly on her heels with Buddy. The dog barked a greeting.

Thank you, Brittany. She'd just saved him from having to be rude to the woman.

"Hi, Dad."

"Hi, kiddo." He reached for his daughter, giving her a hug. Before he'd left for work that morning, he hadn't been able to get two words out of her. But since she'd put in her hours at the restaurant, all that had changed. And he knew why.

"Come on." She tugged on his arm. "I've got a surprise waiting for you."

"What kind?"

"If I told you, then it wouldn't be one."

That made sense. "Where's Jennifer?"

"She went down to the pool."

Sure enough when they walked in the condo, he could see Brittany had opened the sliding door off the living room leading to the patio. It overlooked the harbor, a sight he never tired of. At a glance he could see chips, dip and sodas waiting on the wrought iron table. Her old dad was being set up for something.

"Give me a second and I'm all yours." Instead of sailing, he'd thought they could take in an early movie. The latest James Bond was out, something they'd both enjoy.

"Don't take too long."

"I won't."

Rick headed to his room. A minute later, he walked out on the veranda in khakis and a polo shirt.

"This looks good."

"I made it myself. The guacamole is Abby's recipe."

Of course it was. He'd been waiting for her name to pop up. Brittany hadn't disappointed him.

"It's delicious." He couldn't stop with just one nacho. After popping open his can, he sat opposite her. "Okay. Something's on your mind. What is it?"

She put the soda she'd been drinking on the table.

"While I was washing dishes, Chet told me you went over to see Abby on Friday night. When I asked Jennifer, she said you went for a walk."

Rick drained his cola in one go. "I did both. In case she was ill, I wanted to find out so you'd understand why she didn't show up. She would never intentionally hurt your feelings."

"I know. Chet said you've been to the restaurant twice to see her."

Did he now… "That's right. As your father, I needed to check things out for myself."

"Chet says you have the hots for Abby."

Hell. "Chet shouldn't be talking to you about things that are none of his business or yours. I hope you don't ever gossip with your coworkers."

"I don't."

"That's good. It's a nasty habit to get into. More grief is caused by it than you can imagine. I know because it happens at my work, too."

"Don't worry." She finished munching another chip. "But is it true?"

"About what?" he dissembled.

"About Abby?"

"If you mean do I find her attractive and friendly, then yes. Who wouldn't?" Rick didn't know where to start. "I know one thing. You're lucky to be working for her. She runs a tight ship. And you seem to have made a very favorable impression. I'm proud of you, honey."

"Thanks, Dad." She finished the rest of her drink. "Guess what?"

Here it comes. "What's that?"

"The reason she didn't work Friday night was because her in-laws e-mailed her. They want her to fly to Switzerland at the end of June for a family party. She got hung up trying to make plane reservations."

The Chappuis family. Apparently Abby didn't want to ever forget she was their daughter-in-law.

He bit down so hard on a chip, he ground his teeth.

"She always spends her vacations with them. It's when she does her ordering for the restaurant and brings back new dresses for the waitresses. She said she'd get me a blue one in my size. By then, I'll be able to wait tables."

He grimaced. His daughter was getting too entrenched. "That's very nice, but you'll hardly have time to wear it before we move back to Escondido."

Her expression grew sober. "I know. She said when I leave, I can keep it for a souvenir."

Souvenir or not, Rick knew neither of them would forget Abby. "Lucky you."

"I know."

At the thought of not seeing her again, he lost interest in the dip. "Shall we get going? I thought we'd see a film, then grab a hamburger on the way home." He started clearing the table so Jennifer wouldn't have to.

"Okay." She followed him into the kitchen with the rest of the dirty dishes. "But before we leave, could I ask you something?"

"Shoot."

"I'd like to do something nice for Abby to thank her for giving me the job. Do you think we could take her sailing on Sunday? I'll make the picnic."

Why not? Knowing she'd been wearing her deceased husband's wedding ring for six years, he was confident she'd turn down the invitation. "If that's what you want, we'll make it a foursome."

"Four—who else is coming?"

"Liz."

"Liz!" she cried.

"I invited her earlier today."

His daughter looked crushed. "I didn't know you still liked her."

"I never stopped, but the move put us on hold."

Sorry to burst your bubble again, kiddo, but this time it's for my sanity.

"ABBY? Can I talk to you for a minute?"

She looked up from the computer in her office to see Brittany in the doorway. The teen had just finished her shift and had changed out of her white uniform to her jeans and T-shirt. She looked flushed with excitement.

"Sure. Come on in."

Brittany approached the desk. "Would you like to go sailing with us on Sunday? I've already talked to Dad about it."

Which meant the invitation hadn't come from him. Rick had wanted the situation to get back to some kind of normal with his daughter, but surely *normal* didn't include outside activities.

"I wish I could, but I already have plans to spend the day with my family."

"Oh…" The light faded from Brittany's eyes. "I was thinking of your schedule when I picked Sunday. It doesn't have to be then. We go sailing almost every day. Dad bought us a small boat called a Flying Lateen. He can do everything himself, and is teaching me."

She and her father had the tans to prove it. Abby bit her lip, torn because she wasn't immune to Brittany's disappointment. That girl got to her every time.

"Tell you what," she said, making a split decision. "Maybe one afternoon this week or next I could go with you for an hour after you get off work."

"How about right now? Dad won't care when. You told me Tuesday is the least busy night at the restaurant."

Abby chuckled inwardly. Brittany had a mind that didn't forget anything. Like her father, if she couldn't do something one way, she managed to find another way. Both had too much charisma. It wasn't fair. "Even so, I would have to arrange in advance for Sylvia to cover for me."

"Sylvia's in the kitchen. I'll ask her." The girl was off like a shot before Abby could stop her.

After three weeks of getting to know her, Abby was beginning to understand what a dynamo lived beneath Rick Jakeman's roof. His little offshoot demonstrated all the intelligence and drive that had made Rick a successful land developer.

It wasn't long before she heard footsteps in the hall. Brittany raced back into the office, winded. "She said she'll be glad to do it!"

Abby couldn't control a thrill of excitement. "In that case I'd better turn off the computer and hurry upstairs to change. What should I wear?"

"I'm going to wear what I've got on."

"That's easy. Why don't you wait out in front. I'll join you in a minute."

"Okay." Brittany filed out the door ahead of her.

On the way up the stairs, Abby felt like a teenager who'd been asked to a party where she knew the hottest guy at school was going to be there.

After burying her husband and suffering a miscarriage, she hadn't expected to feel this young again. It took her completely by surprise.

RICK HAD JUST DRIVEN into the garage when his cell phone rang. Brittany. "Hi, honey."

"Hi, Dad. Where are you?"

"Headed toward the elevator. Sorry I'm running a little late."

"I am, too." He smiled. His daughter, the tycoon. "How about I meet you at the marina?" she added.

He blinked. "I thought you weren't keen on taking the boat out today."

"I've changed my mind. We can get tacos after."

The winds of change blew faster than he could keep up with.

Abby must have accepted the invitation for Sunday, the last thing he'd expected. That was the only explanation to account for his daughter's mood.

There was no way Liz could come with them now. He'd never be able to explain Abby. Any way you looked at it, Liz would feel like an unwanted third party. The problem now was to manufacture a damn good reason for uninviting her.

"Sounds like a plan. See you soon."

Once he'd informed Jennifer of their arrangements, he changed into shorts and a T-shirt with Buddy looking on. The day had been exceptionally hot. The dog would be better off staying out of the heat.

He rubbed behind his ears. "After we get back, I'll take you for a walk."

Five minutes later, he reached their small boat, then thought he must be hallucinating. Seated inside with his daughter was the woman responsible for the disruption of his formerly peaceful existence.

Their charming hairstyles were identical. Brittany was in the denims and yellow T-shirt she'd worn to school. Abby had put on a pink one with a pair of jeans her figure did wonders for.

His daughter smiled up at him. "Abby's busy on Sunday so I invited her today."

Abby eyed him tentatively. "I hope it's all right."

"Of course. Welcome aboard," he murmured. While he waited for his heart to stop slamming against his ribs, he hunkered down to undo the ropes.

"You need to put on your life preservers," he reminded them.

"I know," Brittany said, "but it's so hot we were waiting for you first."

His gaze sought Abby's. "Have you done any sailing?"

"No, but I've always wanted to."

"Then you're in for a real treat," he said.

"Dad can do all the work himself. He's teaching me."

"You're a fortunate girl," Abby said, struggling to get into the life jacket.

By the time he jumped in the boat, everyone had fastened their preservers.

"What do you two say we sail up to Laguna and have dinner at El Charro?"

Brittany looked as if she was on the verge of exploding. "Have you eaten there before, Abby?"

"Not for several years. That sounds fun."

"Good," Rick said. "It's settled. Stand over there and hang on. We're going for a ride."

He used the motor to take them beyond the protection of the bay, then shut it off. The swells were perfect for this outing. While Abby watched, Brittany helped him undo the white sail with its royal-blue stripe.

As soon as the breeze filled it, the tug on the boat caused their guest to let out a surprised cry. She gripped the railing tighter. Rick laughed. So did she. A beautiful sound he'd never heard come out of her before. In the full sun her eyes glinted the green of a south sea grotto. He felt as if he was already flying before the boat took off across the water.

Brittany and Abby chatted like two old friends totally at ease with each other, their long matching braids hanging down their backs. One brunette, one champagne. Rick liked the sight before him. He liked it very much.

Halfway to Laguna, he let Brittany take over. He knew she

was anxious to show off in front of her favorite person. Now it was his turn to stand next to Abby. Their arms brushed. He felt her warmth.

"What do you think?" he asked.

"It's exhilarating. After being landlocked in Escondido, no wonder you wanted to come here for the summer."

Landlocked. The very word. He slanted his gaze at her. "You live right by the marina, I'm surprised you haven't done any sailing."

She was staring out to sea. "I've been too busy."

"Not even when your husband was alive?" He found he wanted to know everything about her.

"After our wedding, we moved to San Marcos to open a tiny restaurant in a strip mall."

Just then Brittany waved to him. He waved back. "You're doing great!" he called. "I drive through San Marcos all the time." Odd to think she'd once lived that close to Escondido.

She nodded. "It wasn't until after he died that I moved to the coast."

Rick sucked in his breath. He was relieved to hear that her memories had nothing to do with Oceanside. "What brought you here?"

"The ocean. I was born in San Diego and missed the water. A Realtor I was working with told me there was a business opportunity in Oceanside on the pier. A pizzeria had just closed. If I could swing the loan, it would be a sweet deal. So I pounced on it."

"I…I have to confess…I did a little research on you," he said, watching as her eyes widened. "Discovered your restaurant was featured in Oceanside's *Fine Cuisine Guide* last December. That's a real accomplishment. Bravo."

"*Merci.*" She flicked her gaze to him. "So what did *you* think of our fondue?"

He couldn't help staring at the voluptuous curve of her mouth. "Superb. Just the right amount of kirsch. A touch underplayed so it doesn't overpower."

"So you're a connoiseur." A trace of a smile formed on her lips. She had no idea how provocative she was.

"I've attended enough business dinners to know the difference between an American facsimile of fondue, and an authentic Swiss dish. The fendant was unequaled."

"I'm glad you enjoyed your meal."

A rosy flush that had nothing to do with the sun tinted her cheeks. The desire to press his lips to the little pulse throbbing at her throat was almost overwhelming.

"I understand you're leaving for Switzerland soon."

She nodded and looked away. "Next week."

He was missing her already. "Who runs Chez André when the owner's away?"

"Sylvia."

"Ah. Good. Brittany likes her."

"Your daughter likes everyone," Abby said, smiling over at the teen, who was taking her captain's duties very seriously. "It's a wonderful quality. She'll go far in life with such a positive nature. You know what the good book says about the peacemakers."

"I'm sure it hasn't escaped your notice that she *loves* you."

Abby looked down at the water. "She'd love anyone who gave her her first 'real' job."

"Maybe. But in all these years, she's never invited a woman to do anything with us. You, Abby Chappuis, are the only person who holds that distinction."

She laughed nervously. "You shouldn't have told me. When she discovers I have feet of clay like everyone else, you'll know she's finally growing up."

A small change in wind direction made them look again at Brittany, who'd been handling the boat like a pro.

"You're a fabulous sailor!" Abby called to her.

Brittany broke into a smile. An infectious smile. "Thanks, but I think Dad better take over. It's getting tricky now that we've reached Laguna."

So they had.

He'd been miles away. But once they'd eaten dinner, he'd try to figure out what Abby was hiding. Because he knew in his gut something lay much deeper beneath the surface.

CHAPTER SEVEN

EL CHARRO PROVIDED some of the best fine dining in Laguna. Located on a rise that overlooked the Pacific, the large, elegant restaurant with its palm trees and flowering gardens was a real showplace.

"If you and your wife will come this way, Mr. Jakeman, we have a table for you now."

Abby waited for Rick to correct the man. Instead he put his hand at her wrist—his touch felt like a current of electricity—and guided her through the tables as the host led them to an inside table next to a bank of windows with a spectacular view of the ocean.

When they were seated outside beneath the striped awning, he said, "Could you direct my daughter out here when she finishes in the powder room? You can't miss her. She and my wife have the same hairdo."

"Yes, sir." The man handed them menus. "I'll send your waiter over."

"You're terrible," Abby grumbled the second the host walked away.

Rick stared pointedly at her left hand. "If you insist on wearing your wedding ring, prepare to be linked to the wrong man."

"I'm assuming it didn't take you as long to remove yours," she said in her defense, smarting from the remark.

"I never had one to worry about," he said offhandedly. "Brittany's mother and I didn't marry."

While she digested what he'd just told her, Brittany came and sat down. Her eyes flicked back and forth between the two of them, as if she sensed tension.

"Sorry I took so long, There was a lineup."

Abby was glad for the interruption. She assumed Brittany knew the truth. Maybe she never talked about her mother to avoid the inevitable questions people asked.

"No problem, honey," Rick said.

Another college-age guy approached their table. "Hi, everybody. My name's Derek. I'll be your waiter." He put salsa and chips on the table.

Abby felt Rick's eyes on her. "What do you ladies feel like eating this evening?"

"I think I'll have the Playa del Sole," she said.

"Me, too," Brittany chimed in.

Her father chuckled. "Do you even know what it is?"

Brittany wrinkled her nose. "Not really, but Abby's a chef, so she knows what to order."

"In that case we'll make it an even three," he said to the waiter.

"Would you care for wine with dinner?"

"None for me," Abby spoke up. "Just water."

"You're sure?" Rick asked, eyeing her over the small vase of fresh flowers. From another room he could hear the sounds of a mariachi band.

"I have to close up tonight, so I need to keep a clear head."

By the sudden set of his jaw, it appeared she'd irritated him again.

"Dad? Can I have a Coke please?"

"Make that one Coke and an iced tea with lemon." Rick handed the menus back to Derek.

To Abby's relief the band began to play in their section, preventing in-depth conversation. By the time the group took a break, the three were ready to go back to the boat. They reached Oceanside as twilight faded into night.

Abby helped them secure the boat, then they walked along the dock to the shore. She slowed down and turned, smiling at both of them.

"Thank you for a marvelous outing. I haven't enjoyed myself this much since I can't remember when. See you at work tomorrow, Brittany." She wanted to hug her but didn't dare.

"I'll be there."

"'Bye for now."

A jumble of nerves, Abby took off for the restaurant. Rick Jakeman was an enigma. There were moments when being with him set her on fire—and they weren't even touching. But there were other times when he seemed to close off and she felt to blame. They were in a strange relationship that needed to end.

Much as she adored Brittany, she couldn't let the teen into her heart any further.

It was a good thing Abby was flying to Geneva next week. She needed to put some distance between them and get her head on straight.

She let herself in the service entrance in time to say goodnight to the waitresses. When she found Sylvia, she slipped a big tip into her pocket. "I appreciate your taking over on such short notice."

"Anytime, Abby. I'm almost through here."

"Okay. I'll be in my office."

Chet came in while she was tallying the night's receipts.

"Want me to stay and help?"

Oh, dear. For some time now she'd been aware of his interest, but had hoped he'd realize she saw him only as an employee.

"I appreciate that, Chet, but you go on. I know you've got studies." She kept running the numbers.

"Did you have a good time with Brittany's father?"

He'd come close to the line several times. Tonight he'd overstepped it. Her hand stilled on the machine. She lifted her head. "What's going on with you, Chet?"

"I'm trying to find out if there's any chance for me."

"Chance for what?"

His lips tightened. "I've been hinting at asking you out for a long time."

She let out a sigh. "Then you realize I've been ignoring those hints because you're a good worker and I wouldn't want to lose you." Abby sat back in her swivel chair. "Romance in the office doesn't work. Besides, I'm too old for you."

"But not too young for Brittany's old man?"

There was movement at the door. "Rick!" she gasped. He was here? How much had he heard?

"You owe your boss an apology."

Obviously he'd heard enough.

Brittany's father made a daunting adversary. "If I were the owner, which I'm not, I'd sack you right now."

A curse flew out of Chet's mouth. Angry, he glanced back at Abby. "I don't plan to give you the chance because I quit." He stormed out the door.

Still in shock, she looked up at Rick who stood there with his hands on his hips in an aggressive stance. "He's been needing that lesson for a long time," Rick finally said, shifting where he was, beginning to look uncomfortable.

"A good dishwasher is hard to come by," she said, shaking her head. The man had no right.

Rick looked back to where Chet disappeared "I'm sorry... Since I'm to blame for bringing things to a head, would you allow this old man to offer his services until you can find a replacement?"

Abby laughed. She couldn't help it. "Am I to deduce that the crack commercial developer is a jack-of-all-trades?"

His smile turned her heart over. "I washed dishes at a diner to help put myself through college. It's like riding a bike. You never forget. Brittany can bring me up to speed. With the two of us, the restaurant won't feel a ripple."

She cocked her head. "What will the Jakeman company do without its commander and chief?"

"I'm a good delegator."

Her smile slowly faded. "Why did you come over here?"

He took one last look back down the stairs. "Do you wish I hadn't, *Mrs.* Chappuis?"

The atmosphere sizzled between them like a live wire snaking along the ground.

"No, of course not. Since you're willing. I won't say no." Abby got to her feet, but her legs barely supported her. "Why did you come over here now?"

"In case you hadn't noticed, I can't seem to stay away from you. Does that tell you anything?"

A panicky feeling swept over her. "Sit down for a minute. I have to say good-night to Sylvia."

"I'll come with you to make certain Chet left."

Secretly relieved he was staying, she rushed past, careful to avoid touching him. Her dishwasher had become increasingly difficult over the past month. When he'd stalked out a few minutes ago, it worried her he might still be around waiting to talk to her.

She wanted to believe Chet ran on a short fuse, nothing more. But you never really knew what another person might be capable of. When André was alive, this kind of situation hadn't arisen.

Sylvia was on the verge of leaving. Her attention darted to Rick, then Abby. "What happened with Chet? He tore out of here without saying good-night."

"He quit."

The other woman gave her a knowing glance. "I see…. Well, for what it's worth, it's for the best."

Abby nodded.

"You didn't hire Brittany any too soon. If you want, I'll take over the three nights of his shift until you find someone else."

"What would I do without you?"

"I was going to ask you the same thing. I need this job."

After locking the door behind the other woman, Abby turned to discover Rick on his cell phone. When he finally hung up he said, "I called one of my assistants—"

"At night? At home?" Abby asked.

"It's okay," Rick replied. "Barb's used to being on call for me.

Anyway, she knows an all-night locksmith with a mobile unit. The man will be here within fifteen minutes."

She could only marvel at his quick thinking. He ran circles around other men. "Thank you."

"It's the least I can do. How about I buy us a cup of coffee while we wait?"

She couldn't refrain from smiling. "Why don't you come up to the apartment and I'll fix us some."

Abby made a detour to the office for her purse, then hurried up the dimly lit stairs. At the top she had to stop and get out her key. Aware of Rick standing so close behind her, she fumbled trying to get it in the lock and it fell.

As she turned to retrieve it, he caught her in his arms. Several steps higher than him, she could look straight into his eyes, their faces mere inches apart. The desire she saw in his eyes nearly melted her bones.

"I don't know about you," he whispered huskily, "but I have to do this or go a little mad."

His mouth closed over hers. He propelled her back against the door while he coaxed her lips apart. Caught with her guard down, she didn't have time to think or breathe. There was only this ecstatic sensation whipped up by their hunger for each other.

She clung to him as one kiss slowly turned into another. Her hands slid up his chest to his shoulders. When that didn't bring him close enough, she wound her arms around his neck. Without conscious thought, her body melted into his hard-muscled frame.

This was what she'd been wanting. His touch drove Abby insane. Consumed by needs she'd thought dead after all these years, she realized they'd only been lying dormant until Brittany's father arrived. A man who didn't want to like her, but didn't mind kissing her senseless.

A moan escaped her. What was she doing kissing him back like this as if her life depended on it?

"You're so damn beautiful, you can't even imagine. I want

you, Abby. I've never wanted a woman so much in my life. You want me, too, please don't deny it."

"I'm not, but we can't do this—" she said, trying to escape his mouth.

"We already are," he came back fiercely before devouring her once more.

But they weren't in any kind of relationship you could put a name to. This was how you got into trouble. No words. No understanding. No commitment. Just sensual fullfillment. Crushed in Rick Jakeman's arms.

Wedding or no wedding, Brittany's mother had flung herself into the same position. Abby could understand the woman. She was on the verge of giving into her feelings…while she still had André's ring on her finger!

His cell phone rang and she tore her lips from his.

He kept her locked against him while he answered it. She was out of breath, but he sounded in perfect control.

"That was the locksmith," he said against her lips when he disconnected, before giving her a hard, swift kiss. "He's outside knocking on the front door. I'll let him in." Reluctantly, he let her go and disappeared down the stairs.

Grateful for the respite to fix her lipstick and get herself under control, she joined them a minute later. Before long the service door and the front locks had been changed.

"Here's your new key for both, and a duplicate."

Abby shook the man's hand. "Thank you for coming on such short notice. How much do I owe you?"

"Your husband's already paid me. Good night."

After he went out the front door Abby saw the devilish blue gleam in Rick's eyes. Staring pointedly at her ring, he raised his hands, palms facing her.

She took a deep breath. "About what happened on the stairs—"

"It was long overdue," he interrupted her. "I'm not going to apologize for something we both enjoyed so much. If I didn't have a daughter to get back to, I'd insist on staying for that cup of coffee."

He kissed two fingers and pressed them to her swollen lips. "Later, Mrs. Chappuis."

CHAPTER EIGHT

BEFORE NOON the next day Rick walked over to Brittany's school. He watched the kids pouring out of the high school. When he saw his daughter, he waved. "Hi, honey!"

She looked shocked as she ran toward him. "Dad, how come you're not at work?"

Who was the parent here? "I thought I'd take time off to be with you."

Her face paled. "What's wrong? Did something happen to Buddy…or is it Abby?"

If Rick hadn't known before…

"Actually, this has to do with Chet."

Brittany's expression grew watchful. "What about him?"

"Last night I went over to the restaurant to make certain Abby got home safely, but Chet didn't like it, so he quit."

"Whoa, Dad—"

"Since I'm the reason she's shorthanded, I volunteered to be your assistant washing dishes until she finds a replacement. We need to get there on time."

Rick started walking faster. She hurried to keep up with him.

"You're going to work with me?"

"That's right. Is that okay?"

"I love it! Did Abby say you could?"

"I'm pretty sure she's not going to mind the help. You'll have to show me the ropes, though. I haven't washed dishes in a long time."

"You mean, since you worked at Shorty's Diner." Brittany never forgot anything.

"Think I can handle it?"

"Dad." She laughed. "Who's going to do your work?"

"I've left Ray in charge until further notice. Abby's going to need us all week, including evenings and Saturday."

His daughter's quiet smile was telling.

They made good time and walked around the back to the service entrance. She pushed the red button. In a minute, one of the waitresses let them in. Though the restaurant had just opened for lunch, the place was already humming with activity.

After introductions were made, he waited while Brittany stowed her backpack and changed into her uniform. Then they walked down the hall to the kitchen.

The dishwashing area was at the far end, away from the chefs' work space. Rick was glad there was no sign of Abby yet. He wanted to be hard at work when she noticed there was a new man on the job.

A lump of pride lodged in his throat to see the professional way his daughter did her work. She had other tasks to fill besides dishwashing. If he didn't know the truth, he would have thought she'd been an employee here much longer. She was good at this. Almost as good as she was at sailing.

It wasn't often a parent could be objective when it came to their children, but this gave Rick a chance to see his daughter through new eyes. Her poise at such a tender age had to be one of the qualities that had impressed Abby enough to hire her in the first place.

"Okay, Dad. One of your jobs is to clean the forks and the *caquelons* over at this sink. Turn them facedown to dry on these cloths. Be careful, they're ceramic."

"I'll treat them like a newborn baby."

Her laughter warmed his heart. A month ago, she'd been so upset he didn't want her to work, he'd wondered if he'd ever hear it again.

His adrenaline pumping in anticipation of seeing Abby, he rolled up his shirtsleeves and got busy. In between cleaning pots, he helped Brittany load and unload plates and wineglasses. On his fourth trip to the sink he saw a vision in blue with gold hair enter the kitchen.

Abby came to an abrupt halt, staring at him in disbelief. She clearly hadn't taken him seriously last night.

There was no smile of acknowledgment or welcome from her. Had he overstepped his bounds? It was too late to worry about that now. From here on out they were physically and emotionally in each other's faces.

She turned to talk to Brittany until one of the waitresses motioned to her from the hall. Once she'd left the kitchen, his daughter hurried over to him.

"When the lunch crowd leaves, we always get a break. Abby wants us to go upstairs to her apartment."

Rick had an idea Abby planned to fire him, in the nicest possible way, of course. In the bright light of day she regretted her lapse of control and would use Brittany as a shield to keep him at bay. She was a past master at protecting herself, but it was a little late for that.

Last night they'd been too impatient to make it over the threshold of her inner sanctum. Now that he'd discovered the desire wasn't all on his part, the compulsion to find out what there could be between them wouldn't let him go.

At this point it was immaterial whether she'd wanted or meant to get beneath his skin. Neither of them had chosen to go this route willingly, but Rick could see it was going to be a fascinating journey to…wherever they ended up.

A FEW MINUTES AFTER Abby had gone to her apartment to freshen up, she heard a knock on the door. With pounding heart she hurried across the living room to open it to the two people who'd become frighteningly important to her in a very short period of time.

"Come in." Thankful for Brittany's presence, she was able to avoid Rick's eyes without seeming obvious. "Sit down."

Rick took the upholstered chair, and Brittany opted for the

couch next to Abby. She looked around the room. "It's funny to think of you living inside a restaurant. I bet you feel safe."

Abby didn't know whether to laugh or cry. Memories of last night on the stairs with Rick heated her cheeks. "For the most part I do. That's one of the reasons I asked you to come up here. I need to talk to you about Chet."

"Dad said he quit."

"Yes. He was angry when he left. As a precaution your father arranged to have the locks changed at both restaurant doors last night."

Brittany's eyes widened. "You think Chet has his own key?"

"It happens, honey," her father said. "The locks were changed as a precaution."

"You think he'll come back when no one else is here, huh."

"It's possible." Concerned, Rick flashed Abby a glance before looking at his daughter again. "Unfortunately, some men just won't give up if they've been turned down by a woman."

Her head swung around to Abby. "I could tell he really liked you."

"Well, he's gone now. I just wanted you to be aware in case he comes in the restaurant to try to talk to you."

"Don't worry. I'll avoid him. Besides, Dad's going to be here."

With that comment Abby got to her feet. "That's the other thing I wanted to talk to you about. You've met Tony who works nights."

Brittany nodded. "He's the one who trained Chet."

"I've asked him to train a new applicant, Paul, for the rest of this week. If all goes well, Paul will start working with you on Monday. Until then, Tony will come tomorrow to help fill in at noon for the rest of this week."

Rick stood, eyeing her directly. "Sounds like a lot of pressure for Tony. Why don't you let me finish out this week with my daughter? It will ease my guilt for creating this situation in the first place. I didn't do too badly today, did I, honey?"

"Dad's a lot faster than Chet!"

Abby fought not to smile. She eyed Rick helplessly. "I couldn't ask you to do that."

"But Dad wants to," Brittany cried.

"I confess I like working here better than my other job," he said.

Just thinking about being around him for the rest of the week filled her with too much excitement.

"Dad's already put Ray in charge of his office," Brittany implored. "It'll be fun all three of us working together. You won't have to pay Tony extra and you won't have to pay Dad at all!"

Abby chose the wrong moment to glance at Rick. The dangerous glint in his eyes said there were forms of payment other than money. Her body went weak as she thought about a repeat of last night. If Brittany weren't involved, Abby would be tempted.

But Rick's daughter meant everything to him and to her. She didn't want Brittany hurt, so she didn't dare succumb again. The two of them would be going back to Escondido at the end of the summer. Better not to start something that could destroy Abby once they were out of her life. Keep it light.

"In that case, Rick," she said, putting a smile on her face, "I'll be happy to have you on board for the rest of the week. Though I know Brittany could handle it by herself, I'm sure she'll enjoy working with you. Thank you."

"My pleasure. Now, I think Brittany and I better get downstairs and finish our jobs. Come on, kiddo."

To Abby's dismay she didn't want them to go, but there was nothing for it except to walk them to the door. Just as they started to leave, Brittany turned to her. "Thanks," she whispered. As natural as breathing Brittany reached out and hugged her. Abby reciprocated, no longer able to withhold her heart from Rick's daughter.

Over the teen's shoulder she felt the pull of his gaze twisting her emotions even more.

"What do you do with your time between four and six?" he asked in his deep voice.

"Relax before the next onslaught."

His half smile was so sensual, she actually trembled. "How about I treat you and Brittany to a frozen banana before we call it a day?"

Don't say yes, Abby. Everything's growing too complicated.

"That sounds good."

THURSDAY MORNING Rick put in a call to Liz's law firm. Brittany had just left for class. While he waited for her to come on the line he paced the floor of the terrace thinking about what he would say. Buddy followed him, hoping for a leftover from breakfast.

On principle Rick didn't approve of lying in any form. And Liz would be hurt no matter what he told her. He had to tell her the truth.

"Rick? Forgive me for making you wait. I was in a meeting, but when I heard it was you, I made my excuses. You can't imagine how much I'm looking forward to Sunday. I've missed you horribly."

He came to a standstill, unable to tell her the same thing. Since Abby had come into his life, everything had changed. After last night he felt reborn.

"Liz…I'm afraid I'm going to have to cancel."

"Oh, no. Something unavoidable at work?"

"Not at work, no." Hell, he hated having to do this.

"But something *is* wrong. Wait. I get it. You've…met someone else, haven't you?"

His breathing felt constricted. "Liz…"

The pained silence coming from her end made him feel terrible.

He hesitated. "When I brought Brittany here, I had no idea this was going to happen."

More silence.

Rick cleared his throat. "It's…serious."

He heard her sharp intake of breath. "At least…at least you're honest. I'll give you that."

"I'm sincerely sorry, Liz. Please believe me when I say that I've enjoyed the time we've spent together."

"But not enough to stay in Escondido," she said in a tear-filled voice. "Good luck, Rick." She hung up.

Slowly he put down his phone. He hated to hurt her this way. But all he could think about was Abby. And he couldn't feel guilty when he thought about her.

Since Tuesday, he'd only seen her coming and going. She was very clever the way she managed to avoid being alone with him at the restaurant. The game of hide-and-seek had gone on long enough. With a plan in mind, he got ready for work early.

"Jennifer?" he called from the front hall. "I'm off. See you around four-thirty. Have a good one."

"You, too!"

I intend to.

Taking pity on the dog, he gave him half a piece of toast from the kitchen before leaving the condo. Being old and half-blind, eating was about Buddy's only joy left in life. Except for Brittany, of course.

After the way he'd seen Abby hug Brittany back at the apartment, Rick suspected her feelings for his daughter were stronger than the normal boss-employee relationship, too. Somehow his little girl had gotten to the owner of Chez André. He'd bet his life she'd never hired anyone that young. Today, while no one else was around, he intended to get to the bottom of her unprecedented job offer.

Once he reached the pier he was disappointed to discover she hadn't opened yet. Too impatient to wait, he phoned the restaurant. Frustrated because he was told to leave a message, he walked around to the service entrance and pressed the buzzer. Five minutes later, still no results.

He frowned. The woman had the right to sleep in. Heaven knows she deserved it. Rick understood what it was like to carry the burden of a business on your shoulders. That's why he was taking this semivacation for the summer here in Escondido.

While he stood there pondering what to do next, a car turned down the alley. As it drew closer he spotted Abby at the wheel. He walked over to the driver's side. Her window was already down.

He put his hands on the opening and leaned forward. "Good morning."

"Rick—" She sounded a trifle breathless. Her eyes searched his for an overly long moment. "What are you doing here?"

"I came to see you before we had an audience. Where've you been this early?"

"I took some clothes to the cleaners for my trip next week."

He preferred not to think about that. "Are you in a hurry to open up?"

She checked her watch. "No. The suppliers won't be here for another hour."

"Good. Let's go down to the beach." It was a short walk.

"All right." Her voice didn't sound quite even. "I'll have to park the car first."

"Which garage is yours?" There was a bank of them on the other side of the alley.

"Number five."

"I'll open it."

In another minute, she joined him. They walked down the alley that led to a path to the beach. The air was so warm the mist had all but disappeared. Rick could see a dozen surfers out beyond the breakers. A few people were jogging along the sand, but for the most part they were alone.

Abby's hair had been tied back in a scarf, a purple one. She wore a sleeveless white blouse and shorts with purple polka dots. The woman smelled divine and looked good enough to eat. The urge to kiss her made his lower limbs heavy.

By tacit agreement they took off their sandals. After Rick rolled up his pant legs, they let the water do its worst.

She spoke first. "What did you want to talk to me about?"

"Brittany. Why did you really hire her?"

She slowed down and turned to him. As she shielded her eyes, he caught the glint of her wedding band in the sun. He hated the reminder. "If I tell you, it will betray a confidence."

He stiffened. "I'm trying to understand what drove my daughter to get a job. It's not that I don't want her to have one, but there's some kind of disconnect here. She's the same, yet not the same since our move. Frankly I'm at a loss. It would mean a lot if you could shed some light on it."

Abby stood with the foam swirling around her long shapely legs, obviously weighing what he'd said. "Let me ask you a question first. What did she tell you was the reason?"

They stared at each other. "Brittany doesn't want a housekeeper living with us anymore. She thinks I treat her like a baby. When I insisted Jennifer come with us to the beach, she went into orbit about it. I figured she must have gone job hunting so she wouldn't have to be home with Jennifer. Is that what she told you?"

"Not exactly. I didn't realize you have a housekeeper with you right now. Brittany never mentioned this Jennifer to me." She bit her lip. "When I asked your daughter why she wanted to work, she told me about this guy at school."

A guy?

"Go on," he urged.

After she'd finished telling him all about the senior student's slight, he rubbed the back of his neck in frustration. "Good grief. A few potshots at me and my money did all this damage?"

Abby eyed him with compassion. "She's at a sensitive age, and you've raised a daughter with a strong social conscience. I think it's to her credit she decided to do something positive. A less confident child would probably sit around all summer brooding over a guy with a chip on his shoulder."

"So you saved the day."

"You wish I hadn't?"

"I didn't say that," he muttered.

"You didn't have to," she said soberly. "To answer the rest of your question, I gave her the job because of the way she presented herself. If I had a daughter, I'd want her to be exactly like Brittany."

That's what he'd thought. In the next breath he grasped her shoulders, bringing her so close their mouths were only inches apart. "Why don't you have a daughter or son of your own? Weren't you able to conceive, or were you putting it off?"

Her eyes filled with tears. "When the accident...happened, I was seven months' pregnant. If our little boy had lived, he'd be six years old."

"Abby..." He crushed her against him, rocking her in his arms. Her body shook with silent sobs.

"When they both died, *I* died."

Now he understood why the ring stayed on her finger.

She might have responded physically to him the other night, she might even sleep with him. But that's all it would be. Just as it had been with Rachel.

Some men were destined to repeat their mistakes. He'd be damned if he was going to be one of them. He felt her try to ease away.

"Sorry I've fallen apart on you. How embarrassing." With a little more strength she pulled free of his arms and wiped her eyes.

"I have to get back." She started for the path. He followed. "I hope what I've told you has helped."

His hands formed fists. "You have no idea."

CHAPTER NINE

AT FIVE AFTER FOUR on Friday, Abby breezed in the kitchen, handing each of the staff an envelope before their break. Rick watched as she approached Brittany last.

"It's payday." She thrust the envelope in the teen's hands.

"Thank you."

"You don't need to thank me. You've earned it. Don't spend it all at once."

"You *know* I won't," his daughter confided sotto voce, but Rick heard her.

Since no one else opened their envelopes, he noticed Brittany didn't, either. She turned to him. "I'll change my uniform and meet you out front."

He nodded.

After she darted off, Abby lifted her eyes to him. Since the emotional scene on the beach yesterday when she'd bared her soul to him, she'd reverted to the professionalism of owner and manager.

"Thank you for your help this week. As I said earlier, Brittany could have handled it just fine, but there's nothing like a father to give her that added confidence... Thanks for the other night, too. It made me realize how much I miss André to handle certain situations."

Don't say any more, Abby. You're killing me.

"Have a fun weekend sailing."

This was beginning to sound like a goodbye speech.

"Oh, and tell Brittany I'll see her a week from Monday. Any problems she might have, Sylvia will take care of them."

When she turned to leave, he felt as if he'd just been slammed in the gut by the jib. "I thought you weren't flying to Switzerland until next Wednesday."

She looked back at him. "I decided that if I'm going for a few days, I might as well go for a whole week. Luckily I was able to get a flight leaving in the morning."

Nothing could be plainer than that. She wanted out of here, as far away from Rick as possible.

"In that case, let me wish you *bon voyage,* Madame Chappuis."

He left her standing there and strode toward the hallway. When he walked out of the restaurant, Brittany was already in front. She'd opened her envelope.

"Look—there's a check for you, too." She handed it to him.

Pay for four days' work.

Four days to get nearer to her.

Her timing couldn't have been more perfect.

"I just love Abby," Brittany said.

I know.

Halfway to the condo, she asked, "Can we drive to the bank? I want to deposit it into my account."

"Tell you what—let's pack a bag and drive to Escondido for the weekend. You and Danice can take it to the bank tomorrow. Maybe get together with some friends?"

She stopped walking, her face screwed up in confusion. "But I don't want to go to Escondido."

"The problem is, I think Jennifer would. Maybe it's time for you and me to be on our own."

"You mean…no more housekeeper for me?" Brittany appeared shell-shocked.

"After seeing the exceptional way you've been doing your job at Chez André, you've convinced me you don't need one."

"Oh, Dad!" She threw herself into his arms, almost knocking him over.

"I take it that makes you happy."

"This is the best summer of my life!"

Wish that I could say the same, kiddo.

"Can we go grocery shopping this weekend? I want to make a farewell dinner for her."

"I'm sure that would please Jennifer."

"Oh…no…well, I guess I should, but I meant Abby! She's leaving for Switzerland on Wednesday, so I want to invite her for Tuesday night. That's her slow time at the restaurant so I know she'll come."

"Honey, Abby's plans have changed."

"What do you mean?"

Here we go again. Hell.

"She's decided to go in the morning."

"What? She didn't tell me. What happened?"

He smothered a groan. "Something came up and she has to leave sooner." *She wants to get away from me.* "She asked me to tell you that she'd see you a week from Monday."

They entered the apartment building and walked to the elevator. On the way up to their floor she said, "That's ten days away…"

The pain in her expression turned her eyes a darker shade of blue, if that was possible. "Did Liz ask you to spend the weekend with her? Is that why you brought up Escondido?"

What was going on in her mind?

"No," he said emphatically. "As a matter of fact, I broke everything off with her yesterday on the phone."

"You did?"

Rick took a deep breath. "To go on seeing her would be a waste of her time and mine."

She followed him out of the elevator to the condo. "Does Abby know that?"

Perplexed, he said, "I'm not following you."

"You must be blind if you don't know how much she likes you. That's why Chet got so mad. Cheryl said Abby has never given him or any man the time of day until you came along. Did you and Abby have a fight?"

"What?" he blurted, still reeling from the revelation.

"Dad. She *knows* you have a girlfriend."

"How?"

"You must have told her, because she mentioned it to me. Maybe she's hurt and that's why she decided to leave early."

Rick stared hard at his daughter. Brittany's pride had been stung by a guy. That's why she'd been so willing to come to the beach for the summer. Anything to avoid more pain. Was Abby doing the same thing?

He shook his head trying to figure it all out. "I'm afraid you're jumping to conclusions without knowing the whole story, honey."

Brittany trailed him into the kitchen. "Like what?"

"First off, Abby and I didn't have a fight." Not in the sense she meant. "Second, and most importantly, she's still in love with her husband. When the accident took his life, it also took their unborn child's."

"She was going to have a baby?" Her voice throbbed.

"Yes. A boy."

"Oh, no—" Suddenly she was sobbing in his arms. "She'd make the best mother on earth."

Agreed.

Finally she pulled away from him. "Dad?" She gazed up with beseeching eyes. "Is that why you never got married? Because you loved my mother too much?"

Brittany was old enough to handle the truth. It was time to tell her. But not here.

"Let's drive to Escondido and take Jennifer home. Then you and I will go to our house with Buddy and have a long talk."

He could tell how torn she was. Rick knew his daughter. She wanted to see Abby before she left, but it was better this way.

"Okay." She wiped her eyes. "Maybe we could take Jennifer to dinner somewhere on the way while you tell her the news. Let's buy her a pretty plant or something for a goodbye gift. I'll pay for it."

His daughter was growing up before his very eyes. "You know what, kiddo? I love you."

"Ditto."

Four hours later, his daughter found him in the study. She'd been on the phone with her friends making plans. Buddy was right behind her. "Can we talk now?"

He turned off the computer and moved over to the couch. "To answer your earlier question, I loved your mother very much, otherwise we wouldn't have had you.

"When I realized I was in love with her and asked her to marry me, she turned me down."

Brittany jumped off the couch. "She didn't want to marry *you?*"

"Let me finish. We met in college. Rachel had some liberal attitudes that developed as a result of her parents' strict rules. But it was a revelation to me she didn't want to get married. I thought I could change her mind, but it didn't happen."

"My mother didn't want to marry *you?*" She sounded incredulous and hurt. How he loved this daughter of his.

"You don't understand. She loved me, but I was too traditional for her. We just weren't compatible, honey. I didn't see her again until she told me she was pregnant. That changed everything for me. I wanted you and told her I'd do whatever it took to help raise you."

Brittany threw her arms around him and hugged him for a long time.

"When you were born," he finally said, "it was love at first sight for both of us. We worked out visitation so I could be with you as often as possible… Then your mom…got cancer."

She eased herself out of his arms. "That's so awful."

"Yes, it was… I promised her—and myself—I'd be the best father I could."

"You are!" She hugged him again. "I love you. I'm not like my mother. I'm going to get married like Abby did, and have babies."

Abby. Always Abby.

His eyes smarted. "I want that for you, too, but not for a long time."

She laughed before straightening up again. "Dad? Do you mind if I sleep over at Danice's tonight? She begged me."

Under the circumstances Rick thought it was an excellent idea, never mind that he would be alone in the house, prey to the yawning emptiness he couldn't do anything about.

"It's fine. I'll drive you."

ABBY PULLED OUT the last small load of clothes from the dryer, then folded them into the suitcase on the chair in her bedroom. Her heart was a heavy stone in her chest.

After the way she'd fallen into Rick's arms, how could she have behaved like the bereaved widow the next morning? During those passion-filled moments she'd been an equal participant, giving him kiss for kiss, never wanting to stop. She hadn't been able to get enough.

He had to be laughing now. She needed to talk to him and explain herself. But her hope that Rick would have come by last night or this evening to finish their conversation had never materialized. He hadn't attempted to delay her in the kitchen earlier today. No phone call tonight.

He was a man who enjoyed the woman of the moment. He hadn't married Brittany's mother. He'd been seeing a woman when he'd moved to Oceanside. When he left to go to back to Escondido at the end of the summer, it would be out of sight, out of mind. On to the next romantic interlude.

Not so for Abby. What a convoluted irony that, after years of mourning André, she was leaving for Switzerland to try to forget Rick Jakeman—a man Brittany had brought into Abby's life, changing it dramatically.

Much as she wanted to call him, she couldn't find the courage. She had no doubt women had been chasing him for years. Abby didn't intend to be one of them.

With nothing more to do until morning, she went into the bathroom and brushed her teeth. As she came back into the bedroom, she heard the end of a message being left on her answering machine. Maybe it was Sylvia with a few last-minute questions.

Abby rewound the tape and listened. Her heart leaped when she heard Brittany's voice. "I just wanted to say goodbye. I'm going to miss you."

Hearing those words brought a lump to Abby's throat.

"If you have time, please call me back. Here's my cell phone number."

Without hesitation Abby reached for her phone and pushed the digits.

"Abby?" the teen answered in a hushed tone.

"Brittany—what's wrong? I can hardly hear you."

"I'm in Danice's bathroom and don't want her to hear me."

She frowned. "You're in Escondido?"

"Dad said I didn't need a housekeeper anymore so we drove Jennifer back home."

Incredible.

"We're going to stay here until Sunday night. It's going to be the two of us from now on."

Why was she telling Abby this?

"I found out he broke up with Liz, so I was going to have you over for a farewell dinner on Tuesday night, but Dad said you're leaving earlier."

Her hand tightened on the phone. "That's right."

"He's really upset—like Chet."

Abby's mouth went dry. "What do you mean?"

"I heard about your baby. Because you lost everything, Dad said you'll never love anyone else but your husband. The thing is, I found out tonight that my mother didn't marry my dad, because she didn't believe in marriage. He said she killed his love. She wasn't anything like you, Abby."

A sob rose in Abby's throat.

"You like Dad, don't you?"

"O-of course."

"I mean, you really like him. I've seen the way you look at him. It's the same way he looks at you." There was a pause. "Why do you have to go to Switzerland right now? I think Dad thinks

you don't like him. I think that's why he decided to drive us—
Uh-oh...Danice is calling me. I've got to go. Have a good time,
Abby. Please come home safe. Please."

She hung up before Abby could say goodbye. Maybe it was
better. She wouldn't have been able to get a word out.

Lying awake most of the night gave her time to think. Her
mind replayed every look and conversation with Rick. With the
new knowledge his daughter had imparted over the phone, Abby
began to understand the mixed messages she and Rick had been
giving off.

Throughout their relationship, nothing had been exactly as it
had seemed. *Except* for the way she'd felt when his mouth was
on hers.

The chemistry between them—the love she had for Brittany—
that was real. *That* was truth. There was no mistaking it for anything else. You only got a few chances in this life, but it had taken
Brittany to open Abby's eyes before it was too late. It was time
he knew she'd fallen in love with him. She wouldn't wait any
longer to tell him.

With pounding heart, she got up to shower and dressed. She
picked out her cream suit with café-au-lait piping—her favorite.
She pulled her hair back into a tortoiseshell clip, leaving a few
ends to curl around her jaw. She wanted—no, needed—to look
perfect. After fastening her pearl earrings, she applied mascara
and lipstick. With her heightened excitement, she didn't need
blush.

At six, she went to her office to check something in one of
the files, then she left through the service entrance with her
suitcase. She'd gassed up her car the day before and was ready
to go.

When she reached the Coast highway, she followed the signs
to the interstate. Instead of turning north to L.A., though, she
headed south to the junction for Highway 78. The traffic was
hideous.

It was close to eight before she ate breakfast in San Marcos.

Around nine, she reached Escondido's city limits. At a convenience mart she asked for directions to Cherry Cove Drive, then drove on, riding a fresh surge of adrenaline.

CHAPTER TEN

"BUDDY'S DYING?"

"I'm afraid so, honey. The vet said to bring him in. I knew you'd want to go with me."

After a sleepless night, Rick had driven over to Danice's house to get Brittany. He'd wrapped Buddy in a blanket and laid him on the backseat of the car.

His daughter got in next to the dog. "Buddy...Buddy..." She sobbed.

"We knew it was going to happen one of these days."

"Maybe he just wanted to come home to die."

Out of the mouths of babes.

"You could be right. A few minutes ago, I found him in his favorite place in the dining room where the sun shines in from the terrace."

"We shouldn't have moved to Oceanside. He would have lived longer and—" She didn't finish what she was about to say, but she didn't need to. Rick could finish it for her.

And we would never have met Abby who was off-limits for us.

Suddenly Buddy let out an eerie moan.

"Dad?" she croaked. "H-he's gone...."

Rick checked the dog's breathing to confirm it.

"I don't think I can go back to my job now." The tears poured down her splotchy cheeks. "Buddy hated it when I left him all day. I didn't even stay with him last night." Her body shook. "I think he died of a broken heart, and it's my fault."

"Of course it isn't—"

There were degrees of pain. Rick thought he'd passed through all of them, but he was wrong.

A few minutes later, they arrived at the vet clinic and he confirmed it for them. Taking Rick aside, he said, "You can let me dispose of him, or you can bury him in your yard. It's not legal, but I wouldn't worry about it."

Once again they bundled up the dog. Brittany held him while Rick drove. It was almost noon when they pulled around the back of the house. The day was already a scorcher.

"Let's take him in the house out of the sun. This evening when it's cooler, we'll bury him in the garden. That'll give you time to think of the right words to say. I'm sure Danice will want to come say goodbye."

As Rick moved the dog next to the hearth in the family room, they heard the front doorbell ring.

"Maybe that's her now." Brittany got up from the floor, tears dripping down her face. "I'll get it."

While he stood there looking down at Buddy, he heard his daughter cry Abby's name. Rick's lungs constricted.

No. He must have misheard. She was on her way to Switzerland.

When Brittany didn't come back, he walked through the house to find out what was going on. His psyche wasn't prepared for the breathtaking sight that greeted him.

There was Abby, hugging Brittany, who was sobbing her heart out to her. "I know how you feel, sweetheart. I've lost two dogs myself."

"I loved him so much."

Over his daughter's heaving shoulders, those gorgeous green eyes sought his approval while she gave his child a mother's comfort.

Right now he didn't ask any questions. They could wait.

All he knew was that she'd come. This had to be some kind of miracle because, so help him, Rick had reached the rock bottom on ideas of how to get them through the rest of this day.

"Is Buddy here so I can see him?" she asked Brittany, but she was looking at Rick.

He nodded. "In the family room."

The three of them walked through the Tudor-style home to the back of the house. Brittany ran over and lifted the blanket. Abby sank on her knees to look at the dog.

"Oh...he's adorable. Just like one of those black Scottie dogs wearing a red-and-green sweater you sometimes see on Christmas cards."

"That's what I always thought, too," Brittany said, still crying. "Are you going to have a funeral for him?"

"Tonight, when it's cooler. I wish you could come, but you probably have to leave for the airport, huh?"

Rick stopped breathing while he waited for her response.

She rose to her feet. Without looking at him she said, "After you called me last night to say goodbye, I decided this wasn't the best time to go to Switzerland so I canceled my trip."

His head lifted. Brittany must have phoned her from Danice's house. What in the hell had she said to make Abby change her plans?

"Does André's family know?" he asked.

"Yes."

"Are they upset?"

"Disappointed maybe."

"And what about you?"

Abby eyed him. "What do you think?" She threw him the same challenge he'd once directed at her.

"I can tell you right now this family's going to get through Buddy's passing in better shape than I'd supposed. Brittany," he said, without looking at his daughter, "why don't you go upstairs and call Danice. I'm sure she'll want to know what's happened."

As her footsteps faded, Rick held out his arms. "Come here, Abby."

She came instantly. When she kissed him, he felt a completeness, a joy that was earth-shattering.

He lost track of how long they stood entwined. Every kiss promised more.

"Are you for real, or am I dreaming this gorgeous woman just walked through the door into my life?" he asked in a husky voice.

"What would you prefer?" she whispered provocatively against his lips. "The dream or the reality?"

"Both."

"I've never chased a man in my life. You're the first. Just so you know, I've removed my wedding ring." She covered his face and neck with kisses. "If that makes you nervous, tell me now."

"Do I act nervous?" He reached for her left hand and pressed his lips to her ringless finger. "What exactly did my daughter say to you?"

Rick could see her throat working. "That we're in love."

"She's right about that." His hands cupped her flushed cheeks. "As you pointed out, she's a smart girl. What else did she say?"

"She begged me to come home safely. After we hung up, I thought about that for a long time. Accidents happen. I know that better than anyone." She kissed his hands. "It frightened me to think something might happen and I'd never get the chance to tell you what you mean to me."

"Tell me now," he demanded. "You've got one minute, then I'm taking you somewhere in the house very private and I'm going to show you how *I* feel."

She leaned closer, pressing her forehead against his. "I—I never thought there could be anyone after André. Different men asked me out. But I poured myself into my work. Then one day, along came your daughter."

She lifted her head so she could look at him. "Call it fate, destiny. Whatever it was, I was drawn to her. And then I met you... The night the two of you walked home after eating dinner at the restaurant, I saw you through the upstairs window. It killed me not to be with you. I was struck by the realization that I'd fallen in love with you. But I was afraid I was only a fleeting interest in your life."

"Now you know differently," he murmured against her throat.

"Brittany set me straight last night. I love that daughter of yours. I love you, Rick. You have no idea how much."

"Abby—"

By now he'd undone the clip and her hair fell loose around her shoulders. He buried his face in it.

"The first morning we met, I knew you were going to change my life. You'd already changed Brittany's."

Her adoring gaze played over his features. "The way to your heart was through your daughter? How blessed am I that no one else got there first."

"Is it okay if I come in?"

Rick laughed as he turned Abby around, his arms encircling her slender waist, her back firmly planted against his chest. "Enter at your peril."

"Dad—" Brittany came in smiling, then swung to a full stop. "Oh… Whoops…are you two— I mean…I guess everything's okay now."

"It'll be even better after we're married."

"You're kidding!" she cried.

He kissed the back of Abby's neck. "You *are* going to be my wife, aren't you?" he whispered. "I want a baby with you. How does that sound?" He felt her tremble. "I take it that was a yes."

Brittany stepped closer. "After you're married, will it be all right if—" She hesitated.

"If you call me Mom?" Abby helped her out. "I can't wait. Come here, darling."

LATER THAT EVENING, Rick ushered Abby out to the flower garden. They hadn't let go of each other all day. It was as if they were afraid to be apart even for a moment. But he had to release her long enough to conduct the funeral Brittany was waiting for. The three of them stood around the little grave.

He'd dressed for the occasion in a dark suit and tie. Abby had never seen anyone so handsome.

"Buddy? We're gathered tonight to honor you. You gave us

fifteen years of love. I bought you when Brittany was just a year old and you loved my little girl from the first moment. You understood without words that it was your job to guard her with your life. That's what you did. We'll always miss you."

Abby heard his voice crack and felt the tears come. "Brittany? It's your turn, sweetheart."

With surprising composure she smiled at her father then cleared her throat.

"This morning Dad and I lost our best friend. All day I've been thinking of what I wanted to say to you." She sniffed and unfolded the paper she was carrying.

"Dear, Buddy
In life I loved you dearly, in death I love you still
In my heart you hold a place no one could ever fill
If tears could build a stairway and heartache make a lane
I'd walk the path to heaven and bring you back again"

She looked up from the paper. "I won't ever think of this as a sad time because when you went to heaven today, I know you sent me the present I've always wanted. A mom."

While Abby smiled through her tears at the darling girl who was going to become her daughter, Rick put his arm around Brittany.

"Buddy? We just want you to know that Abby and I are planning a September wedding. We'll have the reception out here so you can be a part of it. We know you would have loved to live long enough to take off with a piece of wedding cake—"

"Dad!"

At that point Abby couldn't resist stepping into Rick's arms. The three of them were going to be a family.

Joy.

* * * * *

For mothers everywhere
who nurture others' dreams into realities

BABY STEPS
Anna DeStefano

Dear Reader,

When I began thinking about what motherhood meant, my wacky writer's mind locked onto an unlikely motif from my favorite fairy tale—*Snow White and the Seven Dwarfs*.

You see, Snow White not only took over the care and nurturing of an entire band of little people, she picked the crankiest, most cantankerous of the dwarfs as her special project—Grumpy. Grumpy wasn't bad in her eyes, just misunderstood. With a little extra effort, he could become all he and the other dwarfs needed him to be.

And Snow White was up for the challenge. I think she understood how scary it was for Grumpy to trust again. How much he must have been hurt to have developed such a hard, hands-off shell. They had a lot more in common, these two, than the reader first realizes. Snow White was determined not to give up until Grumpy let love in again, and by helping him she never really let love go herself.

It's Grumpy who ends up leading the charge that destroys the wicked witch—saving both Snow White and her prince in the process. In fact, if it weren't for Grumpy, Snow White's happily ever after might never have happened. Amazing stuff.

I hope you enjoy my very contemporary interpretation of this timeless fairy-tale theme. Mothers of every kind out there, know that you have my admiration. Being a Mother of the Year is as simple as opening your heart and making a difference in a child's life. And it's just that complicated. Loving so deeply makes you all fairy-tale princesses in my book!

Please come visit me at www.annawrites.com. And join the fun and fabulous giveaways at annadestefano.blogspot.com.

Anna DeStefano

CHAPTER ONE

"LILY, THE CHICKEN bottoms aren't fat enough. Do you have any more stuffing?"

"If I had a dollar for every time someone's asked me that…" Lily Brooks looked up from her portable sewing machine and handed over a bag of cotton batting. "And for the last time, Ashley. They're *hens*. Happy mothers, all."

The stars of her Mother's Day surprise for the school's upcoming Spring Fling.

"Okay, then." Ashley Lawson crammed a brown corduroy bottom with more white filling. "I don't think top-heavy *hens* falling over and smothering live chicks is what Ms. Emory had in mind when you suggested doing something special for the K-third-grade moms."

"Good point." Lily grabbed a handful of cotton, plumped the nearest chicken's tush to find the hidden Velcro seam and pried it open. "I'm going for memories the families can look back on and cherish. Not scarring children for life."

She'd pitched the idea of a booth where carnival attendees could stop and play with baby chicks, then smile for commemorative photos that the younger kids could decorate for a Mother's Day present. Another *fabulous* idea, the assistant principal, Gayle Emory, had cooed. *I'm sure you'll pull it off as effortlessly and successfully as you do everything else.*

Lily stuffed and sighed.

She'd lined up a local farmer to provide the chicks, rented a tent from the same company providing the dunking booth and she and her best friend, Ashley, would be spending their lunch hours for the next two weeks *effortlessly* sewing and painting a picturesque barnyard motif for other women to enjoy with their kids.

A perfect idea that would take forever to execute.

She glanced around the cluttered, colorful art room. Ashley put her energy into exploring and enjoying the school day. Getting the most out of each moment. Planning and worrying that everything was perfect wasn't her style. Lily had the corner on that obsession.

She tossed a chicken at her carefree friend.

Ashley giggled and lobbed the stuffed bundle onto the growing pile. "So, what's next?"

"Mr. Palmer offered to bring enough animals for a petting zoo, if we could find the space for him to set up a corral." Last year, Lily had been his granddaughter's third-grade teacher, and she'd encouraged Molly's parents to test her for dyslexia. Since starting treatment, the formally shy, withdrawn child had blossomed, and the Palmer family was convinced Lily was their angel's fairy godmother. "But I'm not sure—"

"Do it!" Ashley ran her hand over the bolts of bargain-bin fabric Lily was morphing into replicas of living, breathing, pooping stable inhabitants. "Sewing everything would be a safer solution, but a little chaos is a good trade-off. It might get crazy, mixing things up with the kids and real animals, but everyone will love it!"

Crazy…mixing things up…

Panic surged through Lily at the mere suggestion. She was starting to hate that about herself.

"Maybe…maybe it wouldn't be too out of control," she said. "As long as we're careful about which animals Mr. Palmer brings."

"Dakota, stop running in the hallway!" a familiar voice boomed, a split second before a whirlwind dressed in jeans, T-shirt and an Atlanta Falcons cap blurred through the doorway and took aim for Lily and Ashley's poultry assembly line.

"Look out!" Ashley dove left.

Lily ducked right. "Hey!"

The boy hit his knees and slid beneath the table, catching a table leg with his sneaker. Corduroy and butt stuffing flew into the air. The table clattered to its side. Their hen-assailant kept on sliding, until he'd crashed into the easel Ashley had set up to teach the second-graders coming in after lunch.

"Ow!" he yelped.

The wooden frame collapsed on top of him.

"Are you ladies okay?" His pursuer's gaze connected with Lily's. Tyler knelt on one knee, held out his hand and helped her to her feet.

His frown warmed to a smile in response to her nod. When he turned toward Ashley, Lily forced herself to let go and head for the struggling heap of little boy and art supplies in the corner.

"Nice touchdown, kiddo." She extricated the easel, then the blank canvas that had been propped on top of it. The kid's shaggy, dark hair partially obscured the bright blue eyes glowering up at her. "I bet you're a champ on the ball field."

"What do you know about it, stupid!" His insult missed its mark. His scowl was simply too adorable to pull it off.

"Dakota, you know better than that!" Tyler corrected. He stepped to Lily's side. Impossibly tall. Impossibly handsome. Silent Springs' favorite PE teacher. "Apologize to Mrs. Brooks for your bad manners."

The child struggled to his feet, which were covered in unlaced, hole-riddled sneakers that didn't square with the rest of what appeared to be spanking-new clothes. A hint of embarrassment, maybe even regret, touched his hostile expression. Then everything but anger disappeared.

"Why do you care how I talk to your wife?" Dakota demanded. "Everyone in school knows you two aren't even living together anymore."

"BECAUSE SHE'S A teacher," Tyler Brooks explained to his gym-class truant. Lily was also the most beautiful woman Tyler had ever met, not that now was the time to make that point. "And even if she wasn't, she's an adult. Don't talk to adults that way, period, and you might tunnel out of detention before the end of the school year."

"Oh, okay," the kid spit back. "But Nathan Grover can call me a *bastard* all he wants!"

"Of course he can't."

"Nathan called you what?" Lily stepped closer. A petite dynamo, she was barely taller than the kids she taught.

"Some of the boys were playing four square, and Dakota's our new all-star." Tyler dragged his attention away from his wife's peaches-and-cream complexion and dark auburn hair, and nudged Dakota's shoulder. "Seems Nathan doesn't take kindly to losing, so—"

"So! He cheats. And he calls me names when you're not looking. And—"

"You kicked him, Dakota, right before you bolted out of the gym without a pass." Tyler watched his wife circle a gentle arm around the fourth-grader's shoulder. Caught up in the day's latest injustice, the child forgot to resist the nurturing that came as naturally as breathing to Lily. "No matter what someone else does, there's no excuse for—"

"Defending myself?" Dakota's gaze slid to where Lily's hand rested on his shoulder. He sidestepped until they were no longer touching.

"There's no excuse for hitting." Lily folded her arms across her chest. She caught Tyler's smirk and shot him an *eat me* look, because she knew that *he* knew how much she wanted to still be hugging the kid. "And there are smarter ways to defend yourself. You let Nathan goad you into losing your cool, and you're the one who gets caught. Meanwhile, he looks as clean as a whistle?"

"Screw you!" Dakota made a beeline for the door.

Luckily, Tyler had a long reach—a handy thing on a basketball court, where he'd made many of his best high school memories. An essential for a career in corralling hyperactive school children into organized physical activity. He snagged Dakota and turned him around.

"First." He tightened his grip when the boy tensed for another sprint. "Apologize to Mrs. Brooks and Ms. Lawson. Second, help clean up their—" Tyler gazed at the piles of fuzzy white stuff, brown fabric and what looked like overweight chickens strewn about the floor "—whatever. Then you and I are meeting Nathan at the AP's office for a little chat."

"Nathan?" Dakota peered up at Tyler.

"He started the fight, didn't he? He's going to stand up for his part in what happened."

Mr. Confrontation looked younger, suddenly. Confused. Tyler smiled over his student's head, catching his wife's nod of approval. He squeezed Dakota's shoulder and shoved him forward.

"S-sorry," Dakota said to Lily and Ashley.

Sincerity and belligerent ten-year-olds…an unnatural combination if Tyler had ever seen one. The kid began clearing his mess, mumbling under his breath. Something about how stupid adults were.

That kind of spunk was a good thing, Tyler reminded himself, not a pain in the ass. A child like Dakota learned to be tough from the cradle. Had to stay that way just to get through the day. Tyler understood that better than most. More than he cared to.

Lily motioned him closer to the door.

"New student?" Her brown eyes drank him in. When they were in their nineties, she'd still be able to bring him to his knees with just one look.

"Dakota started with Alma Rushing's class on Monday. He's having a little trouble settling in with the other kids."

"So it would seem." Lily held his gaze until he was the one to look away, hiding the need to pull her closer. "Sounds like he and Nathan's problems are more than just boys being boys in PE. You're going to make sure that Ms. Emory gives him a break?"

"Yeah, I'll handle it."

"You always do."

He frowned at the accusation in her tone, then started when she took his hand, reaching for him for the first time since she'd moved out. Their fingers tangled together out of habit. A perfect fit.

"You're amazing when you're fighting for one of your kids." Her smile was hesitant, as if she wasn't sure of its welcome. "You're going to make a great father."

Tyler's throat stung against the urge to start a conversation they couldn't have. Not there. Enough of their personal issues had already followed them to school, if even his newest student knew about their separation.

Temporary separation.

It had only been two weeks. It just felt like forever.

He squeezed her fingers and kissed them. Kept the rest to himself. The sparkle in her eyes dimmed at his nonresponse.

"Ready for our appointment at four?" she asked.

It wasn't really a question.

"How about I meet you there, as soon as I get things settled in the gym?"

It wasn't really an answer.

With a worried nod, Lily turned to help clean up whatever she and Ashley had been working on. Tyler dove in, too, his mind racing with the two battles looming before him that afternoon. And he'd be damned if he felt ready to tackle either.

He had to find a way to get Dakota to fight for his second chance. Then he had to convince his wife to accept the truth that had come as a crushing blow to them both, before what was left of their marriage slipped away.

CHAPTER TWO

"BUT YOU SAID my blood pressure had stabilized," Lily glanced to Tyler for support. She received a grim frown instead.

She shifted in her chair to face their fertility specialist.

Alone.

Why did it feel like she was doing this alone, when—

"We want a baby, Dr. Gruber. As long as there's a chance IVF can work for us, we're willing to try—"

"As long as it's safe," Tyler interrupted. "If not, we'll find another way."

"I feel fine, I just—"

"Can't walk up and down the stairs half the time, without having to sit down you're so dizzy." Tyler bent forward in his chair and braced his arms on his thighs. "Your heart races as if you're having panic attacks, Lily. You're blood pressure bottoms out—last time while you were driving, and you woke up in a ditch."

"But I'm feeling much better." It sucked to be looking to the doctor, instead of her husband, for support. "You said things are better."

"Yes," Dr. Gruber agreed with a total lack of enthusiasm. "Since you stopped your protocol of progesterone and Clomid, your symptoms have leveled off a bit. Still, we need to monitor your condition for a longer period of time. I wouldn't call the side effects you've experienced fine. Going back on the medication before we learn more could be life threatening."

"We knew there would be risks," she argued.

Fertility treatments came with warning after warning. But there'd been nothing in the pamphlets Lily had memorized about the strain on her marriage. Or her childhood sweetheart living in their home while she'd spent the past two weeks at Ashley's apartment, because she couldn't bear to look at the man she loved.

"It's worth it," she insisted. The same thing she'd kept telling herself, as she lied about the exhaustion and nausea and vertigo that hadn't gone away as much as she needed the doctor and Tyler to believe. "We'll do whatever we have to do."

"Not if it means risking your health." Tyler's worried gaze caressed every curve of her face. "I want you home and healthy, whatever we have to do to make *that* happen. If that means not trying to have a baby for a while, or you taking some time off work to get your strength back, we'll deal with it."

"But…no!" She looked back and forth between her reluctant husband and her reluctant doctor. "You said we're good candidates for in vitro fertilization."

Gruber's cautious nod wasn't what she'd call encouraging. "Given the extent of your endometriosis and the fact that your challenges conceiving haven't responded to drug treatment alone, my recommendation would typically be to increase the strength of the hormone therapy and start you on a regimen working toward IVF." He shook his head. "But—"

"Then let's get started."

She didn't want to hear any more *buts*. She wanted to go home and put all the worrying behind them and get back to making her and Tyler's dream of having a baby a reality.

"Not every woman's body can tolerate the treatments," Dr. Gruber reasoned. "IVF would likely mean more side effects for you. Volatile mood swings. Unpredictable weakness. Equilibrium problems. The likelihood of your body being able to tolerate in vitro after the difficulties you're already having would be—"

"As slim as me actually conceiving naturally?"

I'm sure you'll pull it off as effortlessly and successfully as you do everything else, Ms. Emory's voice whispered through her mind.

When it came to creating someone else's fairy-tale Mother's Day moment, Lily was the woman for the job. It was fighting for a family of her own that she was failing at.

"This isn't the end, honey." Tyler leaned closer, her white knight. Her Prince Charming. There'd never been any challenge he couldn't conquer. "Together, we're going to make it work."

She flinched, terrified by how much she wanted to believe him. How much she needed him to still be in this with her.

"R-really?" she whispered. "You mean, you really want to keep trying? I know things are a mess, but this time we'll know what we're up against. I'll be more careful and try harder to—"

"No." He cupped her cheek and thumbed away the tears spilling over her lashes. "I mean, we'll find a way to be parents that doesn't put your health at risk. We'll get free of all this for a while and talk about our options."

Free?

Alternatives?

What he wanted to do together was give up.

Don't leave, he'd begged her two weeks ago, after Gruber recommended not refilling the prescriptions her body needed to get pregnant. She'd wanted to keep trying, to push the doctor for more time. She and Tyler had argued that night. He'd flushed her remaining medication down the toilet, charging full-steam ahead, ready to make the best out of their bad situation, while she became hysterical.

I hate you, she'd yelled as she'd packed her bags.

It had been a lie, but saying it had made what she'd had to do next possible. The same thing she had to do now.

"I'm…" She pushed to her feet. Tyler's hand steadied her when her knees nearly gave out, just like he'd always been her support, every time she'd needed him since they were kids. "I…I can't do this."

She fled.

"Lily." Tyler caught up with her in the crowded reception area. He held out the purse she'd left behind. "We need to talk about this."

"We've already talked about it." She couldn't, wouldn't, look at him.

"No, we've argued, and we never argue about anything. This is disappointment, I know. But it's not just about you. Try to see it from my perspective, too."

Her laugh shocked them both.

"Your perspective?" She yanked her purse away. Heads around the room turned to watch the show. "Your *perspective* is that this disappointment is no big deal. My body's given up on me being a mother, and so have you. Of course that makes me a neurotic mess because I want to keep fighting, but—"

"I don't think you're neurotic, but you're not even trying to—"

"I'm trying to have a b-baby." She choked on the word and longed to be back at school with Ashley, overstuffing chicken butts and watching her husband take care of his students and dreaming of what he'd be like with their own kids. "*Your* baby. And I need your support. But every conversation we've had lately ends up being about why you want to stop. *I'm* not the one with the problem."

The lie felt like a scream coming out, even though she was whispering.

"I want you to stop hurting yourself," Tyler argued, "because you think it's your only option...*our* only option. The treatments aren't working. They're making you sick. There could be long-term side effects that I'm not willing to risk, and our marriage is falling apart because you won't even consider moving on to other possibilities."

"I...I can't." She covered her heart with trembling fingers. "I'm sorry I'm not as strong as you, Tyler. I've wanted to have a baby my whole life. I'm willing to make whatever sacrifices are necessary for that to happen, but you're done. Explain to me how I'm supposed to move on from that."

He blinked, and for a second she thought she'd made a dent in the boundless confidence that had helped him *handle* every challenge in his life since he'd been a scared little boy like

Dakota. Then her husband pasted on his best can-do expression and was once more the survivor who never let anything get to him. He led her into the hallway, ignoring her resistance.

"I'd give anything to have a baby of our own to raise and love and spoil." He rested his forehead against hers. Another time, a lifetime ago, he'd have pecked a kiss on her nose. Tickled her softly until she giggled, then he'd have laughed, too, until they both felt better. "This is hard for me, even if I can't show it the way you want me to. I've known I wanted kids with you since that night our senior year when our parents thought we were at the church social, but we slipped over to Culligan's pond instead and went skinny-dippin'. But there are other ways to make our family a reality."

She backed away. Tried to, at least, but Tyler held fast. "Let me go. I need to be by myself for a while."

"We've tried that, too." The softness was gone from his voice. His words held an edge she'd never heard before. "We've done this your way. It's time to give mine a try. I scheduled another appointment for us this afternoon, and we're going to make it. Together."

THE GRAYSONS, the sign beside the doorbell read.

As if the rumbling of nonstop activity coming from within wouldn't have told Tyler all he needed to know. How often after becoming an adult had he marveled at the Graysons' success fostering upward of five children at a time? A quiet, unassuming couple, they'd chosen a life of chaos—one they and the kids they helped thrived on.

The kind of chaos that had saved Tyler after he'd lost both his parents too young.

Welcome, added the mat beneath his and Lily's feet. It came complete with a smiley face that kept on smiling no matter how many times it was trampled on.

And Tyler had been welcome, from age six until he left to work his way through college and beyond. Marsha and Joshua Grayson had become his parents in every way that mattered—

whenever he'd needed a reality check to break him out of the cycle of anger and hatred that could have destroyed him, and every time he'd needed a hug or advice or a pat on the back to assure him he was okay.

"This is the appointment you're so determined we make?" Lily fidgeted with her wedding band as he rang the bell again. "I can't hang out with your family right—"

"Marsha and Joshua aren't the ones we're meeting with." Though they'd generously offered their kitchen as a neutral place for Tyler and Lily to find some common ground.

"What's going on?" Lily stepped back, clearly wanting to be somewhere else. Anywhere but sharing air with him. "I'm not up for one of your surprises, Tyler."

The door swung inward before he could reply. A Frisbee flew out and they ducked in unison.

"Nice reflexes." Joshua Grayson chuckled as he swept an arm inward. "Bring that beautiful lady on in here. Marsha's got cookies and tea ready in the kitchen, and I'm trying to corral the kids upstairs to do their homework, so you two can have some peace and quiet."

Stepping out of the warm spring day into the cool, shadowy den felt like slipping backward in time. Tyler let the sensation of belonging wash over him. The assurance that this would always be his home. A place he was connected to, if not by blood then by love and respect. The Graysons' home had changed him. Made him believe he could reach for success—for something as special as a life with Lily Jones.

Four youngsters of varying ages were scrambling to gather book bags and toys from the war zone the Graysons' den typically resembled. Lily smiled at the mayhem. A genuine smile he'd missed seeing, so much it hurt.

"Hey, Tyler." A lanky teenage boy brushed by on his way outside, grabbed his Frisbee from the hedge of boxwoods lining the walk, then loped back in. "Hey, Lily."

"Have you grown again, Matt?" Lily asked as he flicked the Frisbee to a buddy who'd already headed upstairs.

"Probably." He took the steps two at a time, the last of the kids to clear the room. Silence descended, the sound of it almost deafening.

"It's all the cookies Marsha keeps baking," Joshua explained. It had always been *Marsha* and *Joshua* since Tyler first came there. Not *Mr.* or *Mrs.*, or *Mom* or *Dad.* Just simple folks offering simple acceptance. "The kids eat their weight in them, then they shoot up another inch. By summer, no one will be able to wear their spring clothes. The shopping carnage will be brutal." He wiped a hand over a horrified expression. "It's enough to wear a man down. Gotta do something about those cookies."

"You eat as many as the kids." Lily linked her arm with Joshua's and let him steer her toward the kitchen. "Marsha's cooking is magical, everyone knows that. Nothing to do about magic but to grab your share and enjoy"

"Well, today you get first dibs." Joshua's easy-going tone didn't jive with the concerned look he shot Tyler.

He could tell. They all could.

Behind Lily's smiles, she was suffering, and she was having a harder and harder time hiding it. And that more than anything had convinced Tyler to give this afternoon a try.

"You two better be staying for supper, is all I have to say," Marsha insisted once they'd reached her domain, the spacious kitchen that was the center of the Grayson home. She stood at the table, elbow deep in a pile of laundry. One piece at a time, she briskly separated and folded the mess into stacks, one for each bedroom. "There's enough roast to feed an army, which means that, once the kids are served, there should be a few scraps left to tempt you to hang around for a bowl of apple cobbler."

The last sock sorted, Marsha brushed her hands and opened her arms for the hug no one in Silent Springs dared resist. Lily let herself be enveloped by Marsha's special brand of gentle honesty. Tyler felt a spurt of jealousy when Lily relaxed into her embrace.

"You always did smell so good, child." Marsha studied the lines of sadness curling at the edges of Lily's smile. "And you're so beautiful, inside and out. You've made our Tyler a very happy man."

Lily wiped at the corners of her eyes. Joshua joined them, his hand cupping her shoulder and rubbing, completing a circle of support Tyler had seen the couple build for countless children.

"The two of you had already taken care of Tyler's happiness before I came into the picture," Lily argued.

"We were a start." Marsha nodded and let go. She lifted an armload of clothes and headed for the floor-to-ceiling utility shelves beside the kitchen door. "But Tyler's picture was always meant to be bigger than us. You were the next step, the one to take him to the life he was meant to have."

Tyler grabbed the rest of the laundry and followed, never feeling less in control of his life. Once Marsha finished sorting the T-shirts and shorts and socks and underwear into the colorful bins stacked on the shelves—to be picked up by their owners before bedtime—she reached for his pile. Her smile was full of fond memories. This had been their chore from almost his first day there, back when he'd just wanted to be left alone and Marsha had been equally determined to show him that sharing time with someone again didn't have to hurt.

The doorbell rang, breaking the silence that had fallen over the room. Tyler relinquished the last of the clothes and hugged Marsha's shoulder. "That's for me." He winked at his wife's confused expression, then headed toward the front of the house.

"Those cookies on the platter are for your meeting," Marsha explained to Lily as he went. "I'll get the tea, then we'll make ourselves scarce."

"What meeting?" Lily wanted to know.

Tyler kept walking, determined to see this through. He was aware that he didn't have the Graysons' knack for gently easing people into things they didn't think they could handle. Helping them work through problems they didn't want to face. He was a fixer. He kept things moving. Pushed past whatever disappointment stood in his way and focused on the next opportunity.

I'm not up for one of your surprises, Tyler.

He knew he should cancel the meeting. Use the obvious excuse that he was an idiot who didn't have the first clue what his wife needed. But what if Lily was never ready to accept the truth? What if the new dream he wanted to paint for their future, their family, wasn't possible?

What if he quit pushing, and ended up losing her for good?

CHAPTER THREE

"I'M SORRY." Lily knew she didn't sound sorry, but at least she wasn't screaming at her husband in front of the social worker Tyler had invited over for a chat. "I…I forgot I have a previous engagement."

She stood and would have walked out the back door, except that's where the Graysons had disappeared to, to give them some privacy with the children's-services caseworker. The couple's consideration in helping Tyler trap Lily into—how had he put it, *facing difficult choices*—wasn't nearly as heartwarming as Marsha's earlier offer of cookies, pot roast and homemade cobbler.

"If you'll excuse me," she said to the room in general.

She headed toward the front of the house to find her purse and keys. A small body darted across the den. A scurry of motion racing for the front stairs confirmed that not all of the kids had stayed out of sight as instructed. A crash, followed by a childish "Ouch!" stopped her.

"Everything okay?" she asked as she reached the little body that had collided with the hall table and knocked both it and himself to the floor.

The moment of déjà vu was completed when she found herself for the second time that day setting furniture to rights and helping Dakota Miller to his feet. She'd heard the Graysons had recently taken in another child, but she and Tyler hadn't talked enough lately for her to be up on all the details.

"We've simply got to stop meeting this way." She looked the

little boy over, saw no obvious injuries and resisted the urge to give the kid a reassuring hug.

"He's here to take me back to the group home, isn't he?" Dakota demanded. He still wore his red-and-black Falcons cap, this time turned tough-guy backwards.

"Who?" She glanced toward the kitchen. "Mr. Kramer?" Then it clicked. "No, sweetie. The children's-services coordinator is here to talk with Mr. Brooks and me. It has nothing to do with the Graysons or what happened at school today. No one's taking you anywhere."

Dakota's blue eyes narrowed. Their color was so similar to Tyler's, Lily couldn't help but stare.

"He's here for you?" Dakota sputtered. "But you and Mr. Brooks are mad at each other. Everyone at school says so. And you want them to give you a kid?"

"What? No!" Her sharp refusal echoed up the stairs. Rustling noises came from the second-floor bedrooms, muffled voices, but thankfully none of the other kids emerged from homework exile. "I don't want to… The meeting was just to get some information and see what it would take if we decided to foster children like the Graysons do."

So, why did you run from the conversation before it even got started?

"We're not like puppies, you know." Dakota squared off, his you-can't-hurt-me glare pulling Lily's head out of her own problems. "They don't just give kids away to everyone. Even screwups like me."

So much for sprinting to her car and driving far, far away from Tyler and his latest solution to their problems. She knelt on one knee so she and Dakota were eye-to-eye.

"No," she said. "They give great kids like you to families like this one, because the Graysons are the best there is."

The kind of family Tyler had thrived with.

Dakota backed away so fast he knocked into the table again. He kicked the sturdy piece of oak, crimson staining his cheeks from either embarrassment or anger, she couldn't say which. It was equally impossible to tell which was causing the suspicious sheen making his eyes sparkle.

"Great kids don't get thrown away and dumped in a group home, until some loser place like this opens up." He edged toward the door that opened to the backyard. "Throwaways don't get second chances after screwing up at school like I have this week. Like I care," he sneered. "Tell that man I can't wait to go back. The Graysons are so lame, I can't wait to get out of here!"

He yanked the door open and bolted outside. Dust bunnies kicked up in the beams of sunlight as he ran, like the animated puffs of smoke cartoon characters left in their wake. Lily stared after Dakota, wondering what the child's reaction would be when he came across his *lame* foster parents cuddling on the back porch swing.

Tyler appeared at her side.

"When you're scared, it's a lot easier to run," he said, "than it is to stay and fight."

She met his troubled gaze, even though she wanted to shove his latest pearl of philosophical wisdom back down his throat.

"Not everyone's as good at getting on with it as you are, Tyler." She fought back the anger that made her want to run every time they were close. "You didn't tell me Dakota was Marsha and Joshua's newest lost boy."

That's how Tyler had jokingly referred to himself back in middle school, when they'd first become friends. The Graysons had a reputation for taking on cases that other families wouldn't. Usually angry little boys. They saw it as their chance to do the most good.

"Dakota's only been here a few days." Tyler closed the back door. "All I know is he's a tough character who isn't attached to anything but that Falcons cap and the tennis shoes his grandmother bought him. He refuses to let Marsha replace them. I've only seen him at school before today. I haven't made it by for dinner the last few weeks."

Not since she'd moved out. She'd disrupted everything in

their ordered world, including their regular visits to this crazy, loving household.

"Do Marsha and Joshua know?"

"That we're having trouble having a baby? Of course."

"That you're giving up on me being a mother and already researching Plan B."

"I haven't given up on anything. Accepting that having a baby of our own isn't the only way for us to be parents isn't giving up."

"Well, I can't accept it, Tyler. I'm not made like you. I can't just—"

"Let go and move on?" His hand curled around hers and his grip firmed when she tried to pull away. "I know you can't. Just like I know this is about more than whether or not we should keep trying to have our own child. This isn't the first time you've insisted on feeling responsible for something out of your control, Lily. Ever since Carter, you've—"

"I have to go." She reached for her purse. "Make my apologies to Mr. Kramer."

"Don't leave." He followed her to the front door. "I realize this was a surprise. Too much too soon, no matter how excited I am about the prospect of fostering. But it's going to be okay. We can—"

She lifted her hand for him to stop.

"I want to have a baby, Tyler. More than anything, I want to give you a child. So unless you have some solution for helping me do that, you'll have to forgive me for not feeling *okay*." She heard the words come out of her mouth, heard the selfishness of them, and shook her head. "I'm sorry. I know I should be handling this better. It's not you. I'm the one who's messed up."

"No, you're hurting, and I'm pushing too hard." Her fairy-tale prince sounded desperate. Pleading. "This was a bad idea. *I'm* sorry. I'll get rid of Mr. Kramer so we can talk. Please, don't go."

But she already had the door open. Then she was sprinting down the walk, escaping out a different door than Dakota but running just the same.

Tyler was merely facing facts. It was how he lived his life, how he'd survived his childhood. But for her, letting go of their dream of a family felt too much like giving up. Like failing. Too much like...

Carter...

It felt like losing Carter all over again.

She slid into her car and headed for the school and the now-empty art room, instead of to Ashley's apartment. Instead of heading to her own home. She slapped her hand on the steering wheel. Maybe a healthy dose of sewing and painting for the Spring Fling would take her mind off memories she thought she'd buried a lifetime ago.

Don't bet on it, her conscience snickered.

She saw again the worry and confusion and hurt on her husband's face and pressed the accelerator.

MARSHA WASHED the remains of pot roast and mashed potatoes off another plate, rinsed and handed it to Tyler to dry.

They'd been working side by side in silence for the past fifteen minutes. Joshua was on wash-up duty of another kind, upstairs supervising shower rotation and the nightly room check that prevented weekend cleaning marathons no one had patience for.

"Mr. Kramer seemed encouraging," she finally said.

"What's not to like?" Tyler took the next drippy plate and went to work with an age-worn towel that had been around as long as he had. "Two teachers who love kids. Nonexistent restrictions on the type of child we'd be willing to take in. Open to whatever classes and training are required. And we've already passed endless background checks to work in the public school system."

Marsha kept washing while she listened and waited.

"Of course," Tyler added, "it's not a stroke in our favor that Lily and I aren't living together at the moment."

Marsha nodded. "Josh and I gathered there was a reason you two had made yourself so scarce. Figured you'd get around to talking about it when you were ready."

And Tyler naturally had hoped he'd work things out before

that kind of talking became necessary. He set the plate aside and grabbed the sponge to wipe down the stove and countertop.

"Lily's messed up about not being able to have a baby. We both are, and I can't seem to help her through it. I can't even get her to slow down at work long enough for her body to recuperate from the last round of fertility drugs. Now she's taken on planning the Spring Fling and some kind of petting zoo she wants to bring in. How's she supposed to get better with all that going on, on top of teaching her class?"

Marsha slid the cobbler pan into the soapy water to soak, then dried her hands.

"Maybe Lily's not as ready for things to get better as you are." Her expression was a shade short of the kind of disapproval that had once left him quaking in sneakers more tattered than Dakota's. "If I'd known you were surprising her with this thing with Kramer, I never would have set it up for you, let alone become a cookie-baking coconspirator."

"I'll make sure she knows you and Joshua had nothing to do with it."

"Which means Josh and I can move on to worrying about whether the two of you will get through this with your marriage intact. Infertility can trash even the strongest relationship. Josh and I nearly didn't make it."

But they had, and look at the life they'd made. What Tyler's life had become because they hadn't quit.

"Lily won't listen to reason," he said.

"It's a difficult thing, feeling as if you've failed at something as important as giving your husband a piece of himself that will live on, long after the both of you are gone."

Tyler linked his arm around Marsha's shoulder.

"You've given him so much more. And look at what you've done for me and every other kid who came here."

"I know. And we're so proud of you, Tyler. Proud of all you kids." She hugged him back with the same gusto she gave to everything else. Then she took back her sponge and tossed it at him, sending it bouncing, to the floor. "But that doesn't mean it was easy, giving up what we'd hoped our life was going to be. Change that big is a hard thing to accept, especially…"

"Especially for someone who's been through what Lily has." What she'd never really talked about with anyone. Not her mother. Not even him.

"I think she's always felt responsible for what happened to her brother." Marsha waited until she had Tyler's full attention. "Lily's one of the hardest-working, most loving people I've ever met. She's wonderful for you, anyone can see that. But…"

"She's so careful." He put his hands into his pockets. "She needs everything and everyone around her to be okay, and if they're not—"

"She takes it all on her shoulders." Marsha sighed. "There were a dozen kids swimming in the lake that day."

"But Lily was supposed to watch Carter."

"She couldn't have known her little brother would hit his head when he jumped in."

"Doesn't matter." Tyler could still feel the panic when they'd realized Carter hadn't come up for air. "She wouldn't stop looking for him until her mother dragged her away." She would have kept diving until they'd lost her, too. "Then she just sat there on the end of the dock until they brought Carter up."

"It was horrible." Marsha's voice filled with the tears of that long-ago memory. The entire community had mourned along with the Jones family. "You're the only one she'd let near her. You two were already inseparable, even in sixth grade."

Tyler had tried to help her then, too, but nothing he'd said would convince her. *It's my fault,* she'd kept whispering. She had been told to look out for Carter, and he was gone. And now she was breaking her heart over yet one more loss that she couldn't fix, no matter how hard she tried.

"How do I help her?" he asked the woman who'd seen him through the darkness and anger that could have swallowed his life. "Lily can't get past losing her chance to have our baby, any more than she ever really got over what happened to Carter. And if she can't find a way to let it go…"

How was she going to believe in their marriage again, when every time she looked at him, she saw failure and him giving up on her, instead of the amazing things they could still do together?

"You listen to her, son." Marsha ran a soothing hand down his back. "Until she's ready to hear anything but what's in her own head, you listen, and you try to get her to understand that you're hurting, too."

"I have. I—"

"You ambushed her with children's services, just to make sure she felt good and trapped in circumstances she doesn't want to face!" Marsha thunked the side of his head with her palm. "I said tell her how *you're* feeling, not pressure her to hurry up and see things your way."

He swallowed and realized he was shaking his head again.

"I…" He tried. "I feel…"

The words wouldn't come.

"You don't even know, do you?" Marsha's smile slipped away. "You learned how to do damage control so young, and you've conquered everything since. Class president. Most Likely to Succeed. Varsity basketball captain and MVP. Teacher of the year. You have a solution for everything and never stop fighting until you find the answer you need."

"What's wrong with that?" he demanded, a rush of defensiveness adding extra punch.

"Nothing. Unless solving this problem has become a substitute for letting yourself feel the disappointment that—"

"Of course I feel it!"

"Does Lily know that?"

Yes! he almost snapped back. But then his mind replayed a slice of their last argument.

I'm not made like you, she'd said. *I can't just—*

Let go and move on?

Marsha went to work on her soaking cobbler pan.

"Lily's problems aren't yours to fix, Tyler. She loves you. But push her too hard before she's ready, and you'll cause more problems than even you can solve."

CHAPTER FOUR

"MRS. BROOKS?"

Lily looked up from the sheet of lamination she'd been trimming into multiplication flash cards, then stood as Mr. Kramer stepped into her classroom. Tiny bits of plastic slid off the pile of scraps she'd amassed, sparkling in the fluorescent light from the overhead fixtures.

Brushing at the shavings that clung to her navy sundress, she checked the clock above the whiteboard. In less than fifteen minutes, the first of her students would start trickling in.

"Mr. Kramer." She rounded her desk, smiling as she shook the social worker's hand. "I...I'm sorry I had to leave so abruptly yesterday afternoon. Tyler and I appreciate you coming all the way out to the Graysons, just to give us a rundown on the county's foster program."

"Not at all." Mr. Kramer was a shorter than average man, though he still towered over Lily, with a receding hairline and a little more than average around the middle. His eyes were kind and he had a way of talking that should have put her at ease. "Your husband sounded very motivated when I spoke to him over the phone, and it's always my pleasure to help new couples take their first steps toward becoming foster parents."

First steps...

"Yes, well..." She toyed with her dress and the shiny leftovers of the mindless work she'd distracted herself with for hours that morning. "If there's something else you needed to tell us, my husband should be in the gym by now. He's the best person for you to talk with…I mean, he's collecting all the information about—"

"I left Mr. Brooks a stack of pamphlets yesterday afternoon," Mr. Kramer assured her. "Brochures to read through. He has all the information you'll need to begin the first of the training classes."

Classes?

"Well, then, I don't understand. I…" She really needed to sit down.

She should have eaten when she'd gotten to Ashley's last night, instead of staying up answering her friend's questions because she'd worried her by not showing up until well after midnight.

"I'm not here to pressure you about fostering, Mrs. Brooks. It's an important decision I wouldn't dream of rushing anyone into." Mr. Kramer's reassuring smile flattened. He cleared his throat. "There's actually another matter I need your input on, and I was hoping you might have a few minutes before class began. I normally wouldn't bother you at work, but I've just met with Gayle Emory, and if the situation's escalating as quickly as I fear it is, time is of the essence."

Lily's mind flashed to the memory of shaggy brown hair, angry blue eyes and an angelic face framed by a frown and a backwards Falcons cap.

"Dakota?"

"Dakota Miller, yes. He's just recently moved in with the Graysons, after having quite a bit of difficulty at the group home that cared for him last. And I understand there was an altercation here at school yesterday that you witnessed."

"I…" She'd promised the child Mr. Kramer couldn't possibly be investigating something as inconsequential as a fight between two boys in the gymnasium. "I didn't see what happened during PE, but I did get the chance to speak with Dakota afterward. It seemed like a relatively minor incident from what my husband told me. What—"

"Yes, the fighting isn't that out of character for Dakota, though

I'd hoped moving to a home as stable as the Graysons' might curb some of his hostility. It's the running that concerns me most."

"Running?"

"I understand he bolted from gym class after the fight. Before his grandmother turned him over to children's services, Dakota had a history of running away from home."

"His grandmother gave him away? I… Can people do that?"

Mr. Kramer grimaced. "It's not an ideal situation, but the woman's in her seventies, her daughter's in and out of rehab for drug problems, and Dakota's acting out had progressed to a point where the county had to get involved. A more stable environment was advisable. I suggested a group home."

"A group home?" Nothing stable about that, if the stories Tyler told were any indication.

"Only until a private situation could be arranged. The Graysons were my first choice for Dakota, and I was hoping their influence would help settle him down. But—"

"I don't think one isolated incident at school means the Graysons' home isn't working out." Lily wiped at the beads of perspiration on her forehead. Chills raced down her arms.

"No, but he ran from the house last night while I was still there."

After he'd stormed away from her.

"Is he still missing?"

"A neighbor spotted him heading for a nearby park, and Mr. Grayson found him there and brought him home. But my concern is that his inability to attach to his surroundings is escalating rather than improving. Did you have enough of a chance to observe Dakota yesterday to shed any light on whether or not he's settling in here?"

"I've only spoken with him a couple of times." And both times he'd seemed determined to hate the world and everyone in it. "He's not one of my students. My husband—"

"Yes, I spoke with Mr. Brooks last night, after Dakota returned and things had settled down. He suggested that I follow up with you."

Mr. Kramer seemed a tad confused that she and Tyler hadn't spoken of it. Lily mentally kicked herself for ignoring her husband's calls on her cell.

"Yes, of course," she hedged. The room seemed to be shifting under her feet. She made it to the nearest desk and slid into the seat. It was unfortunate that the world didn't seem to realize that meant it should stop tilting around them. "I'd be happy to help any way I can."

Mr. Kramer sat in the desk beside her. "Are you feeling all right?"

"I'm fine," Lily whispered. "Just…a little dizzy."

Except dizzy and *a little* didn't go together. Not for her. Not since her body had decided to reject every fertility drug known to man. She grabbed the edge of the desk. Her vision faded to a narrowing white.

"Mrs. Brooks?" Mr. Kramer's voice grew staticky. Whatever he said next made no sense at all.

"Lily?" Was that Ashley? "I'll go get Tyler."

No! Lily wanted to say. She'd be fine, as soon as she…put her head down for a minute…found a way not to pass out…got back on her feet before Tyler got there…

Countless minutes later, the sound of someone running into the room penetrated the buzzing in her ears.

"Mr. Brooks!" Mr. Kramer sounded relieved. Poor man. "She was fine, then she seemed to—"

"Lily?" Tyler knelt beside her. "Honey, can you hear me? What's wrong?"

My body. Lily tried to raise her head, but could only manage to turn it sideways until she could see his worried frown. *My body's what's wrong.*

"I'm so sorry." She hated how weak she sounded. How weak she clearly was. "I'm so sorry, Tyler."

"CAN I GET YOU anything?" Tyler asked from the doorway of their bedroom.

Lily looked so beautiful, propped up on their pillows, her

glossy brown hair spilling over her shoulders. Beautiful, and miserable.

"This isn't necessary," she said. "I feel fine now."

"I had to carry you to the car back at school."

"No, you carried me because you were overreacting."

Overreacting, hell!

He'd been terrified.

"I suppose the doctor was overreacting, too, when he insisted you either had someone watch you overnight or checked yourself into the hospital."

Tyler had pushed her into a visit to Dr. Gruber's, where there'd been no gentle advising this time. No wiggle room. There would be no further fertility treatments, until her symptoms had subsided for a full six months.

"Doctors are forced to be overly cautious," Lily argued. "Lawsuits. Malpractice insurance. Gruber's covering his ass. There are other specialists, and—"

"Not for us, there aren't." Tyler shook his head. "You scared me to death today. I thought…I thought I was losing you. Your pulse was racing out of control. Your blood pressure was still dangerously low at Gruber's almost an hour after you fainted."

"*Nearly* fainted."

"Lord knows what kind of permanent effects all this will have on your body. We're done, Lily."

"No kidding!" She pulled her legs from beneath her favorite blanket and swung them to the ground. "The handwriting on the wall is clear enough for even me to read, Tyler."

He sat beside her, leery of her sudden acquiescence. "Does that mean you're ready to talk?"

"No." She flinched. "But I am ready to get out of here."

"And go where? Ashley won't be off work yet, and the doctor wants someone with you for at least twenty-four hours."

"I'll go to my mother's, then." Anything, it seemed, was preferable to staying there with him. "She's home during the day."

"Rose will want to know what's going on. If the kids at school have figured out we're living apart, you can bet someone as active in the community as your mother has. How much do you want to bet she'll have a passel of questions you'll want to run from as badly as you want to run from me?"

Tyler heard himself cornering her. He was sitting with the woman he'd love for the rest of his life, side by side on the bed he hadn't been able to sleep in since she'd left, and he'd never felt more like a bastard. Then he realized she was silently crying. Not turning to him. Not asking for comfort. Facing the pain alone.

"Damn it." He cuddled her against his side. Drew her head to his shoulder. "I'm so sorry, honey. For everything. I know it's hard, but—"

She pushed off the bed, away from him, her tears still falling as she headed for the master bath.

"Lily?" He stood but didn't crowd her further. "Please talk to me. Stay, so we can figure this out together."

She hesitated, then turned back.

"There's nothing to figure out. You don't know what it's like. You've never failed at anything in your life."

"Neither have you, honey." She had the biggest heart in Silent Springs. When it came to her family and her friends and her students, she never gave up until everyone was taken care of.

She couldn't be giving up on them now.

"When it comes to what's important," she argued, "I'm a big, fat failure, Tyler. Don't kid yourself."

"We're not failing. We're doing what we have to, to keep you safe."

"Well, safety's not always ours to guarantee, is it?"

Her shout wasn't what propelled Tyler forward—it was the haunted look in her eyes. He'd seen it before, at the end of a weather-worn dock, on an overcast summer day twenty years ago.

"Lily." He raised a hand to her cheek. "Being willing to destroy your health to make a baby we aren't meant to have isn't going to bring Carter back."

She slapped his hand away.

"Don't bring my brother into this," she said on a choked whisper. "You lost your parents. You've survived the kind of tragedy I can't even imagine. But I...I don't know how... I feel so powerless. And if you really understood that, you'd be helping me find another way to have a baby, instead of pushing me to settle for failing all over again."

BUNNIES. Lily checked her list from Mr. Palmer. Fluffy little things. No possible harm there, just keep tiny fingers out of the cages.

Ponies. *Check*. Potentially messy, but what was a petting zoo without ponies?

Potbellied pigs. *Check*. Wilber was a crowd favorite every time.

Hoot owl? Strike that one. Shrieking wasn't exactly the warm, fuzzy effect she'd promised.

Llama. *Llama?* The answer was in the question.

Peacock. Too exotic.

Flamingo. Cute, but the tall, gangly freaks of feathered nature didn't exactly say, *I Love You, Mom*. Too Spring Break, Daytona.

"What are *you* doin' here?" an accusing voice asked from the bottom of the bleachers.

Lily jumped, very nearly throwing her list of barnyard fun at Dakota. The paper slid from her shaking fingers and floated to the ground at his feet. She'd forgotten for a moment that she'd wandered outside during her planning period. She glanced up to find that Tyler had noticed Dakota's absence from the kickball game. Their gazes met and held, reminding her that it wasn't just the sunny day that had drawn her to the PE field.

They hadn't spoken since last night's argument. She'd been horrible to him, when he'd been trying to listen for a change. Trying to understand. She'd stayed instead of going to her mother's, but facing her husband and their problems *together* hadn't been possible.

So Tyler had slept in the guest room. And as a reward for his thoughtfulness, they'd shared a strained breakfast and silent drive to school, and now she'd deposited herself under his nose for the past half hour. To maybe get the chance to talk things through once his class went back inside? To torture him from a distance? Given her uncharacteristic ambivalence, it was a toss-up.

Dakota picked up her crumpled list and scanned the page.

"I'm talking to Molly Palmer's grandfather about bringing a petting zoo to the Spring Fling." She stepped down the bleachers until she was standing on the grass beside him. "He has a farm about a mile or so from the Graysons' place, actually, and he's offered us our choice of animals. He needs to know which ones would work best for the carnival."

Dakota took a second look.

"You marked off all the cool ones." He stared up at her. "Grown-ups are so lame."

She snatched her paper back with a very unteacherlike yank and double-checked her choices while she counted to ten. "You should stay home today," Tyler had said when they'd gotten up that morning. Her only response had been taking a quick shower, applying minimal makeup and donning her brightest top and skirt—both a cheery pink.

She was fine. She could handle school, even if she couldn't face anything else. Her work, her kids here, were the one part of her life that was still the way it was supposed to be.

So why was she a breath away from snapping at an adorable fourth-grader who was only being a typical fourth-grader? Grown-ups *were* lame, no doubt about it.

She sat on the lowest bleacher.

"Ms. Emory wants to keep things low-key. It's better to stick with the animals that are—"

"Boring?"

"Calmer." She checked her watch. Her class had story time in the library for another half hour. "Don't you need to get back to your game?"

"What's wrong with flamingos?"

"The petting zoo's part of a Mother's Day theme. Flamingos

don't exactly fit." Catching Tyler's attention, she waited for him to call his student over.

Instead, he waved and blew his whistle to have the team that was kicking switch with the one in the field. He traded several high fives with passing children, smiling and encouraging everyone.

That was why she'd come outside, she realized, when she could have reviewed Mr. Palmer's list over a cup of tea in her classroom. Tyler's enthusiasm for life, for others, was infectious even from a distance. Despite weeks of being away from him and a long night of uncomfortable silence, she'd been drawn here. To see him smile, and see how much he loved working with kids. Maybe even to find a way to accept what he'd been trying to tell her for so long.

…*being willing to destroy your health in order to make a baby we aren't meant to have isn't going to bring Carter back…*

The paper was torn from her hand.

"Pigs?" Dakota snorted. "Stinky pigs say Mother's Day to you? And what's wrong with owls? They're fluffy like bunnies."

Lily craned her neck so she could see the other end of the field, where the teachers sometimes sat and watched their classes play.

"Mrs. Rushing's not here," her heckler informed her. "We've got a stinky substitute, and she has *allergies.* She's inside somewhere, probably talking with the principal about me."

That didn't sound good.

"Rough day?"

Dakota glanced to where his classmates where cheering and rooting one another on. "The substitute thinks I'm a flamingo."

Lily blinked.

"Mrs. Rushing's substitute thinks you're a leggy, hot-pink bird?"

Dakota's eyes narrowed at the smirk she hadn't been able to swallow. "She'd rather have a class full of bunnies."

His eyes fell to her list. He shoved it back at her.

"I'm not even a stinky pig," he said. "Maybe I'd fit in better if I went to live with the flamingos."

Lily realized her mouth was hanging open. She covered it while she gave a small cough and fought to regroup. Either she really shouldn't have come to school today and she was imagining things, or a fourth-grader was actually standing in front of her spouting a spur-of-the-moment analogy that was twisting her heart around his little finger.

Keep him talking, Lily. Focus on the child. Help him before children's services takes over and unsettles his life even more.

She took a chance and smoothed a hand down his arm. When Dakota scowled but didn't bolt, she pulled gently, urging him to sit.

"There's nothing wrong with flamingos. Or...owls."

He flopped onto the bleachers and kicked at the dirt at his feet. "Right. That's why you scratched them off your list."

"But a classroom isn't a petting zoo."

"Yeah, they *have* to take you at school, whether you belong or not."

Tyler smiled over again. Encouraging. Adoring. So insistent that she was the amazing woman he'd married. How did he do that with just a twitch of his lips? How could she believe him, when deep inside she felt as much of a misfit as Dakota?

"You belong at Silent Springs." She pulled her pen from her pocket and checked one of the lines she'd crossed off so casually. "You and the flamingos."

Dakota pushed to his feet, eyeing her as if she were as strange as the pink birds she'd just agreed to include along side the family-friendly chicks. His chin wobbled as his eyes filled.

"Who needs you!" he choked out, backing away. "Screw you and your stupid zoo!"

"Dakota!" a woman admonished as he fled across the field.

Lily turned to see Mariah Caldwell approaching—Alma Rushing's substitute.

"He's okay," she assured the part-time teacher. "I upset him, and—"

"He's been disruptive all day." Mariah shook her head and puffed at the bangs that always seemed to be rebelling against whatever she did to style them. "I don't know how Alma deals with him."

"He's just settling in." Lily tried to sound as if she believed that was all there was to it. "It's only his first week here, and with the Graysons."

"Marsha and Joshua?" Mariah glanced from Lily to the kick-ball game. Dakota was sulking near the rest of his team but still standing separate, awaiting his turn at the plate. "He's a foster child?"

"He's smart as a whip," Lily added. "Just not about how to stay out of trouble."

"*Courting* trouble seems to be his specialty."

On cue, Dakota shoved a kid who'd been laughing at him— Nathan Grover.

"Oh, no," Lily groaned, taking off.

Nathan took a swing at Dakota, missed, then Dakota's fist showed him exactly how it was done. Both boys ended up on the ground, rolling and punching.

"Stop it now!" Tyler lifted them to their feet at the same time. He held the kids far enough apart that the punches they were still throwing only made contact with his thighs. "Stop it!"

A shake got their undivided attention.

"That's it." Mariah grabbed a handful of Dakota's jacket. "You and me, in Ms. Emory's office—now!"

Lily caught Nathan's sneer as his classmate was dragged away. She shot Tyler an *oh, hell, no!* look.

"You, too." She set off after the *stinky* substitute, pulling Dakota's bully with her.

CHAPTER FIVE

"WE HAVE A no-tolerance policy for physical violence." Ms. Emory's disapproving stare nailed the child standing to Tyler's right. "This isn't the first time you've put your hands on another student, Dakota, and you've only been at Silent Springs for a week."

"They were both fighting." Tyler nudged Nathan closer to the AP's desk from where the fourth-grader was sulking beside Lily.

Ms. Emory's eyebrow's flattened as her attention shifted Nathan's way.

"Is that so?" she asked. "Who threw the first punch?"

"I saw the Miller boy shove Nathan first," Mariah Caldwell answered. She'd hung back by the door. When both Tyler and Lily's heads snapped around in surprise, she crossed her arms and swallowed. "But I...I was talking with Lily by the bleachers. I could have missed somethi—"

"Nathan was taunting Dakota," Lily said. "And this was after I'd upset Dakota when he spoke with me. It looked as if Nathan knew Dakota was angry and decided to take advantage of the situation."

Tyler nodded in agreement, when what he wanted was to drag his wife into the hallway and ask why she'd been there watching his class in the first place.

"Nathan's made a habit of teasing Dakota this week," he added.

"Has that been your observation, as well, Ms. Caldwell?" Ms. Emory asked.

"I...I've only had the class for the morning," Mariah answered. "All I can say is that Dakota's behavior has been very disruptive."

"But you *couldn't* say what's been upsetting him to the point that he's acting out?" Lily turned on the shy substitute, her accusation laser sharp, the gentleness she normally showered on everyone evaporating.

Tyler clasped her hand and squeezed, then made himself let her go.

Ms. Emory caught the gesture before shifting her attention to the boys. "You two wait outside for a few minutes."

The kids shuffled away. But Tyler caught Dakota eyeing Lily as if he couldn't believe a teacher had gone to bat for him. When the door closed behind them, Ms. Emory motioned to the guest chairs in her office.

"Let's have a seat." She took her own behind the desk. "Ms. Caldwell, why don't you tell me what you've observed between these boys the few hours you've had them this morning, so you can return to your class. I believe the librarian's now watching them along with Mrs. Brooks's students?"

"Yes." Tyler stretched his legs in front of his chair, crossing them at the ankles. Okay, so he'd moved them as close to Lily's feet as he could manage. If that made him desperate, so be it. "I dropped them by on my way here."

Lily shifted in her chair, sitting taller and drawing away from him.

"Mrs. Rushing left work to keep the kids busy." Mariah, still standing, had her back braced against the door. "That's taken most of my attention today. All I can tell you is that Dakota's rarely in his seat, and he's been incredibly distracting to the other children while they complete their assignments. Then he turned PE into a wrestling match."

"Did he complete his work?" Lily's voice was more confrontational than Tyler had ever heard it.

"What?" Mariah pushed her glasses up her nose.

"Before he began wandering around and bothering you and the other kids, did he complete his work?"

"I…I guess, but—"

"Then maybe half the problem, Nathan Grover's bullying aside, is that Dakota's bored." Lily flinched when Tyler touched her arm, asking her to back off, no matter how badly he wanted to cheer her on. "With a little more direction, maybe he would—"

"*He's* the bully." Mariah kept her eyes trained on Gayle. "He's an unhappy kid, and I doubt he's interested in my or anyone else's direction. But I'm just a substitute. If you'd like someone else to take Alma's kids for the rest of the day…"

"Of course not," Ms. Emory soothed. "Why don't you go collect your class. Let the librarians know someone will be along for Ms. Brooks's students as soon as possible."

Mariah's glance toward Lily and Tyler was an odd mixture of annoyance and sympathy. She left, shutting the door behind her and leaving the tension in the AP's office behind.

"How are you feeling, Lily?" Ms. Emory's attention dropped for a moment to where Tyler still held his wife's arm. "After yesterday's crisis, I half expected you to take the remainder of the week off to rest."

"I FEEL FINE." Lily assured her boss. She was getting tired of trying to convince people of that, herself most of all. "I'm perfectly okay being back today."

"You just challenged another teacher in front of two students." Ms. Emory picked up her pen, tapped it on her desk a few times, then set it back down. "A substitute teacher, Lily, whom you then accused of intentionally ignoring a disruptive student because she didn't want to deal with him."

"I only suggested that part of Dakota's problems settling in here might be that he's gifted and not being challenged in the classroom." Lily swallowed the next rush of words pushing to get out. She looked to Tyler for support, then told herself to knock it off. "Even if that's not the case, any child with the amount of disruption in his life Dakota's had to deal with might reasonably be expected to behave the way he has!"

After several seconds of the AP's skeptical silence, Lily realized she'd shouted the last sentence.

"What does your doctor say?" Ms. Emory waited. When Lily didn't respond, the AP turned to Tyler for her answers.

And, damn it, if Lily didn't, too.

She held her breath. If she'd ever needed her husband on her side it was now, no matter how worried he still was. She knew it didn't make sense that helping Dakota had become so important to her so quickly, but he had.

"The doctor's given Lily a clean bill of health." Tyler's gaze locked with Lily's as he stretched the truth. "She's cleared to work, as long as she feels up to it."

"And I feel fine." Lily didn't remember Tyler taking her hand, but the feel of his fingers nestled between hers was heaven.

"Given yesterday morning's episode—" Ms. Emory's expression was as concerned as it was confused "—I wouldn't say *fine* is exactly the right word. And you've had similar episodes over the last six months, Lily. You've missed quite a bit of work because of the side effects of your fertility treatments."

"Personal time she's accumulated over the last ten years," Tyler pressed.

"Of course." Ms. Emory folded her hands and nodded. "I'm happy for my teachers to take whatever medical leave they need." Her focus shifted to Lily. "Your health is what's most important. If you need more of a break, that's not a problem. But when you're here, I have to know that I can depend on you to continue doing the same fine work as always."

"That's exactly what she has done today," Tyler insisted, backing Lily up even though he'd wanted her home himself. "I've seen Lily with Dakota, the way he responds to her. Mariah's right. He's an angry, confused little boy. But Lily's created an instant rapport with him. And Nathan Grover does pick on the kid. What happened today is just as much Nathan's fault as Dakota's."

"Except Dakota instigated the physical outcome," Ms. Emory reminded them. "And it's not the first time in a single week that he's become overly aggressive with his peers."

"A child displaced the way he was will naturally have more difficulty attaching to a new situation and making new friends." Lily caught Tyler's nod. Remembered all the reasons her husband was so careful to hide his emotions, even from her. "It takes a special person to be able to face the obstacles Dakota's has, then to start over someplace new."

"And it takes a special teacher to see the gifts buried beneath the grumpiness and misbehavior of a student who needs as much help as this one." The speculative glint in the AP's eye was Lily's only warning. "Since it's my observation that you need some downtime, and we have quite a situation on our hands with young Mr. Miller, I'm wondering if you spending some one-on-one time with him might not be the best solution for all involved."

"That's a great idea," Tyler blurted out.

"What!" Lily leaned forward. "I have my own class to teach. A Spring Fling to plan. And—"

"An assistant principal who at the moment isn't convinced you need to be at school at all. You can't seem to go five minutes without shrieking at me or one of my staff."

"But my class…"

"I have a list of substitutes who can help out while you work with Dakota. In fact, I'm going to ask one to cover your class for the rest of the afternoon."

"The carnival, I—"

"Lily," Tyler reasoned, "I think you should—"

"I know exactly what you think!" And she'd actually believed he was back on her side.

"Let's not worry about the carnival right now." Ms. Emory pushed to her feet. "If need be, I'm sure Ashley Lawson wouldn't mind taking over the final planning."

"But, I…" Lily stood, too. The arguments kept tumbling out. The panic. "I'm close to having things—"

"Lily," Tyler said beside her. "I think you should listen—"

"Like you always listen?" She turned to him and fought to breathe.

"I need to deal with Dakota and Nathan." Ms. Emory headed

for the door. "It sounds like they both would benefit from spending the rest of the day at home. A couple of weeks of afternoon detention beyond that. You two talk for as long as you need. Come back in the morning, Lily. You can let me know your answer then. If you think you're up for it, we'll arrange to have you start with Dakota tomorrow."

"Tomorrow?"

"Either that, or I'm afraid we're going to have to find another solution for the young man. It sounds as if Nathan's behavior has been questionable, but that doesn't change the fact that a mainstream classroom clearly isn't the best place for Dakota right now."

"That's not giving him much of a chance." Tyler braced his hands on his hips. "He just arrived at Silent Springs. The Graysons are only starting to work with him."

Ms. Emory grimaced. "From what his children's-services caseworker said, that situation doesn't seem to be working, either, regardless of Marsha and Joshua's track record."

"Dakota needs more time." Lily felt Ms. Emory's reasoning, the walls, closing around her. No matter how much she longed to sprint for the door—away from Tyler—she couldn't run this time. She couldn't let Dakota down. "He's a bright, lonely child who's spinning out of control due to circumstances that aren't his fault."

"Yes, and his experience in this school seems to be making matters worse, not to mention disrupting the learning environment for everyone else. I'm sorry." Ms. Emory seemed genuinely regretful. "Everyone's doing the best they can to help him, but sometimes there's simply nothing to be done if the child's not ready to take the help he's given."

"If he wasn't ready," Tyler argued, "why would he be reaching out to Lily the way he is?"

"A valid point." The AP glanced between Lily and Tyler. "I'll speak with the Graysons when they come to pick Dakota up. I'll ask if they'd be open to Lily working one-on-one with the child until he's ready to rejoin his class. If they aren't, or if you're not feeling up to that, Lily, I'll have no choice but to give Mr. Kramer a call. It might be best to transition Dakota back to the group home he came from, and whatever learning environment he'd settled into there, sooner rather than later. I'll have the school secretary schedule us an appointment first thing tomorrow. Please, think about it."

The door closed behind the AP.

Lily rounded on her husband.

"WHAT WAS THAT!" Lily demanded as she backed away from Tyler.

"That was me supporting you." Tyler edged around her, physically blocking her escape. "Isn't that what you wanted?"

"You just agreed with Ms. Emory that I'm not capable of taking care of my own class!" accused the woman who'd looked at him just a few minutes ago as if he was her hero.

"Because you need some more time, Lily!" He inhaled to curb the urge to keep yelling. "It's not a character flaw. We're both hurting. Just because I can see possibilities for our marriage and our life beyond having kids doesn't mean I don't feel the disappointment as deeply as you do."

School—work—wasn't the place for this conversation. But she avoided him everywhere else, so school it was.

"You always could do that," she said, surprisingly calm, almost sounding like the dreamy young woman he'd asked to share his life.

Tyler remembered holding his breath when he'd proposed. He hadn't believed he deserved anyone as light and loving and perfect as Lily. He realized he was holding his breath now, terrified he was losing that light for good.

"I could always do what?" he asked.

"Adjust, to whatever you had to. Handle anything— disadvantages I can't even imagine."

"Not having to fight for everything you've had in life doesn't make you any less a champion."

She snorted. "Some champion. I…I feel as if I'm just standing by, watching everything slip away…"

Like she'd watched Carter slip away.

"Everyone's weak sometimes, Lily. Sometimes we all lose big, no matter how hard we fight. I'm no exception." Marsha was right. He'd pushed Lily to move on before she was ready, rather than letting her feel what she needed to. "I was just like Dakota when I lost my parents. A part of me still is."

Her beautiful features clouded at the roughness in his voice.

"What do you mean?" She reached for him, instinctively offering the support he needed to keep talking.

"A part of me still doesn't believe I can hold on to the things I want most." What was it she'd said about feeling powerless? He took the hand of his best friend, the best part of himself, and dug deep for the truth that might help her understand. "That if I stop fighting, everything will disappear again, the way my family did. Almost as if they weren't real. As if what you and I have isn't real."

"Of course we're real."

She was drowning in her own doubts, but that didn't stop her from reassuring him. That was the amazing way Lily's heart worked.

His perfect Lily.

"Every day you're in my life, I believe that a little bit more," he whispered. "But the fear still creeps back in, and I've let it come between us. I've been so worried about losing you, I haven't been listening to what you need. I've been pushing you to accept my solution and not trying hard enough to accept what you're dealing with. The same way Dakota keeps pushing when he's scared. He's not a bad kid. You can see that. You understand him, the way you've always understood me. That's what I was trying to tell Ms. Emory. And so were you, before you panicked about being pulled away from your work for a while."

"But…he has the Graysons." Lily's eyes shimmered with confusion.

"Dakota doesn't trust them, honey. Not yet. But I think he's starting to trust you. Yes, I was excited about Ms. Emory's offer, partially because I want you taking things easier around here for a while. But I can see how much you could help Dakota, too."

"I…" She looked so scared. "I don't think I can."

"I know," he said, hating her self-doubt but accepting that he couldn't fix it. All he could do was love her and support her and hope it was enough. "But you wouldn't be doing it alone. I'd have your back. Whatever you need, I'll be there if you'll let me."

"I…" She stepped around him to the door. "I'm sorry, I can't… I…I'll call Mom to take me home."

Tyler watched her leave and fought the instinct to follow. To try and make her trust him and keep fighting for them. For Dakota.

She needed time. She needed him to believe she could handle this. If he didn't stop trying to slay her dragons for her, she might never believe she was strong enough to face them herself.

I'm a big, fat failure, Tyler…

He'd been as honest as he knew how. All he could do now was hope the love he'd let himself believe in—Lily's love—was strong enough to get them both through this.

CHAPTER SIX

LILY SAT in the passenger seat of her mother's ancient Ford and stared at her house. Tyler was in there, wondering where she was. He hadn't hounded her on her cell the way she'd expected. He'd called her parents' at their home, according to her father, to be sure Rose was with her. But her father hadn't divulged their trip to Dr. Gruber's.

I'm sorry, she'd said to Tyler as she'd run out on him.

Both the fertility specialist and her mother had said the same thing. Rose, over and over again, on the drive home.

I'm sorry.

Thank you was all Lily could remember saying to the doctor. She'd actually thanked the man.

She'd asked him for the truth one last time, after refusing to hear it during all the appointments she and Tyler had made together. Then she'd proceeded to cry all over her mother when Gruber confirmed what she already knew. And she hadn't stopped crying since.

Silent tears. Useless—just like all the years of trying and praying and believing she could make her and Tyler's dreams happen. Just like all the expensive treatments and endless checkups that had resulted in one disappointment after another.

"You said Tyler's already accepted the diagnosis." Her mother's touch was as gentle as her voice. "He loves you, Lily. The two of you will get through this."

Lily wiped at the wet trails running from the corners of her eyes. "Yes, he's accepted it."

Tyler knew how to make a success out of what was possible,

instead of mourning what couldn't be changed. It was an amazing outlook, considering everything he'd survived. And he was trying so hard now, to really understand what she was going through. Which she'd blasted him for last night.

"Can you accept it?" her mother asked, voicing the question Lily had been trying to answer since leaving the AP's office. "I was hoping that wanting to see Dr. Gruber was a sign you were ready to try."

"So was I." Lily stared at the dashboard.

"So controlled." Rose's finger tipped Lily's chin and turned her face until they were eye-to-eye. "So careful. You've needed everything to be right and perfect and planned down to the last detail for so long. Too long. Keep holding on to life that hard, and you'll strangle all the pleasure out of it."

Pleasure?

Fun loving on the outside, *effortlessly* successful in everything, blessed with a wonderful man who'd made a place for her in his life. That's how the world saw her. But it seemed like forever since Lily had felt pleasure in any of it.

"Losing Carter was a terrible thing for all of us," her mother added. "But—"

Lily fumbled with the doorknob.

"Stop it!" Her mother locked the doors from her side of the car. "We're talking about this. I'm tired of dancing around it. You're father is, too. It's been years, Lily, and you're not the only one who's had to deal with losing him. You're just the last one to let go."

Let go and move on, Tyler had said.

Lily gazed out the windshield, finally accepting that it was her husband's ability to face reality that she'd been running from, not her unfair accusations that he'd given up.

"It's hard," she finally said.

It was exhausting, making sure everything and everyone around her was okay. As if she'd ever had any real control over any of it.

"It's not your fault." Her mother gripped the steering wheel.

"Years of therapy, and the only thing I can say for certain is that losing Carter wasn't anyone's fault."

"Therapy?"

"It's the only way your father and I were able to get through it."

"Mom…"

"Tragedy is hard enough, Lily, without the added pressure of feeling responsible for what happened, or for somehow making up for something that you'll never make right. You'll destroy your life that way. Your ability to love. Your father and I refused to let that happen. Now you have your own choice to make."

As if on cue, the front door opened and Tyler stepped onto the brick steps that led up from the walk. He looked harried. Worried. Hurt.

Amazing.

"Things in this life are never going to be perfect, honey." Her mother unlocked the doors. "And neither will we."

She started the engine.

Lily couldn't move. Her heart was pounding in her throat. Static roared in her ears. Her whole body throbbed, panicked, at the thought of walking into her home and confronting the least-threatening person in her life.

The man she suspected understood her better than she did herself.

She'd been fighting to fill the hollow place in her heart for so long. She'd never let anything close enough, except the dream of having a child of her own. A little boy with gentle brown eyes like…like Carter's.

"I…I don't know what to do now."

Her mother was wiping away her own tears.

"You take small steps," she said. "One at a time. You face what you really want most, and you find a way to believe in it, even if it means you might lose all over again."

Lily's only response was to shake her head. She stepped out of the car.

Her mother drove away, leaving her standing at the curb on her own. But she wasn't alone, not really. Not as long as she still had Tyler's love.

I'll be there if you let me.

She walked toward him, guilt and fear kicking her heart rate even higher. She'd pushed him away so many times. Would he give him one more chance to believe? Could she really take it?

She reached the top of the steps and without a word walked into his embrace, wrapping her arms around him as he folded her close. When she lifted her head and kissed him, she felt him start, heard his breath catch, then his groan tangled with hers. He lifted her to her toes and deepened the kiss.

"Lily," he whispered as he backed into the house and spun her toward their bedroom, kicking the door closed with his foot.

IT HAD BEEN SO LONG since they'd made love and not focused on making a baby.

Lily shuddered as Tyler's need drove hers higher. His hands found the hem of her blouse. His fingers ran beneath the silk and roamed then massaged her back. His strength, his uncontrolled response, was hotter and wilder than ever before. He unhooked her bra, then he was cupping her breasts, kneading and flicking and pinching in a heavenly way that sent her senses soaring.

"Honey, what is it?" he asked around her gasp. "What's wrong?"

"Nothing," she lied.

She nipped at his lip. Drank down his curse of desperation. Reveled in the strength that lifted her and carried her to the bed and tossed her on top of the covers he hadn't taken the time to tidy that morning.

Her husband stood over her, his breathing rough, coming from deep in his chest. His expression hard, needing. He ripped at his clothes as she worked with equal determination to be rid of hers. It had been so long. Too long. But even lost to the physical need consuming them both, his eyes were still so blue, so clear and concerned, her tears made a unwelcome reappearance.

They were both free, skin to skin, his heart pounding against hers. The muscles of his forearms bunched beneath her hands. His fingers cradled her head. His thumbs wiped at the tears trickling down her cheeks.

"What is it, Lily?" His next kiss was the softest thing she'd ever felt. It throbbed through her body, promising so much. Making her want more. "What happened this afternoon? If you're not sure you want this, we can wait until—"

"No!"

She pulled him tighter against her. Her thighs cradled his body to where hers screamed for his touch. Her lips grazed the sensitive flesh on his neck in a caress that she knew could distract him from anything. No matter how completely unsure and confused she still was, she couldn't go one more minute without what she really wanted.

"Make love to me, Tyler," she begged. "Love me, please."

TYLER KNEW he should stop.

Stop! his mind kept telling his hands.

Not possible.

Lily was too sweet and warm, melting against him. Yearning, the desire that had always burned beneath her carefully controlled exterior flaming his even higher.

Lily.

Something was still wrong. He could feel it. They should be talking, about Dakota and the fact that they hadn't really trusted each other since their plans for starting a family had begun to unravel. But all Tyler could do was pull her closer, bury himself inside her and drink her cries of pleasure. Her need.

Lily needed him again. Maybe she'd never stopped. She was in his arms and begging him to love her. Nothing else mattered tonight.

He'd have to trust that they would still be together come morning. That they could still hang on to the future.

TYLER PULLED into his parking spot at the school and killed the ignition.

A part of him wanted to shake his wife, for sneaking out of their bed and out of the house that morning. *And* driving to work on her own when she wasn't supposed to be driving yet. Another part of him was proud of Lily for facing her appointment with Gayle Emory on her own, even though she hadn't told him whether she'd decided to work with Dakota.

Don't be mad. I've got to figure some things out, was all her note had said.

Mad?

He wanted her back in his arms. His bed. After last night, he wanted to hold her close and hide her away and keep her all to himself until she promised to never run from him again. None of which he could do, so he headed for the building instead.

His cell rang as he passed Lily's vintage VW Beetle safely parked several spots from his Explorer. He checked the phone's display and flipped it open, walking up the sidewalk leading to the front of the building.

"Hey, Marsha."

"Dakota's missing again." His foster mother's voice was shaking, something Tyler had heard only a few times in his life. "Josh's out looking for him, but Dakota may have been gone all night. His bedroom window was open, and none of the other kids saw him when they got up this morning."

"Maybe he just left early." The Grayson house was only a few blocks away, and the streets were lined with sidewalks that made it easy for the kids to get to and from school on their own. "I'm at school now. Let me call you back once I know more."

He jogged inside and waved as he passed the receptionist without asking her to buzz him into the AP's office. He raised his hand to knock on Ms. Emory's door. Before he could, it opened, and he came face-to-face with his wife. Lily's expression was strained, but a flicker of the fire that had mesmerized him last night still smoldered in her eyes.

"Tyler!" She pulled him into a hug. "I'm sorry I didn't get you

up this morning, but I needed to do this on my own. And I wante
to run by my mother's on the way to school. She…she helpe
me realize something important last night."

Her tentative smile didn't last once she realized he was shak
ing his head. She frowned and stepped back. Tyler caught he
before she could move out of reach, needing her close still. Need
ing her forever.

"I want to hear about your morning," he assured her. "What
ever you need, I want to make that happen. But we've got to fin
Dakota first. He's run away again."

CHAPTER SEVEN

"IF DAKOTA'S on school grounds," Ms. Emory said. "He's found a new hiding place I don't know about. We have every available staff member looking, but there's no trace of him. Principal White just got off the phone with Mrs. Grayson. The child hasn't returned to the Grayson place."

Panic clenched in Lily's chest. Tyler looked up from his cell call to Joshua and shook his head. No luck finding Dakota near his home, either.

"I'll take another look outside." Lily left the school office, as her need to scream, to throw something, built. She wasn't sure how much longer she could control it.

Just half an hour ago, Lily had agreed to be Dakota's shadow for the indefinite future, tutoring him one-on-one whenever possible. Accompanying him to group activities to observe his interaction with his peers, intervening if appropriate and working with the school counselor and children's-services caseworker to design an individual plan that would give the bright child his best chance of success.

"You'll be like his mother here at Silent Springs," Ms. Emory had said as she arranged for a substitute to take over Lily's class.

Lily bolted for the art room instead of heading out the side door to the grassy area where some of the kids hung out before the bell rang for class. Ashley wasn't there, of course. She was with the rest of the staff, scouring the grounds for a lost little boy who didn't have a real mother to keep up with him. He didn't even have a grandmother who could deal with his special needs.

I don't have anyone.

Lily stared at the table covered with hand-sewn hens tha would be watching over Mr. Palmer's chicks at the Spring Fling Make-believe mothers, because Lily hadn't wanted the kind c mess too many real birds might make out of an otherwise perfec day. The chubby little creations looked back at her with empt eyes, mocking the idea of there being perfect mothers or perfec children in the world. Perfect, safe families. Perfect anything.

Perfect wasn't important. Controlled and careful hadn't kep Lily from failing at having a baby. It hadn't gotten her a ste closer to the happiness she and Tyler deserved, or buried the pa once and for all.

…a little chaos is a good trade-off…

"Lily?" asked the person who had been there through th night, soothing her soul while their bodies had healed the lone liness they'd let grow between them. "We'll find him."

"By hanging around here waiting for him to show up?" Sh turned to face Tyler. "We have to do something more. *I* have t do something."

"It's not your fault Dakota ran away. Don't take that on, too.

"I could have stayed yesterday and talked with him. I coul have gone over to the Graysons' and let him know I'd be spendin more time with him at school."

"You told Gayle you'd work with Dakota?"

"Like it did any good."

"It'll do a lot of good, once we find him."

"Unless Mr. Kramer decides to send him back to a grou home after this, and then I've lost my chance to—"

"*Then* Dakota will get help from someone else!" Tyler rake a hand through his hair. "Stop taking responsibility for things yo can't fix, Lily. It's pointless and selfish and you know better tha that at school, even if you can't figure it out in our personal life.

"Selfish!"

"Indulgent." His hard stare didn't flinch at her gasp. "You'v been running on guilt over Carter for so long, it's your first in stinct every time something goes wrong. And that's fine. It' normal. But the fact that you won't even try to work past it is selfish."

"You're lecturing me about not handling my feelings!"

"Right. That's my MO. But I'm doing everything I can to knock it off and figure out another way."

"Meanwhile, *I'm* being selfish."

"Beating yourself up isn't going to help Dakota when he shows up here and you're an emotional wreck. It'll just make it harder for the two of you to get to work."

"He's not coming here. Why would he, when he thinks no one will understand him?"

The way she'd been so sure Tyler wouldn't understand her. If Dakota was feeling even a speck of that kind of insecurity, no wonder he kept running.

"You went to bat for him yesterday, Lil." Tyler's expression softened as he used the nickname she hadn't heard since they were kids. "That's a huge first step for him. He'll trust you when the moment's right. You two are a good fit. He'll know that you understand."

"What?" she asked. Something Tyler had said…there was something—

"You and Dakota are connected. You—"

"Fit!"

Maybe I'd fit in better if I went to live with the flamingos.

"Oh, my gosh!" She tugged Tyler with her as she raced out of the art room. "I think I know where he's gone!"

"I HEADED INTO THE BARN for some feed." Mr. Palmer led Lily and Tyler through a corral where several ponies were standing docilely, their tails lazily switching at flies. "And I heard a commotion up in the loft where I keep the hay. When I headed up, this kid yelled down that if I didn't stop, he'd jump. Something about there being no flamingos. Then you folks called from the school. I was getting ready to phone the sheriff."

"Dakota's a student of mine," Lily explained over the harshness of her own breathing. She and Tyler had run all the way from the car. "He saw my list of animals you thought you could bring for the Spring Fling, and he must have come to check out the exotic birds."

"Hell, I don't keep those things here!" They slowed to a stop as they reached the barn. Mr. Palmer nudged his hat back and wiped his forehead with the sleeve of his faded chambray shirt. "I got a friend who works for a traveling zoo up in Rounder, and he hooks me up whenever I need something I don't have here. All the birds except the chickens are his."

"I'm so sorry." Lily peered at the opening to the barn's loft—presumably what Dakota was threatening to jump from. Only one story up, it might not be a life-threatening fall, but she shivered just the same. "I'd like to try talking to him until the Graysons get here."

"Good luck," Palmer grumped. He glanced over his shoulder at the sound of approaching vehicles. "That'll be them there."

Tyler nodded, recognizing at least one of the cars at the same time Lily did. "I'll go. You take care of Dakota."

He squeezed Lily's shoulder before jogging away. She headed for the ladder leaning against the side of the barn.

"Will this reach the loft?"

"Yep." Mr. Palmer squinted. "But I told you, the kid screams bloody murder anytime I try to head up."

"He'll have a lot harder time jumping if I'm coming in through his escape hatch." Lily grunted as she tried to wrestle the ladder into place. "Maybe you could stand by the steps inside, so he'll think twice about scurrying down that way while I'm climbing in."

"I don't know. We should probably wait for the Graysons." Mr. Palmer eyed her peasant skirt and strappy sandals as he helped her with the ladder.

Lily kicked off her shoes and climbed. She checked over her shoulder and saw Tyler returning with Marsha and Joshua, joined by, of all people, Mr. Kramer from children's services.

"Watch the steps inside in case he bolts," she insisted to the hovering farmer. "And ask everyone else to give me a few minutes alone up there."

TYLER RACED to foot of the ladder that his still-weak wife was rushing up. She'd started climbing faster the second she saw him coming.

"Lily!"

Mr. Palmer lifted his hat and slapped it against his thigh. "She said something about wanting a few minutes alone with the kid."

Tyler held his breath. Lily reached the top of the ladder and said something to the child. Then she slipped inside.

Alone.

He turned toward the concerned folks behind him instead of following her.

"She's done a great job with Dakota at school," he explained to Ralph Kramer. "Lily's the one who guessed he'd be here. Give her a little time. If anyone can talk him down, she can."

"I certainly hope so," Mr. Kramer said. "I was pleased to hear Assistant Principal Emory's plan to give Dakota an advocate at school. And I know the Graysons are doing everything they can with the child. But if he refuses to stop running away, if we can't help him attach—"

"Lily Brooks will," Marsha insisted with the same confidence she placed in all her kids, no matter what challenge they faced. "She's an amazing teacher and an instinctive nurturer. Dakota doesn't stand a chance of holding out against love like that."

Tyler nodded and returned his attention to the loft.

He'd been out of line back at the school. He'd accused Lily of letting her past interfere with helping Dakota. No way would she let that happen.

She could do this. And he was going to be right there supporting her—even if it meant clutching the ladder she'd just scaled, and clenching his teeth against the instinct to protect her from the disappointment that would suck her under if this didn't work.

CHAPTER EIGHT

"YOU LIED!" Dakota yelled from the other side of the loft.

A fistful of hay sailed Lily's way as she scrambled off the ladder and tried to crawl to her feet without flashing the fine people below with a charming view of her Friday panties.

"I lied about what?" Kneeling near him, she brushed her hands on her skirt.

"You said he had animals here!" The kid peered down the inside steps—presumably at Mr. Palmer waiting below—then backed further into the corner.

"He does." A considerate cow mooed in the distance, driving her point home.

"Boring farm animals. Everybody has those." Dakota's shoulders sagged. He plopped down in a heap of hay, his head hanging. He peaked at her from under the brim of his Falcons cap. "You said... Where are the cool ones?"

"They—" Lily bit the corner of her lip "—they don't live here, Dakota. They have another home. Mr. Kramer's friend brings them over for events like the Spring Fling."

"So they don't belong in Silent Springs, either."

Lily edged nearer. Sat close enough to touch. Dakota was too engrossed in shredding the straw at his feet to notice. Her arms ached to hug him until some of his loneliness eased. She kept her hands to herself, remembering all the awful times it had felt as if Tyler was crowding her, when he'd only been trying to find a way to reassure her that she wasn't alone.

"How long have you been here?" she asked.

Dakota shrugged. "I couldn't sleep at that place."

"At the Graysons'? Why not?"

"They're going to send me back, aren't they?" His glare dared her to lie and say things weren't as bad as he thought. "Why don't they just go ahead and get it over with?"

The way his grandmother had finally gotten it over with?

"Have you ever stopped to think that maybe the Graysons don't want to send you back?"

Dakota's next look made it clear she was nuts.

"Can't you even try to believe it's possible?" she asked.

A rush of tears filled his eyes.

"What do you know!" He stood, looking wildly around the loft but going nowhere. He swiped at his eyes. "You're just a stupid teacher. What do you know!"

"I know that if I expect things to be bad for long enough, things end up being that way—kind of as if it's what I'd planned all along."

"I didn't plan anything," Dakota's forehead scrunched.

"Well, you're here, instead of at school. You spent the night in a stranger's barn instead of in your new home."

"That stupid place isn't my home!"

"Exactly."

It was Lily's turn to blink while chickens clucked nearby, going about their day as if the world that had hurt this child was a fine and lovely place.

"Do you really want a new family?" Lily reached for his arm. "Or are you planning to hate every home Mr. Kramer sends you to?"

Dakota sat, staring at the hay again.

"The Graysons are downstairs waiting for you." She nudged him with her shoulder the way she'd seen Tyler do. "They're worried, Dakota, and they want to take you home."

His chest heaved in and out.

"I'll just mess up again," he mumbled. "Just like before."

"You will if you keep running away because you're afraid to try."

His watery gaze rose to hers. "I always mess up."

"With your mom?" Lily let her own tears fall, hoping they'd reassure Dakota that he wasn't hurting alone. When he nodded, she asked, "With your grandmother?"

Another nod, smaller than the last.

"Maybe they're the ones who messed up, Dakota. Or maybe things just got so bad that no one could have made them better, no matter how much they loved you."

His forehead wrinkled even more than before.

"Teachers really are lame." His shoulder nudged hers back.

"No doubt about it." Lily suppressed a mile-wide grin at his tiny show of acceptance. "But you can't live in a hayloft for the rest of your life, wanting to be with silly pink birds because they sound safer than people. And I don't think you really want to go back to the group home you lived at before the Graysons."

"So?" was the best his ten-year-old wisdom could produce.

"So, I guess you're going to have to find a way to want to be somewhere else. *With* someone else. You know, with people who want to take the time to know you and like you and take care of you."

"Who, the Graysons? Why would they want a messed-up kid like me?"

Lily blinked at the hope and fear behind his disbelief, realizing just how important this moment was. There in a shadowy loft on a warm spring day, talking to someone else's child, she'd never felt more like the mother she'd hoped to be.

So, this is what mothers were created to do. What Dakota had never had, and what Rose had always been for Lily's entire life, including last night when she'd all but shoved Lily out of her car. Someone to give hope and shine light into the shadows, until a child, even a thirty-one-year-old one, learned how to see the success they were born to be.

Lily had felt the same emotions as Dakota, dueling inside her since…forever. Since losing her brother.

And *she'd* had loving, adoring parents to help her. She'd had Tyler.

Everyone's weak sometimes, Lily. Sometimes we all lose big, no matter how hard we fight.

But Tyler had fought through the weakness. And with his patience and love, she would, too. So would this child.

"You have to let someone new want you, Dakota," she finally said. "You have to let them see beyond what's already happened. Which means *you* have to let the past go. It doesn't always have to be the way it was with your mother and grandmother."

And for her it didn't always have to be about control and planning things to death and desperately forcing everything to be perfect.

"You…" He clutched straw between his fingers. "You could want me…maybe you could…you know, you said you and Mr. Brooks were talking with Mr. Kramer about doing what the Graysons do. So…maybe…"

Lily covered those restless hands with her own and waited until he looked up.

"Of course Mr. Brooks and I would want you," she assured the little boy who'd helped her realize how long she'd been running, too. "I've told Ms. Emory that I'll work with you at school, just you and me for as long as it takes for you to believe you belong there, too. But you already have a new family that wants you. A new home. People who'll love you for who you are now. But you have to learn how to trust them enough to let them."

He swallowed. Glanced toward the stairs. Didn't budge an inch. But he didn't let go of her hand.

"It's your choice, Dakota. It's your life. So what if you're a flamingo?" She winked at his surprised snicker. "I think maybe I am, too. Maybe that's why we get along so well. Because I understand how things can get messed up, and that there's nothing wrong with being different. Unless we decide to make being different the reason we give up on having what the chickens have."

He squinted as he tried to follow her *lame* attempt to expand on his analogy. "And what…what do the chickens have?"

She nodded toward the ladder, where Mr. Palmer was watching from below. Down where the Graysons and Mr. Kramer were waiting for Dakota, and Tyler was waiting for her. Where happy little barnyard birds were clucking away, content that they belonged, and trusting that they and their friends would be okay no matter what might go wrong.

"I'm not sure," she admitted. "But I'm ready to give it a try. How about you?"

She stood and held out her hand. Still squinting at her, likely debating if she'd gone a few feathers past flamingo, he let her help him up. That gesture alone, such a simple show of trust, made her long to give him a bone-crushing hug that would ruin everything. Flipping up the bill of his cap would have to do.

He tensed, then in midscowl surprised her by taking the hat off. It took several heartbeats before she realized he was holding the sweat-stained thing out to her.

His prized possession.

"Take it." He shoved it into her hands. "I..."

His eyes were shiny again, and that just wouldn't do when he faced the chickens, so Lily took the hat and then did what she'd seen work for Tyler when gentle persuasion wasn't enough. She grasped the boy's shoulders and turned him toward the steps.

You take small steps, her mother had said. *One at a time.*

"I'll be right behind you." With a gentle nudge, she let go.

Wiping at her own eyes, she held her breath as Dakota took the first step down. He looked back once, to catch her putting his cap on. She nodded and waited, her heart racing as he disappeared below.

TYLER SAW himself in the scared young man that slowly turned from the bottom of the barn stairs to face his future. There was strength and too-old wisdom in those shadowed eyes. But there was innocence still. A promising flicker of hope.

Dakota walked slowly toward where the Graysons were waiting just outside the barn, eyeing Ralph Kramer who stood beside them. Tyler's attention shifted to the woman making her way down the same steps Dakota had. He reached for Lily's arm before Mr. Palmer could. By the time her feet hit the ground, the good-natured farmer was ambling away to get on with his day.

They turned to watch as Joshua held his hand out for Dakota to shake.

"Ready to go home, son?" Joshua hugged Marsha to his side.

Both adults smiled down at the boy, relaxed, calmly waiting. Like they could wait forever for Dakota to puzzle out the answer. Tyler had every confidence they could.

And then Dakota reached for Joshua's hand.

"I…I'd like to go home now." He gave a small shake. Looked to Marsha next, then Mr. Kramer. "If…if that's still okay."

"Well, of course it's okay," Marsha announced. She offered no mushy, sappy hug that the kid would hate if he was anything like Tyler had been—even though she'd been wringing her hands, worried sick, up until the moment Dakota emerged from the loft. She turned and headed for the cars. "Let's get going. I'm two loads of laundry behind already, and this boy needs to be in school."

Joshua followed in her wake, guiding Dakota at his side. "You'll learn," he said with a conspiratory wink. "Marsha and her laundry. A smart man never wants to get in the way of that."

Ralph Kramer waved, on his way out, as well. Tyler found himself chuckling. He looked down to where Lily was laughing beside him, only to realize it was sobs shaking her shoulders instead.

"Lily?" He folded her in his arms. Over the top of her head—Dakota's Falcons cap, actually—he asked, "Honey, what's wrong?"

She clung to him. She'd done such an amazing job with Dakota, Tyler had forgotten for a moment about all the rest. He shifted back, trying see her face, expecting more of the confusion and the fear and the hurt that he couldn't make go away. But one look at her radiant smile, the promise and the hope there, and he was crushing her into another hug.

"Lily?" he asked, almost afraid to believe.

"Take me back to school," she whispered, "so I can see what

Dakota's up for today." She slipped her hand in his. "Then I want to go home and hear more about what Mr. Kramer left us to read."

"Are you sure?" What was he saying! "I mean…that's great, but…"

She shook her head, as she wiped the last of her tears away. "I don't need to be sure anymore." There was that smile, lighting up her face and laying claim to his heart all over again. "I need to feel what I did upstairs, Tyler. And I need to hear you laugh. And I need to…"

"Let go?" he asked, holding on tighter.

"Yeah," she agreed.

Yeah.

His new favorite word.

He walked with her to the Explorer, following her lead, playing it cool the same as she was, meanwhile his head was spinning.

"Nice hat, by the way," he said once they were seated.

She took it off and held it to her heart as if it were the finest bouquet of roses.

"I…I had no idea…" she said. "I knew what the Graysons did. I saw the world they made possible for you. But I never realized what it must have meant to them, to be there when you learned how to trust again. If that's not being a parent, a mother, I…I don't know how I could have seen it as failing. It would be such a privilege…the chance of a lifetime. And I almost…I'm so sorry, Tyler. I had no idea."

"No sorries, Lily." His arms were around her. "As long as you've found your way back to me, as long as you can love the life we can still make, the kids we can help together, you're giving me everything I'll ever need."

EPILOGUE

"I'VE GOT HER," Ashley cried.

Squawk! screeched the flamingo she was trying to corral back into its pen.

"Look out!" Lily warned when the bird faked left then crossed right, leading Ashley toward the—

Shriek!

"...for the peacock," Lily finished as her friend collided with the other bird and people scattered.

Pebbles the flamingo honked her way toward the dunking booth, where Tyler was enjoying the show from his lofty seat above freezing-cold water. Joshua Grayson waved from his place in line. Dante the peacock strutted in the opposite direction, stopping for a drink from the wading pool the younger kids were fishing plastic prizes from. Ashley sat in a stunned sprawl, rubbing her backside.

The spontaneous giggle at Lily's elbow was a beautiful sound. It went a long way toward smoothing over the day's disaster. But Ms. Emory was glowering from the other side of the Spring Fling, so Lily plastered on her best *responsible adult* look and shook her head down at Dakota.

"It's not funny," she insisted.

The animals were everywhere. Poop was everywhere. Parents were snapping pictures and recording the show with their digital cameras. Her guess was *America's Funniest Home Videos* was about to hit the mother lode in animal-disaster material.

"It's cool." Dakota surveyed the chaos that had been unleashed when *someone* opened the temporary pen Mr. Palmer had erected to contain the larger animals. At her speculative glance, he raised his hands in innocence. "Don't look at me. I don't know how they got out. But…" he gave her the devilish grin he knew was her weakness "…it's still cool."

"Got him!" Mr. Palmer shouted, his hands full of Lenny the llama. He started herding the beast, which had kicked over the lemonade stand, back to the farm's trailer. Catching sight of Dakota's grin, he jerked a thumb over his shoulder. "Grab the shovel out of my truck and clean up that mess."

"What?" Dakota's gaze followed the thumb to the steaming piles of llama leftovers scattered about the carnival. "No way am I picking up all that sh—"

"Sounds like you've got a job to do, son." Marsha Grayson appeared beside Lily and Dakota, her eyebrows raised at her youngest foster child's colorful vocabulary. "Helping set up and clean up after the carnival is part of your detention. If you want your afternoons free to take horseback-riding lessons, better fetch that shovel and get to work."

"Man…" Dakota dragged his feet as he headed after the farmer.

But he was going, and he'd do his job. And tomorrow his after-school hours would be free to hang out at Mr. Palmer's as much as he wanted.

"They're becoming fast friends." The hope in Marsha's calm voice wasn't lost on Lily.

"Thanks to you and Joshua, Dakota's starting to believe that he deserves friends." She smiled. "And you're making sure he works off the trouble he's made for himself, so he'll appreciate his time at the farm even more. Nice job."

Marsha waved away the compliment. "Mr. Palmer doesn't seem to mind that Dakota likes to help with the animals. The kid must be doing a good job of staying out of the way over there, because the riding lessons were Palmer's idea. Dakota's making it work on his own."

"Uh-huh." Lily wasn't buying it, but she *was* watching every move the Graysons made, taking mental notes and hoping she and Tyler could do half as well. "We start our introductory class tonight. I hope we're better at being foster parents than I am at creating a picturesque Mother's Day surprise for the carnival."

Marsha took in the families huddled together in hysterics and snapping pictures as Mr. Palmer rounded up the uncooperative Pebbles and Dante and ended the disaster Spring Fling had become.

"You'll do all right," she said as Dakota slipped. He and his brand-new sneakers landed in the pile of poop he'd been shoveling into a wheelbarrow. "Lord, give me strength," she muttered, heading after the child and presumably planning the afternoon's first load of laundry.

"The photographer wants to know if he should pack things up." Ashley stepped to Lily's side, still rubbing her bruised assets. "Looks as if everyone who wants to has finished the art project."

Over by the stuffed hens was the case of soft, fluffy chicks that the kids and parents had flocked to when they first arrived. Digital pictures had been taken and printed and glued to cardstock and decorated by messy little fingers—but that was before the real show had begun. Then *safe* and *conservative* had been abandoned by the families who'd delighted in Lily's petting zoo catastrophe. Even Gayle Emory was laughing now, as Dakota and Mr. Palmer chased the last of the pigs toward the trailer.

"Tell the photographer thank you for me," Lily said. "But I think we're ready to wrap things up."

"It wasn't so bad after all, was it?" Ashley's smile was an all-knowing thing.

"What?" Lily pretended not to understand, momentarily distracted by the kiss Tyler blew to her a second before Joshua hit his mark and dumped Tyler into the water.

Cheers of delight erupted from the crowd they'd drawn.

"Your first taste of choosing chaos over perfection," her friend teased.

First taste. A baby step. A new, imperfect beginning.

Tyler waved as he climbed out of the booth so the next sap— teacher—could take his place. His smile was G-rated, but the heat in his gaze reminded her of how wonderful each private moment between them had had become, now that her obsession with ovulation and fertility and conception was behind them.

"I'm loving every minute of it," she said. "It's not perfect and things are messy, but it's magic. And there's nothing to do about magic but grab your share and enjoy."

* * * * *

Look for LAST WOLF WATCHING
by Rhyannon Byrd—the exciting conclusion
in the BLOODRUNNERS miniseries
from Silhouette Nocturne.

Follow Michaela and Brody on their fierce journey
to find the truth and face the demons from the past,
as they reach the heart of the battle between
the Runners and the rogues.

Here is a sneak preview of book three,
LAST WOLF WATCHING.

Michaela squinted, struggling to see through the impenetrable darkness. Everyone looked toward the Elders, but she knew Brody Carter still watched her. Michaela could feel the power of his gaze. Its heat. Its strength. And something that felt strangely like anger, though he had no reason to have any emotion toward her. Strangers from different worlds, brought together beneath the heavy silver moon on a night made for hell itself. That was their only connection.

The second she finished that thought, she knew it was a lie. But she couldn't deal with it now. Not tonight. Not when her whole world balanced on the edge of destruction.

Willing her backbone to keep her upright, Michaela Doucet focused on the towering blaze of a roaring bonfire that rose from the far side of the clearing, its orange flames burning with maniacal zeal against the inky black curtain of the night. Many of the Lycans had already shifted into their preternatural shapes, their fur-covered bodies standing like monstrous shadows at the edges of the forest as they waited with restless expectancy for her brother.

Her nineteen-year-old brother, Max, had been attacked by a rogue werewolf—a Lycan who preyed upon humans for food. Max had been bitten in the attack, which meant he was no longer human, but a breed of creature that existed between the two worlds of man and beast, much like the Bloodrunners themselves.

The Elders parted, and two hulking shapes emerged from the trees. In their wolf forms, the Lycans stood over seven feet tall, their legs bent at an odd angle as they stalked forward. They each held a thick chain that had been wound around their inside wrists, the twin lengths leading back into the shadows. The Lycans had taken no more than a few steps when they jerked on the chains, and her brother appeared.

Bound like an animal.

Biting at her trembling lower lip, she glanced left, then right, surprised to see that others had joined her. Now the Bloodrunners and their family and friends stood as a united force against the Silvercrest pack, which had yet to accept the fact that something sinister was eating away at its foundation—something that would rip down the protective walls that separated their world from the humans'. It occurred to Michaela that loyalties were being announced tonight—a separation made between those who would stand with the Runners in their fight against the rogues and those who blindly supported the pack's refusal to face reality. But all she could focus on was her brother. Max looked so hurt... so terrified.

"Leave him alone," she screamed, her soft-soled, black satin slip-ons struggling for purchase in the damp earth as she rushed toward Max, only to find herself lifted off the ground when a hard, heavily muscled arm clamped around her waist from behind, pulling her clear off her feet. "Dammit, let me down!" she snarled, unable to take her eyes off her brother as the golden-eyed Lycan kicked him.

Mindless with heartache and rage, Michaela clawed at the arm holding her, kicking her heels against whatever part of her captor's legs she could reach. "Stop it," a deep, husky voice grunted in her ear. "You're not helping him by losing it. I give you my word he'll survive the ceremony, but you have to keep it together."

"Nooooo!" she screamed, too hysterical to listen to reason. "You're monsters! All of you! Look what you've done to him! How dare you! *How dare you!*"

The arm tightened with a powerful flex of muscle, cinching her waist. Her breath sucked in on a sharp, wailing gasp.

"Shut up before you get both yourself and your brother killed. I will *not* let that happen. Do you understand me?" her captor growled, shaking her so hard that her teeth clicked together. "Do you understand me, Doucet?"

"Dammit," she cried, stricken as she watched one of the guards grab Max by his hair. Around them Lycans huffed and growled as they watched the spectacle, while others outright howled for the show to begin.

"That's enough!" the voice seethed in her ear. "They'll tear you apart before you even reach him, and I'll be damned if I'm going to stand here and watch you die."

Suddenly, through the haze of fear and agony and outrage in her mind, she finally recognized who'd caught her. *Brody.*

He held her in his arms, her body locked against his powerful form, her back to the burning heat of his chest. A low, keening sound of anguish tore through her, and her head dropped forward as hoarse sobs of pain ripped from her throat. "Let me go. I have to help him. *Please,*" she begged brokenly, knowing only that she needed to get to Max. "Let me go, Brody."

He muttered something against her hair, his breath warm against her scalp, and Michaela could have sworn it was a single word… But she must have heard wrong. She was too upset. Too furious. Too terrified. She must be out of her mind.

Because it sounded as if he'd quietly snarled the word *never.*

nocturne™

THE FINAL INSTALLMENT OF
THE BLOODRUNNERS TRILOGY

Last Wolf Watching

Runner Brody Carter has found his match in
Michaela Doucet, a human with unusual psychic powers.
When Michaela's brother is threatened, Brody becomes
her protector, and suddenly not only has to protect her
from her enemies but also from himself....

LOOK FOR

LAST WOLF WATCHING
BY

RHYANNON
BYRD

Available May 2008 wherever you buy books.

Dramatic and Sensual Tales of Paranormal Romance

www.eHarlequin.com   SN61786

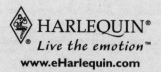

REQUEST YOUR FREE BOOKS!

2 FREE NOVELS PLUS 2 FREE GIFTS!

HARLEQUIN®

Super Romance®

Exciting, emotional, unexpected!

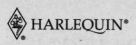

HARLEQUIN®

American ★ Romance®

Three Boys and a Baby

When Ella Garvey's eight-year-old twins and
their best friend, Dillon, discover an abandoned
baby girl, they fear she will be put in jail—
or worse! They decide to take matters into their
own hands and run away. Luckily the outlaws are
found quickly…and Ella finds a second chance
at love—with Dillon's dad, Jackson.

LOOK FOR

Three Boys and a Baby

BY

LAURA MARIE ALTOM

Available May
wherever you buy books.

LOVE, HOME & HAPPINESS

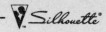

SPECIAL EDITION™

THE WILDER FAMILY
Healing Hearts in Walnut River

Social worker Isobel Suarez was proud to work at Walnut River General Hospital, so when Neil Kane showed up from the attorney general's office to investigate insurance fraud, she was up in arms. Until she melted in his arms, and things got very tricky...

Look for

HER MR. RIGHT?

by

KAREN ROSE SMITH

Available May wherever books are sold.

COMING NEXT MONTH

#1488 A SMALL-TOWN TEMPTATION • Terry McLaughlin
When acquisitions specialist Jack Maguire arrives in Charlie Keene's small town, nobody's safe. Not Charlie and not the family business she's desperate to keep from this Southern charmer…

#1489 THE MAN BEHIND THE COP • Janice Kay Johnson
Count on a Cop
Detective Bruce Walker has vowed never to get involved, never to risk emotional entanglements. But then he meets Karin Jorgenson, and the attraction is so intense, he risks breaking his promise. Can he trust himself enough to show her the real man inside?

#1490 ANYTHING FOR HER CHILDREN • Darlene Gardner
Suddenly a Parent
Raising someone else's children has tested Keri Cassidy, so when trouble strikes too close to home she's quick to meet the challenge. Although sorting out her adopted son's basketball coach seems easy pickin's, she soon finds out there's a lot more to the gorgeous, quiet man—there's a scandal in Grady Quinlan's past. But the spark between him and Keri may be exactly what it takes to start a new future for them all.…

#1491 HIS SECRET PAST • Ellen Hartman
Single Father
If she can only make one more film, it's got to count. And award-winning documentary filmmaker Anna Walsh knows exactly what she has to do. Track down the former lead singer of the rock band Five Star and make him tell her what happened the night her best friend died.

#1492 BABY BY CONTRACT • Debra Salonen
Spotlight on Sentinel Pass
Libby McGannon's ad for a donor lands actor Cooper Lindstrom, and she's thrilled. With his DNA, her baby will be gorgeous! While this is a business exchange, her feelings are unbusinesslike…until she discovers his real reasons for being in Sentinel Pass.

#1493 HIDDEN LEGACY • Margaret Way
Everlasting Love
When Alyssa Sutherland's great-aunt Zizi dies unexpectedly, Alyssa inherits her beautiful house in Australia's north Queensland. But Zizi's legacy also includes a secret.… It's Zizi's friend and neighbor, the handsome young architect Adam Hunt, who helps Alyssa reveal the love her aunt kept hidden all those years.